Robert Browning

Agamemnon

La Saisiaz and Dramatic idyls

Robert Browning

Agamemnon
La Saisiaz and Dramatic idyls

ISBN/EAN: 9783337334017

Printed in Europe, USA, Canada, Australia, Japan

Cover: Foto ©Andreas Hilbeck / pixelio.de

More available books at **www.hansebooks.com**

AGAMEMNON, LA SAISIAZ
AND DRAMATIC IDYLS

BY

ROBERT BROWNING

BOSTON
HOUGHTON, MIFFLIN AND COMPANY
New York: 11 East Seventeenth Street
The Riverside Press, Cambridge
1883

CONTENTS.

AGAMEMNON.

MAY I be permitted to chat a little, by way of recreation, at the end of a somewhat toilsome and perhaps fruitless adventure?

If, because of the immense fame of the following Tragedy, I wished to acquaint myself with it, and could only do so by the help of a translator, I should require him to be literal at every cost save that of absolute violence to our language. The use of certain allowable constructions which, happening to be out of daily favor, are all the more appropriate to archaic workmanship, is no violence; but I would be tolerant for once, — in the case of so immensely famous an original, — of even a clumsy attempt to furnish me with the very turn of each phrase in as Greek a fashion as English will bear; while, with respect to amplifications and embellishments, anything rather than, with the good farmer, experience that most signal of mortifications, " to gape for Æschylus and get Theognis." I should especially decline, — what may appear to brighten up a passage, — the employment of a new word for some old one — πόνος, or μέγας, or τέλος, with its congeners, recurring four times in three lines ; for though such substitution may be in itself perfectly jus-

tifiable, yet this exercise of ingenuity ought to be within the competence of the unaided English reader if he
likes to show himself ingenious. Learning Greek
teaches Greek, and nothing else; certainly not common sense, if that have failed to precede the teaching.
Further, if I obtained a mere strict bald version of
thing by thing, or at least word pregnant with thing, I
should hardly look for an impossible transmission of
the reputed magniloquence and sonority of the Greek;
and this with the less regret, inasmuch as there is
abundant musicality elsewhere, but nowhere else than
in his poem the ideas of the poet. And lastly, when
presented with these ideas, I should expect the result
to prove very hard reading indeed if it were meant to
resemble Æschylus, ξυμβαλεῖν οὐ ῥᾴδιος, "not easy to
understand," in the opinion of his stoutest advocate
among the ancients, while, I suppose, even modern
scholarship sympathizes with that early declaration of
the redoubtable Salmasius, when, looking about for an
example of the truly obscure for the benefit of those
who found obscurity in the sacred books, he protested
that this particular play leaves them all behind in this
respect, with their " Hebraisms, Syriasms, Hellenisms,
and the whole of such bag and baggage." [1] For, over

---

[1] " Quis Æschylum possit affirmare Græce nunc scienti magis
patere explicabilem quam Evangelia aut Epistolas Apostolicas?
Unus ejus Agamemnon obscuritate superat quantum est librorum

and above the purposed ambiguity of the Chorus, the text is sadly corrupt, probably interpolated, and certainly mutilated ; and no unlearned person enjoys the scholar's privilege of trying his fancy upon each obstacle whenever he comes to a stoppage, and effectually clearing the way by suppressing what seems to lie in it.

All I can say for the present performance is, that I have done as I would be done by, if need were. Should anybody, without need, honor my translation by a comparison with the original, I beg him to observe that, following no editor exclusively, I keep to the earlier readings so long as sense can be made out of them, but disregard, I hope, little of importance in recent criticism so far as I have fallen in with it. Fortunately, the poorest translation, provided only it be faithful, — though it reproduce all the artistic confusion of tenses, moods, and persons with which the original teems, — will not only suffice to display what an eloquent friend maintains to be the all-in-all of poetry — "the action of the piece " — but may help to illustrate his assurance that " the Greeks are the highest models of expression, the unapproached masters of the grand style ; their expression is so excellent because it is so admirably kept in its right degree of

sacrorum cum suis Hebraismis et Syriasmis et tota Hellenisticæ suppellectili vel farragine." — SALMASIUS, *De Hellenistica*, Epist. Dedic.

prominence, because it is so simple and so well sub-ordinated, because it draws its force directly from the pregnancy of the matter which it conveys . . . not a word wasted, not a sentiment capriciously thrown in, stroke on stroke ! " [1]   So may all happen !

Just a word more on the subject of my spelling — in a transcript from the Greek and there exclusively — Greek names and places precisely as does the Greek author.   I began this practice, with great innocency of intention, some six-and-thirty years ago.   Leigh Hunt, I remember, was accustomed to speak of his grat-itude, when ignorant of Greek, to those writers (like Goldsmith) who had obliged him by using English characters, so that he might relish, for instance, the smooth quality of such a phrase as " hapalunetai galené ; " he said also that Shelley was indignant at " Firenze " having displaced the Dantesque " Fioren-za," and would contemptuously English the intruder " Firence."   I supposed I was doing a simple thing enough ; but there has been lately much astonishment at *os* and *us*, *ai* and *oi*, representing the same letters in Greek.   Of a sudden, however, whether in transla-tion or out of it, everybody seems committing the of-fence, although the adoption of *u* for *v* still presents such difficulty that it is a wonder how we have hith-erto escaped " Eyripides."   But there existed a sturdy

---

[1] *Poems,* by Matthew Arnold, Preface.

Briton who, Ben Jonson informs us, wrote "The Life
of the Emperor Anthony Pie," — whom we now ac-
quiesce in as Antoninus Pius : for " with time and
patience the mulberry leaf becomes satin." Yet there
is, on all sides, much profession of respect for what
Keats called "vowelled Greek" — " consonanted,"
one would expect ; and, in a criticism upon a late ad-
mirable translation of something of my own, it was de-
plored that, in a certain verse corresponding in measure to the two hundred and fourteenth of the fourth
Pythian Ode, "neither Professor Jebb in his Greek, nor
Mr. Browning in his English, could emulate that match-
lessly musical γόνον ἰδὼν κάλλιστον ἀνδρῶν." Now, undoubtedly, "Seeing his son the fairest of men" has
more sense than sound to boast of ; but then, would
not an Italian roll us out " Rimirando il figliuolo bellis-
simo degli uomini ? " whereat Pindar, no less than Professor Jebb and Mr. Browning, τριακτῆρος οἴχεται τυχών.

It is recorded in the annals of Art,[1] that there was
once upon a time, practising so far north as Stockholm,
a painter and picture-cleaner — sire of a less unhappy
son — Old Muytens ; and the annalist, Baron de
Tessé, has not concealed his profound dissatisfaction
at old Muytens' conceit "to have himself had something to do with the work of whatever master of emi-
nence might pass through his hands." Whence it

[1] *Lettres à un jeune Prince, traduites du Suédois.*

was, — the Baron goes on to deplore, — that much detriment was done to that excellent piece "The Recognition of Achilles," by Rubens, through the perversity of Old Muytens, "who must needs take on him to beautify every nymph of the twenty by the bestowment of a widened eye and an enlarged mouth." I, at least, have left eyes and mouths everywhere as I found them, and this conservatism is all that claims praise for, — what is, after all, ἀκέλευστος ἄμισθος ἀοιδά. No, neither "uncommanded" nor "unrewarded;" since it was commanded of me by my venerated friend Thomas Carlyle, and rewarded will it indeed become, if I am permitted to dignify it by the prefatory insertion of his dear and noble name.

R. B.

LONDON, *October* 1, 1877.

PERSONS OF THE DRAMA.

WARDER.

CHOROS OF OLD MEN.

KLUTAIMNESTRA.

TALTHUBIOS, *Herald*.

AGAMEMNON.

KASSANDRA.

AIGISTHOS.

AGAMEMNON.

THE gods I ask deliverance from these labors,
Watch of a year's length whereby, slumbering through
    it
On the Atreidai's roofs on elbow, — dog-like —
I know of nightly star-groups the assemblage,
And those that bring to men winter and summer,
Bright dynasts, as they pride them in the æther
— Stars, when they wither, and the uprisings of them.
And now on ward I wait the torch's token,
The glow of fire, shall bring from Troia message
And word of capture : so prevails audacious
The man's-way-planning hoping heart of woman.
But when I, driven from night-rest, dew-drenched, hold
    to
This couch of mine — not looked upon by visions,
Since fear instead of sleep still stands beside me,
So as that fast I fix in sleep no eyelids —

And when to sing or chirp a tune I fancy,
For slumber such song-remedy infusing,
I wail then, for this House's fortune groaning,
Not, as of old, after the best ways governed.
Now, lucky be deliverance from these labors,
At good news — the appearing dusky fire !
O hail, thou lamp of night, a day-long lightness
Revealing, and of dances the ordainment !
Hallco, halloo! .

To Agamemnon's wife I show, by shouting,
That, from bed starting up at once, i' the household
Joyous acclaim, good-omened to this torch-blaze,
She send aloft, if haply Ilion's city
Be taken, as the beacon boasts announcing.
Ay, and, for me, myself will dance a prelude,
For, that my masters' dice drop right, I 'll reckon :
Since thrice-six has it thrown to me, this signal.
Well, may it hap that, as he comes, the loved hand
O' the household's lord I may sustain with this hand !
As for the rest, I 'm mute : on tongue a big ox
Has trodden. Yet this House, if voice it take should,
Most plain would speak. So, willing I myself speak
To those who know : to who know not — I 'm blank-
        ness.

CHOROS.

The tenth year this, since Priamos' great match,
King Menelaos, Agamemnon King,

— The strenuous yoke-pair of the Atreidai's honor
Two-throned, two-sceptred, whereof Zeus was donor —
Did from this land the aid, the armament dispatch,
The thousand-sailored force of Argives clamoring
" Ares " from out the indignant breast, as fling
Passion forth vultures which, because of grief
Away, — as are their young ones, — with the thief,
Lofty above their brood-nests wheel in ring,
Row round and round with oar of either wing,
Lament the bedded chicks, lost labor that was love :
Which hearing, one above
— Whether Apollon, Pan, or Zeus — that wail,
Sharp-piercing bird-shriek of the guests who fare
Housemates with gods in air —
Suchanone sends, against who these assail,
What, late-sent, shall not fail
Of punishing — Erinus.   Here as there,
The Guardian of the Guest, Zeus, the excelling one,
Sends against Alexandros either son
Of Atreus : for that wife, the many-husbanded,
Appointing many a tug that tries the limb,
While the knee plays the prop in dust, while, shred
To morsels, lies the spear-shaft ; in those grim
Marriage-prolusions when their Fury wed
Danaoi and Troes, both alike.   All 's said :
Things are where things are, and, as fate has willed,
So shall they be fulfilled.

Not gently-grieving, not just doling out
The drops of expiation — no, nor tears distilled —
Shall he we know of bring the hard about
To soft — that intense ire
At those mock-rites unsanctified by fire.
But we pay nought here : through our flesh, age-
        weighed,
Left out from who gave aid
In that day, — we remain,
Staying on staves a strength
The equal of a child's at length.
For when young marrow in the breast doth reign,
That 's the old man's match, — Ares out of place
In either : but in oldest age's case,
Foliage a-fading, why, he wends his way
On three feet, and, no stronger than a child,
Wanders about gone wild,
A dream in day.
But thou, Tundareus' daughter, Klutaimnestra queen,
What need ? What new ? What having heard or
        seen,
By what announcement's tidings, everywhere
Settest thou, round about, the sacrifice a-flare ?
For, of all gods the city-swaying,
Those supernal, those infernal,
Those of the fields', those of the mart's obeying, —
The altars blaze with gifts ;

And here and there, heaven-high the torch uplifts
Flame — medicated with persuasions mild,
With foul admixture unbeguiled —
Of holy unguent, from the clotted chrism
Brought from the palace, safe in its abysm.
Of these things, speaking what may be indeed
Both possible and lawful to concede,
Healer do thou become ! — of this solicitude
Which, now, stands plainly forth of evil mood,
And, then . . . but from oblations, hope, to-day
Gracious appearing, wards away
From soul the insatiate care,
The sorrow at my breast, devouring there !

Empowered am I to sing
The omens, what their force which, journeying,
Rejoiced the potentates :
(For still, from God, inflates
My breast, song-suasion : age,
Born to the business, still such war can wage)
— How the fierce bird against the Teukris land
Dispatched, with spear and executing hand,
The Achaian's two-throned empery — o'er Hellas'
      youth
Two rulers with one mind :
The birds' king to these kings of ships, on high,
— The black sort, and the sort that's white behind —

Appearing by the palace, on the spear-throw side,
In right sky-regions, visible far and wide, —
Devouring a hare-creature, great with young,
Baulked of more racings they, as she from whom they
      sprung !
Ah, Linos, say — ah, Linos, song of wail !
But may the good prevail !

The prudent army-prophet seeing two
The Atreidai, two their tempers, knew
Those feasting on the hare
The armament-conductors were ;
And thus he spoke, explaining signs in view.
" In time, this outset takes the town of Priamos :
But all before its towers, — the people's wealth that
      was,
Of flocks and herds, — as sure, shall booty-sharing
      thence
Drain to the dregs away, by battle violence.
Only, have care lest grudge of any god disturb
With cloud the unsullied shine of that great force, the
      curb
Of Troia, struck with damp
Beforehand in the camp !
For envyingly is
The virgin Artemis
Toward — her father's flying hounds — this House —

The sacrificers of the piteous
And cowering beast,
Brood and all, ere the birth: she hates the eagles'
     feast.
Ah, Linos, say — ah, Linos, song of wail !
But may the good prevail !

Thus ready is the beauteous one with help
To those small dew-drop things fierce lions whelp,
And udder-loving litter of each brute
That roams the mead ; and therefore makes she suit,
The fair one, for fulfilment to the end
Of things these signs portend —
Which partly smile, indeed, but partly scowl —
The phantasms of the fowl.
I call Ieïos Paian to avert
She work the Danaoi hurt
By any thwarting waftures, long and fast
Holdings from sail of ships :
And sacrifice, another than the last,
She for herself precipitate —
Something unlawful, feast for no man's lips,
Builder of quarrels, with the House cognate —
Having in awe no husband : for remains
A frightful, backward-darting in the path,
Wily house-keeping chronicler of wrath,
That has to punish that old children's fate ! "

Such things did Kalchas, — with abundant gains
As well, — vociferate,
Predictions from the birds, in journeying,
Above the abode of either king.
With these, symphonious, sing —
Ah, Linos, say — ah, Linos, song of wail!
But may the good prevail!

Zeus, whosoe'er he be, — if that express
Aught dear to him on whom I call —
So do I him address.
I cannot liken out, by all
Admeasurement of powers,
Any but Zeus for refuge at such hours,
If veritably needs I must
From off my soul its vague care-burthen thrust.

Not — whosoever was the great of yore,
Bursting to bloom with bravery all round —
Is in our mouths : he was, but is no more.
And who it was that after came to be,
Met the thrice-throwing wrestler, — he
Is also gone to ground.
But "Zeus" — if any, heart and soul, that name —
Shouting the triumph-praise — proclaim,
Complete in judgment shall that man be found.
Zeus, who leads onward mortals to be wise,

Appoints that suffering masterfully teach.
In sleep, before the heart of each,
A woe-remembering travail sheds in dew
Discretion, — ay, and melts the unwilling too
By what, perchance, may be a graciousness
Of gods, enforced no less, —
As they, commanders of the crew,
Assume the awful seat.
And then the old leader of the Achaian fleet,
Disparaging no seer —
With bated breath to suit misfortune's inrush here
— (What time it labored, that Achaian host,
By stay from sailing, — every pulse at length
Emptied of vital strength, —
Hard over Kalchis shore-bound, current-crost
In Aulis station, — while the winds which post
From Strumon, ill-delayers, famine-fraught,
Tempters of man to sail where harborage is naught,
Spendthrifts of ships and cables, turning time
To twice the length, — these carded, by delay,
To less and less away
The Argeians' flowery prime :
And when a remedy more grave and grand
Than aught before, — yea, for the storm and dearth, —
The prophet to the foremost in command
Shrieked forth, as cause of this
Adducing Artemis,

So that the Atreidai striking staves on earth
Could not withhold the tear) —
Then did the king, the elder, speak this clear.

" Heavy the fate, indeed, — to disobey !
Yet heavy if my child I slay,
The adornment of my household : with the tide
Of virgin-slaughter, at the altar-side,
A father's hands defiling : which the way
Without its evils, say ?
How shall I turn fleet-fugitive,
Failing of duty to allies ?
Since for a wind-abating sacrifice
And virgin blood, — 't is right they strive,
Nay, madden with desire.
Well may it work them — this that they require ! "

But when he underwent necessity's
Yoke-trace, — from soul blowing unhallowed change
Unclean, abominable, — thence — another man —
The audacious mind of him began
Its wildest range.
For this it is gives mortals hardihood —
Some vice-devising miserable mood
Of madness, and first woe of all the brood,
The sacrificer of his daughter — strange ! —
He dared become, to expedite

Woman-avenging warfare, — anchors weighed
With such prelusive rite!

Prayings and callings " Father " — naught they made
Of these, and of the virgin-age, —
Captains heart-set on war to wage!
His ministrants, vows done, the father bade —
Kid-like, above the altar, swathed in pall,
Take her — lift high, and have no fear at all,
Head-downward, and the fair mouth's guard
And frontage hold, — press hard
From utterance a curse against the House
By dint of bit — violence bridling speech.

And as to ground her saffron-vest she shed,
She smote the sacrificers all and each
With arrow sweet and piteous,
From the eye only sped, —
Significant of will to use a word,
Just as in pictures : since, full many a time,
In her sire's guest-hall, by the well-heaped board
Had she made music, — lovingly with chime
Of her chaste voice, that unpolluted thing,
Honored the third libation, — paian that should bring
Good fortune to the sire she loved so well.

What followed — those things I nor saw nor tell.

But Kalchas' arts, — whate'er they indicate, —
Miss of fulfilment never : it is fate.
True, justice makes, in sufferers, a desire
To know the future woe preponderate.
But — hear before is need?
To that, farewell and welcome! 'tis the same, in-
    deed,
As grief beforehand : clearly, part for part,
Conformably to Kalchas' art,
Shall come the event.
But be they as they may, things subsequent, —
What is to do, prosperity betide
E'en as we wish it ! — we, the next allied,
Sole guarding barrier of the Apian land.

I am come, reverencing power in thee,
O Klutaimnestra ! For 'tis just we bow
To the ruler's wife, — the male-seat man-bereaved.
But if thou, having heard good news, — or none, —
For good news' hope dost sacrifice thus wide,
I would hear gladly : art thou mute, — no grudge !

KLUTAIMNESTRA.

Good-news-announcer, may — as is the by-word —
Morn become, truly, — news from Night his mother !
But thou shalt learn joy past all hope of hearing.
Priamos' city have the Argeioi taken.

CHOROS.

How sayest? The word, from want of faith, escaped me.

KLUTAIMNESTRA.

Troia the Achaioi hold : do I speak plainly?

CHOROS.

Joy overcreeps me, calling forth the tear-drop.

KLUTAIMNESTRA.

Right ! for, that glad thou art, thine eye convicts thee.

CHOROS.

For — what to thee, of all this, trusty token?

KLUTAIMNESTRA.

What 's here ! how else? unless the god have cheated.

CHOROS.

Haply thou flattering shows of dreams respectest?

KLUTAIMNESTRA.

No fancy would I take of soul sleep-burthened.

CHOROS.

But has there puffed thee up some unwinged omen?

KLUTAIMNESTRA.

As a young maid's my mind thou mockest grossly.

CHOROS.

Well, at what time was — even sacked, the city?

KLUTAIMNESTRA.

Of this same mother Night — the dawn, I tell thee.

CHOROS.

And who of messengers could reach this swiftness?

KLUTAIMNESTRA.

Hephaistos — sending a bright blaze from Idé.
Beacon did beacon send, from fire the poster,
Hitherward : Idé to the rock Hermaian
Of Lemnos : and a third great torch o' the island
Zeus' seat received in turn, the Athoan summit.
And, — so upsoaring as to stride sea over,
The strong lamp-voyager, and all for joyance —
Did the gold-glorious splendor, any sun like,
Pass on — the pine-tree — to Makistos' watch-place ;
Who did not, — tardy, — caught, no wits about him,
By sleep, — decline his portion of the missive.
And far the beacon's light, on stream Euripos
Arriving, made aware Messapios' warders,

And up they lit in turn, played herald onwards,
Kindling with flame a heap of gray old heather.
And, strengthening still, the lamp, decaying nowise,
Springing o'er Plain Asopos, — full-moon-fashion
Effulgent, — toward the crag of Mount Kithairon,
Roused a new rendering-up of fire the escort —
And light, far escort, lacked no recognition
O' the guard — as burning more than burnings told
    you.
And over Lake Gorgopis light went leaping,
And, at Mount Aigiplanktos safe arriving,
Enforced the law — "to never stint the fire-stuff."
And they send, lighting up with ungrudged vigor,
Of flame a huge beard, ay, the very foreland
So as to strike above, in burning onward,
The look-out which commands the Strait Saronic.
Then did it dart until it reached the outpost
Mount Arachnaios here, the city's neighbor ;
And then darts to this roof of the Atreidai
This light of Idé's fire not unforefathered !
Such are the rules prescribed the flambeau-bearers :
He beats that's first and also last in running.
Such is the proof and token I declare thee,
My husband having sent me news from Troia.

CHOROS.

The gods, indeed, anon will I pray, woman!

But now, these words to hear, and sate my wonder
Thoroughly, I am fain — if twice thou tell them.

KLUTAIMNESTRA.

Troia do the Achaioi hold, this same day.
I think a noise — no mixture — reigns i' the city.
Sour wine and unguent pour thou in one vessel —
Standers-apart, not lovers, would'st thou style them :
And so, of captives and of conquerors, partwise
The voices are to hear, of fortune diverse.
For those, indeed, upon the bodies prostrate
Of husbands, brothers, children upon parents
— The old men, from a throat that 's free no longer,
Shriekingly wail the death-doom of their dearest :
While these — the after-battle hungry labor,
Which prompts night-faring, marshals them to break-
        fast
On the town's store, according to no billet
Of sharing, but as each drew lot of fortune.
In the spear-captured Troic habitations
House they already : from the frosts upæthral
And dews delivered, will they, luckless creatures,
Without a watch to keep, slumber all night through.
And if they fear the gods, the city-guarders,
And the gods' structures of the conquered country,
They may not — capturers — soon in turn be captive.
But see no prior lust befall the army

To sack things sacred — by gain-cravings vanquished !
For there needs homeward the return's salvation,
To round the new limb back o' the double race-
    course.
And guilty to the gods if came the army,
Awakened up the sorrow of those slaughtered
Might be — should no outbursting evils happen.
But may good beat — no turn to see i' the balance !
For, many benefits I want the gain of.

CHOROS.

Woman, like prudent man thou kindly speakest.
And I, thus having heard thy trusty tokens,
The gods to rightly hail forthwith prepare me ;
For, grace that must be paid has crowned our labors.

O Zeus the king, and friendly Night
Of these brave boons bestower —
Thou who didst fling on Troia's every tower
The o'er-roofing snare, that neither great thing might,
Nor any of the young ones, overpass
Captivity's great sweep-net — one and all
Of Até held in thrall !
Ay, Zeus I fear — the guest's friend great — who was
The doer of this, and long since bent
The bow on Alexandros with intent
That neither wide o' the white

3

Nor o'er the stars the foolish dart should light.
The stroke of Zeus — they have it, as men say!
This, at least, from the source track forth we may!
As he ordained, so has he done.
" No " — said someone —
" The gods think fit to care
Nowise for mortals, such
As those by whom the good and fair
Of things denied their touch
Is trampled!" but he was profane.
That they do care, has been made plain
To offspring of the over-bold,
Outbreathing " Ares " greater than is just —
Houses that spill with more than they can hold,
More than is best for man.   Be man's what must
Keep harm off, so that in himself he find
Sufficiency — the well-endowed of mind!
For there's no bulwark in man's wealth to him
Who, through a surfeit, kicks — into the dim
And disappearing — Right's great altar.

                                        Yes —

It urges him, the sad persuasiveness,
Até's insufferable child that schemes
Treason beforehand : and all cure is vain.
It is not hidden : out it glares again,
A light dread-lamping-mischief, just as gleams

The badness of the bronze ;
Through rubbing, puttings to the touch,
Black-clotted is he, judged at once.
He seeks — the boy — a flying bird to clutch,
The insufferable brand
Setting upon the city of his land
Whereof not any god hears prayer ;
While him who brought about such evils there,
That unjust man, the god in grapple throws.
Such an one, Paris goes
Within the Atreidai's house —
Shamed the guest's board by robbery of the spouse.

And, leaving to her townsmen throngs a-spread
With shields, and spear-thrusts of sea-armament,
And bringing Ilion, in a dowry's stead,
Destruction — swiftly through the gates she went,
Daring the undareable.   But many a groan outbroke
From prophets of the House as thus they spoke.
" Woe, woe the House, the House and Rulers, — woe
The marriage-bed and dints
A husband's love imprints !
There she stands silent ! meets no honor — no
Shame — sweetest still to see of things gone long ago !
And, through desire of one across the main,
A ghost will seem within the house to reign ∶
And hateful to the husband is the grace

Of well-shaped statues : from — in place of eyes,
Those blanks — all Aphrodité dies.

" But dream-appearing mournful fantasies —
There they stand, bringing grace that 's vain.
For vain 't is, when brave things one seems to view ;
The fantasy has floated off, hands through ;
Gone, that appearance, — nowise left to creep, —
On wings, the servants in the paths of sleep ! "
Woes, then, in household and on hearth, are such
As these — and woes surpassing these by much.
But not these only : everywhere —
For those who from the land
Of Hellas issued in a band,
Sorrow, the heart must bear,
Sits in the home of each, conspicuous there.
Many a circumstance, at least,
Touches the very breast.
For those
Whom any sent away, — he knows :
And in the live man's stead,
Armor and ashes reach
The house of each.

For Ares, gold-exchanger for the dead,
And balance-holder in the fight o' the spear,
Due-weight from Ilion sends —

What moves the tear on tear —
A charred scrap to the friends :
Filling with well-packed ashes every urn,
For man that was the sole return.
And they groan — praising much, the while,
Now this man as experienced in the strife,
Now that, fallen nobly on a slaughtered pile,
Because of — not his own — another's wife.
But things there be, one barks,
When no man harks :
A surreptitious grief that 's grudge
Against the Atreidai, who first sought the judge.
But some there, round the rampart, have
In Ilian earth, each one his grave :
All fair-formed as at birth,
It hid them — what they have and hold — the hostile
    earth.

And grave with anger goes the city's word,
And pays a debt by public curse incurred.
And ever with me — as about to hear
A something night-involved — remains my fear :
Since of the many-slayers — not
Unwatching are the gods.
The black Erinues, at due periods —
Whoever gains the lot
Of fortune with no right —

Him, by life's strain and stress
Back-again-beaten from success,
They strike blind : and among the out-of-sight
For who has got to be, avails no might.
The being praised outrageously
Is grave, for at the eyes of such an one
Is launched, from Zeus, the thunder-stone.
Therefore do I decide
For so much and no more prosperity
Than of his envy passes unespied.
Neither a city-sacker would I be,
Nor life, myself by others captive, see.

A swift report has gone our city through,
From fire, the good-news messenger : if true,
Who knows ?   Or is it not a god-sent lie ?
Who is so childish and deprived of sense
That, having, at announcements of the flame
Thus novel, felt his own heart fired thereby,
He then shall, at a change of evidence,
Be worsted just the same ?
It is conspicuous in a woman's nature,
Before its view to take a grace for granted :
Too trustful, — on her boundary, usurpature
Is swiftly made ;
But swiftly, too, decayed,
The glory perishes by woman vaunted.

KLUTAIMNESTRA.

Soon shall we know — of these light-bearing torches,
And beacons and exchanges, fire with fire —
If they are true, indeed, or if, dream-fashion,
This gladsome light came and deceived our judgment.
Yon herald from the shore I see, o'ershadowed
With boughs of olive : dust, mud's thirsty brother,
Close neighbors on his garb, thus testify me
That neither voiceless, nor yet kindling for thee
Mountain-wood-flame, shall he explain by fire-smoke :
But either tell out more the joyance, speaking. . . .
Word contrary to which, I aught but love it!
For may good be — to good that's known — append-
     age !

CHOROS.

Whoever prays for aught else to this city
— May he himself reap fruit of his mind's error !

HERALD.

Ha, my forefathers' soil of earth Argeian !
Thee, in this year's tenth light, am I returned to —
Of many broken hopes, on one hope chancing ;
For never prayed I, in this earth Argeian
Dying, to share my part in tomb the dearest.
Now, hail thou earth, and hail thou also, sunlight,
And Zeus, the country's lord, and king the Puthian

From bow no longer urging at us arrows!
Enough, beside Skamandros, cam'st thou adverse:
Now, contrary, be saviour thou and healer,
O king Apollon!   And gods conquest-granting,
All — I invoke too, and my tutelary
Hermes, dear herald, heralds' veneration, —
And Heroes our forthsenders, — friendly, once more
The army to receive, the war-spear's leavings!
Ha, mansions of my monarchs, roofs beloved,
And awful seats, and deities sun-fronting —
Receive with pomp your monarch, long time absent!
For he comes bringing light in night-time to you,
In common with all these — king Agamemnon.
But kindly greet him — for clear shows your duty —
Who has dug under Troia with the mattock
Of Zeus the Avenger, whereby plains are out-ploughed,
Altars unrecognizable, and gods' shrines,
And the whole land's seed thoroughly has perished.
And such a yoke-strap having cast round Troia,
The elder king Atreides, happy man — he
Comes to be honored, worthiest of what mortals
Now are.   Nor Paris nor the accomplice-city
Outvaunts their deed as more than they are done-by:
For, in a suit for rape and theft found guilty,
He missed of plunder and, in one destruction,
Fatherland, house and home has mowed to atoms:
Debts the Priamidai have paid twice over.

CHOROS.

Hail, herald from the army of Achaians !

HERALD.

I hail : — to die, will gainsay gods no longer !

CHOROS.

Love of this fatherland did exercise thee ?

HERALD.

So that I weep, at least, with joy, my eyes full.

CHOROS.

What, of this gracious sickness were ye gainers ?

HERALD.

How now ? instructed, I this speech shall master.

CHOROS.

For those who loved you back, with longing stricken.

HERALD.

This land yearned for the yearning army, say'st thou ?

CHOROS.

So as to set me oft, from dark mind, groaning.

HERALD.

Whence came this ill mind — hatred to the army?

CHOROS.

Of old, I use, for mischief's physic, silence.

HERALD.

And how, the chiefs away, did you fear any?

CHOROS.

So that now, — late thy word, — much joy were —
     dying !

HERALD.

For well have things been worked out : these, — in
     much time,
Some of them, one might say, had luck in falling,
While some were faulty : for who, gods excepted,
Goes, through the whole time of his life, ungrieving?
For labors should I tell of, and bad lodgments,
Narrow deckways ill-strewn, too, — what the day's
     woe
We did not groan at getting for our portion?
As for land-things, again, on went more hatred !
Since beds were ours hard by the foemen's ramparts,
And, out of heaven and from the earth, the meadow
Dews kept a-sprinkle, an abiding damage

Of vestures, making hair a wild-beast matting.

Winter, too, if one told of it — bird-slaying —

Such as, unbearable, Idaian snow brought —

Or heat, when waveless, on its noontide couches

Without a wind, the sea would slumber falling

— Why must one mourn thee? O'er and gone is
    labor:

O'er and gone is it, even to those dead ones,

So that no more again they mind uprising.

Why must we tell in numbers those deprived ones,

And the live man be vexed with fate's fresh out-
    break?

Rather, I bid full farewell to misfortunes!

For us, the left from out the Argeian army,

The gain beats, nor does sorrow counterbalance.

So that 't is fitly boasted of, this sunlight,

By us, o'er sea and land the aery flyers,

"Troia at last taking, the band of Argives

Hang up such trophies to the gods of Hellas

Within their domes — new glory to grow ancient!"

Such things men having heard must praise the city

And army-leaders: and the grace which wrought
    them —

Of Zeus, shall honored be. Thou hast my whole
    word.

CHOROS.

O'ercome by words, their sense I do not gainsay.

For, aye this breeds youth in the old — "to learn
        well."
But these things most the house and Klutaimnestra
Concern, 't is likely : while they make me rich, too.

KLUTAIMNESTRA.

I shouted long ago, indeed, for joyance,
When came that first night-messenger of fire
Proclaiming Ilion's capture and dispersion.
And someone, girding me, said " Through fire-bearers
Persuaded — Troia to be sacked now, thinkest ?
Truly, the woman's way, — high to lift heart up ! "
By such words I was made seem wit-bewildered :
Yet still I sacrificed ; and, — female-song with, —
A shout one man and other, through the city,
Set up, congratulating in the gods' seats,
Soothing the incense-eating flame right fragrant.
And now, what 's more, indeed, why need'st thou tell
        me ?
I of the king himself shall learn the whole word :
And, — as may best be, — I my revered husband
Shall hasten, as he comes back, to receive : for —
What 's to a wife sweeter to see than this light
(Her husband, by the god saved, back from warfare)
So as to open gates ?   This tell my husband —
To come at soonest to his loving city.
A faithful wife at home may he find, coming !

Such an one as he left — the dog o' the household —
Trusty to him, adverse to the ill-minded,
And, in all else, the same : no signet-impress
Having done harm to, in that time's duration.
I know nor pleasure, nor blameworthy converse
With any other man more than — bronze-dippings !

HERALD.

Such boast as this — of the veracious brimful —
Is not bad for a high-born dame to send forth !

CHOROS.

Ay, she spoke thus to thee — that hast a knowledge
From clear interpreters — a speech most seemly !
But speak thou, herald ! Meneleos I ask of :
If he, returning, back in safety also
Will come with you — this land's beloved chieftain ?

HERALD.

There 's no way I might say things false and pleasant
For friends to reap the fruits of through a long time.

CHOROS.

How then if, speaking good, things true thou chance
on ?

HERALD.

For, sundered, not well-hidden things become they.

The man has vanished from the Achaic army,
He and his ship too.   I announce no falsehood.

CHOROS.

Whether forth-putting openly from Ilion,
Or did storm — wide woe — snatch him from the
    army ?

HERALD.

Thou hast, like topping bowman, touched the target,
And a long sorrow hast succinctly spoken.

CHOROS.

Whether, then, of him, as a live or dead man
Was the report by other sailors bruited ?

HERALD.

Nobody knows so as to tell out clearly
Excepting Helios who sustains earth's nature.

CHOROS.

How say'st thou then, did storm the naval army
Attack and end, by the celestials' anger ?

HERALD.

It suits not to defile a day auspicious
With ill-announcing speech : distinct each god's due :
And when a messenger with gloomy visage

To a city bears a fall'n host's woes — God ward
    off ! —
One popular wound that happens to the city,
And many sacrificed from many households —
Men, scourged by that two-thonged whip Ares loves
    so,
Double spear-headed curse, bloody yoke-couple, —
Of woes like these, doubtless, whoe'er comes weighted,
Him does it suit to sing the Erinues' paian.
But who, of matters saved a glad-news-bringer,
Comes to a city in good estate rejoicing. . . .
How shall I mix good things with evil, telling
Of storm against the Achaioi, urged by gods' wrath ?
For they swore league, being arch-foes before that,
Fire and the sea : and plighted troth approved they,
Destroying the unhappy Argeian army.
At night began the bad-wave-outbreak evils ;
For, ships against each other Threkian breezes
Shattered : and these, butted at in a fury
By storm and typhoon, with surge rain-resounding, —
Off they went, vanished, thro' a bad herd's whirling.
And, when returned the brilliant light of Helios,
We view the Aigaian sea on flower with corpses
Of men Achaian and with naval ravage.
But us indeed, and ship, unhurt i' the hull too,
Either some one out-stole us or out-prayed us —
Some god — no man it was the tiller touching.

And Fortune, saviour, willing on our ship sat.
So as it neither had in harbor wave-surge
Nor ran aground against a shore all rocky.
And then, the water Hades having fled from
In the white day, not trusting to our fortune,
We chewed the cud in thoughts — this novel sorrow
O' the army laboring and badly pounded.
And now — of them if anyone is breathing —
They talk of us as having perished : why not ?
And we — that they the same fate have, imagine.
May it be for the best !   Meneleos, then,
Foremost and specially to come, expect thou !
If (that is) any ray o' the sun reports him
Living and seeing too — by Zeus' contrivings,
Not yet disposed to quite destroy the lineage —
Some hope is he shall come again to household.
Having heard such things, know, thou truth art hear-
          ing !

CHOROS.

Who may he have been that named thus wholly with
          exactitude —
(Was he someone whom we see not, by forecastings of
          the future
Guiding tongue in happy mood ?)
— Her with battle for a bridegroom, on all sides con-
          tention-wooed,
Helena ?   Since — mark the suture ! —

Ship's-Hell, Man's-Hell, City's-Hell,
From the delicately-pompous curtains that pavilion
    well,
Forth, by favor of the gale
Of earth-born Zephuros did she sail.
Many shield-bearers, leaders of the pack,
Sailed too upon their track,
Theirs who had directed oar,
Then visible no more,
To Simois' leaf-luxuriant shore —
For sake of strife all gore !

To Ilion Wrath, fulfilling her intent,
This marriage-care — the rightly named so — sent :
In after-time, for the tables' abuse
And that of the hearth-partaker Zeus,
Bringing to punishment
Those who honored with noisy throat
The honor of the bride, the hymenæal note
Which did the kinsfolk then to singing urge.
But, learning a new hymn for that which was,
The ancient city of Priamos
Groans probably a great and general dirge
Denominating Paris
"The man that miserably marries :" —
She who, all the while before,
A life, that was a general dirge

4

For citizens' unhappy slaughter, bore.
And thus a man, by no milk's help,
Within his household reared a lion's whelp
That loved the teat
In life's first festal stage :
Gentle as yet,
A true child-lover, and, to men of age,
A thing whereat pride warms ;
And oft he had it in his arms
Like any new-born babe, bright-faced, to hand
Wagging its tail, at belly's strict command.

But in due time upgrown,
The custom of progenitors was shown :
For — thanks for sustenance repaying
With ravage of sheep slaughtered —
It made unbidden feast ;
With blood the house was watered,
To household — woe there was no staying :
Great mischief many-slaying !
From God it was — some priest
Of Até, in the house, by nurture thus increased.

At first, then, to the city of Ilion went
A soul, as I might say, of windless calm —
Wealth's quiet ornament,
An eyes' dart bearing balm,

Love's spirit-biting flower.
But — from the true course bending —
She brought about, of marriage, bitter ending :
Ill-resident, ill-mate, in power
Passing to the Priamidai — by sending
Of Hospitable Zeus —
Erinus for a bride, — to make brides mourn, her dower.

Spoken long ago
Was the ancient saying
Still among mortals staying :
" Man's great prosperity at height of rise
Engenders offspring nor unchilded dies ;
And, from good fortune, to such families,
Buds forth insatiate woe."
Whereas, distinct from any,
Of my own mind I am :
For 't is the unholy deed begets the many,
Resembling each its dam.
Of households that correctly estimate,
Ever a beauteous child is born of Fate.

But ancient Arrogance delights to generate
Arrogance, young and strong mid mortals' sorrow,
Or now, or then, when comes the appointed morrow.
And she bears young Satiety ;
And, fiend with whom nor fight nor war can be,

Unholy Daring — twin black Curses
Within the household, children like their nurses.

But Justice shines in smoke-grimed habitations,
And honors the well-omened life ;
While, — gold-besprinkled stations
Where the hands' filth is rife,
With backward-turning eyes
Leaving, — to holy seats she hies,
Not worshipping the power of wealth
Stamped with applause by stealth :
And to its end directs each thing begun.

Approach then, my monarch, of Troia the sacker, of
    Atreus the son !
How ought I address thee, how ought I revere thee, —
    nor yet overhitting
Nor yet underbending the grace that is fitting ?
Many of mortals hasten to honor the seeming-to-be —
Passing by justice : and, with the ill-faring, to groan
    as he groans all are free.
But no bite of the sorrow their liver has reached to :
They say with the joyful, — one outside on each, too,
As they force to a smile smileless faces.
But whoever is good at distinguishing races
In sheep of his flock — it is not for the eyes
Of a man to escape such a shepherd's surprise,

As they seem, from a well-wishing mind,
In watery friendship to fawn and be kind.
Thou to me, then, indeed, sending an army for He-
    lena's sake,
(I will not conceal it) wast — oh, by no help of the
    Muses ! — depicted
Not well of thy midriff the rudder directing, — con-
    victed
Of bringing a boldness they did not desire to the men
    with existence at stake.
But now — from no outside of mind, nor unlovingly —
    gracious thou art
To those who have ended the labor, fulfilling their
    part ;
And in time shalt thou know, by inquiry instructed,
Who of citizens justly, and who not to purpose, the
    city conducted.

AGAMEMNON.

First, indeed, Argos, and the gods, the local,
'T is right addressing — those with me the partners
In this return and right things done the city
Of Priamos : gods who, from no tongue hearing
The rights o' the cause, for Ilion's fate man-slaugh-
    t'rous
Into the bloody vase, not oscillating,
Put the vote-pebbles, while, o' the rival vessel,

Hope rose up to the lip-edge : filled it was not,
By smoke the captured city is still conspicuous :
Até's burnt offerings live : and, dying with them,
The ash sends forth the fulsome blasts of riches.
Of these things, to the gods grace many-mindful
'T is right I render, since both nets outrageous
We built them round with, and, for sake of woman,
It did the city to dust — the Argeian monster,
The horse's nestling, the shield-bearing people
That made a leap, at setting of the Pleiads,
And, vaulting o'er the tower, the raw-flesh-feeding
Lion licked up his fill of blood tyrannic.
I to the gods indeed prolonged this preface ;
But — as for *thy* thought, I remember hearing —
I say the same, and thou co-pleader hast me.
Since few of men this faculty is born with —
Their friend, successful, without grudge to honor.
For moody, on the heart, a poison seated
Its burthen doubles to who gained the sickness :
By his own griefs he is himself made heavy,
And out-of-door prosperity seeing groans at.
Knowing, I 'd call (for well have I experienced)
" Fellowship's mirror," " phantom of a shadow,"
Those seeming to be mighty gracious to me :
While just Odusseus — he who sailed not willing —
When joined on, was to me the ready trace-horse.
This of him, whether dead or whether living,

I say.   For other city-and-gods' concernment —
Appointing common courts, in full assemblage
We will consult.   And as for what holds seemly —
How it may lasting stay well, must be counseled :
While what has need of medicines Paionian
We, either burning or else cutting kindly,
Will make endeavor pain to turn from sickness.
And now into the domes and homes by altar
Going, I to the gods first raise the right-hand —
They who, far sending, back again have brought me.
And Victory, since she followed, fixed remain she !

KLUTAIMNESTRA.

Men, citizens, Argeians here, my worships !
I shall not shame me, consort-loving manners
To tell before you : for in time there dies off
The diffidence from people.   Not from others
Learning, I of myself will tell the hard life
I bore so long as this man was 'neath Ilion.
First : for a woman, from the male divided,
To sit at home alone, is monstrous evil —
Hearing the many rumors back-revenging :
And for now This to come, now That bring after
Woe, and still worse woe, bawling in the household !
And truly, if so many wounds had chanced
On my husband here, as homeward used to dribble
Report, he 's pierced more than a net to speak of !

While, were he dying (as the words abounded)
A triple-bodied Geruon the Second,
Plenty above — for loads below I count not —
Of earth a three-share cloak he 'd boast of taking,
Once only dying in each several figure !
Because of such-like rumors back-revenging,
Many the halters from my neck, above head,
Others than *I* loosed — loosed from neck by main
        force !
From this cause, sure, the boy stands not beside me —
Possessor of our troth-plights, thine and mine too —
As ought Orestes ; be not thou astonished !
For, him brings up our well-disposed guest-captive
Strophios the Phokian — ills that told on both sides
To me predicting — both of thee 'neath Ilion
The danger, and if anarchy's mob-uproar
Thy council should o'erthrow ; since it is born with
Mortals, — whoe'er has fallen, the more to kick him.
Such an excuse, I think, no cunning carries !
As for myself — why, of my wails the rushing
Fountains are dried up : not in them a drop more !
And in my late-to-bed eyes damage have I
Bewailing what concerned thee, those torch-holdings
For ever unattended to.   In dreams — why,
Beneath the light wing-beats o' the gnat, I woke up
As he went buzzing — sorrows that concerned thee
Seeing, that filled more than their fellow-sleep-time.

Now, all this having suffered, from soul grief-free
I would style this man here the dog o' the stables,
The saviour forestay of the ship, the high roof's
Ground-prop, son sole-begotten to his father,
— Ay, land appearing to the sailors past hope,
Loveliest day to see after a tempest,
To the wayfaring-one athirst a well-spring,
— The joy, in short, of scaping all that 's — fatal!
I judge him worth addresses such as these are
— Envy stand off! — for many those old evils
We underwent.   And now, to me — dear headship! —
Dismount thou from this car, not earthward setting
The foot of thine, O king, that 's Ilion's spoiler!
Slave-maids, why tarry? — whose the task allotted
The soil o' the road to strew with carpet-spreadings.
Immediately be purple-strewn the pathway,
So that to home unhoped may lead him — Justice!
As for the rest, care shall — by no sleep conquered —
Dispose things — justly (gods to aid!) appointed.

AGAMEMNON.

Offspring of Leda, of my household warder,
Suitably to my absence hast thou spoken,
For long the speech thou didst outstretch!   But aptly
To praise — from others ought to go this favor.
And for the rest, — not me, in woman's fashion,
Mollify, nor — as mode of barbarous man is —

To me gape forth a groundward-falling clamor!
Nor, strewing it with garments, make my passage
Envied! Gods, sure, with these behoves us honor:
But, for a mortal on these varied beauties
To walk — to me, indeed, is nowise fear-free.
I say — as man, not god, to me do homage!
Apart from foot-mats both and varied vestures,
Renown is loud, and — not to lose one's senses,
God's greatest gift. Behoves us him call happy
Who life has brought to end in loved well-being.
If all things I might manage thus — brave man, I!

KLUTAIMNESTRA.

Come now, this say, nor feign a feeling to me!

AGAMEMNON.

With feeling, know indeed, I do not tamper!

KLUTAIMNESTRA.

Vowedst thou to the gods, in fear, to act thus?

AGAMEMNON.

If any, *I* well knew resolve I outspoke.

KLUTAIMNESTRA.

What think'st thou Priamos had done, thus victor?

AGAMEMNON.

On varied vests — I do think — he had passaged.

KLUTAIMNESTRA.

Then, do not, struck with awe at human censure. . . .

AGAMEMNON.

Well, popular mob-outcry much avails too!

KLUTAIMNESTRA.

Ay, but the unenvied is not the much valued.

AGAMEMNON.

Sure, 't is no woman's part to long for battle!

KLUTAIMNESTRA.

Why, to the prosperous, even suits a beating!

AGAMEMNON.

What? thou this beating us in war dost prize too?

KLUTAIMNESTRA.

Persuade thee! power, for once, grant *me* — and
willing!

AGAMEMNON.

But if this seem so to thee — shoes, let someone
Loose under, quick — foot's serviceable carriage!
And me, on these sea-products walking, may no
Grudge from a distance, from the god's eye, strike at!
For great shame were my strewment-spoiling — riches
Spoiling with feet, and silver-purchased textures!
Of these things, thus then. But this female-stran-
     ger
Tenderly take inside! Who conquers mildly
God, from afar, benignantly regardeth.
For, willing, no one wears a yoke that's servile:
And she, of many valuables, outpicked
The flower, the army's gift, myself has followed.
So, — since to hear thee, I am brought about thus, —
I go into the palace — purples treading.

KLUTAIMNESTRA.

There is the sea — and what man shall exhaust
     it? —
Feeding much purple's worth-its-weight-in-silver
Dye, ever fresh and fresh, our garments' tincture;
At home, such wealth, king, we begin — by gods'
     help —
With having, and to lack, the household knows not.
Of many garments had I vowed a treading

(In oracles if fore-enjoined the household)
Of this dear soul the safe-return-price scheming!
For, root existing, foliage goes up houses
Shadow o'erspreading against Seirios dog-star ;
And, thou returning to the hearth domestic,
Warmth, yea, in winter dost thou show returning.
And when, too, Zeus works, from the green-grape
      acrid,
Wine — then, already, cool in houses cometh —
The perfect man his home perambulating!
Zeus, Zeus Perfecter, these my prayers perfect thou!
Thy care be — yea — of things thou may'st make per-
      fect!

CHOROS.

Wherefore to me, this fear —
Groundedly stationed here
Fronting my heart, the portent-watcher — flits she?
Wherefore should prophet-play
The uncalled unpaid lay,
Nor — having spat forth fear, like bad dreams — sits
      she
On the mind's throne beloved — well-suasive Bold-
      ness?
For time, since, by a throw of all the hands,
The boat's stern-cables touched the sands,
Has past from youth to oldness, —
When under Ilion rushed the ship-borne bands.

And from my eyes I learn —
Being myself my witness — their return.
Yet, all the same, without a lyre, my soul,
Itself its teacher too, chants from within
Erinus' dirge, not having now the whole
Of Hope's dear boldness : nor my inwards sin —
The heart that 's rolled in whirls against the mind
Justly presageful of a fate behind.
But I pray — things false, from my hope, may fall
Into the fate that 's not-fulfilled-at-all !

Especially at least, of health that 's great
The term 's insatiable : for, its weight
— A neighbor, with a common wall between —
Ever will sickness lean ;
And destiny, her course pursuing straight,
Has struck man's ship against a reef unseen.
Now, when a portion, rather than the treasure,
Fear casts from sling, with peril in right measure,
It has not sunk — the universal freight,
(With misery freighted over-full)
Nor has fear whelmed the hull.
Then too the gift of Zeus,
Two-handedly profuse,
Even from the furrows' yield for yearly use
Has done away with famine, the disease ;
But blood of man to earth once falling, — deadly,
        black, —

In times ere these, —
Who may, by singing spells, call back ?
Zeus had not else stopped one who rightly knew
The way to bring the dead again.
But, did not an appointed Fate constrain
The Fate from gods, to bear no more than due,
My heart, outstripping what tongue-utters,
Would have all out : which now, in darkness, mut-
    ters
Moodily grieved, nor ever hopes to find
How she a word in season may unwind
From out the enkindling mind.

KLUTAIMNESTRA.

Take thyself in, thou too — I say, Kassandra !
Since Zeus — not angrily — in household placed
    thee
Partaker of hand-sprinklings, with the many
Slaves stationed, his the Owner's altar close to.
Descend from out this car, nor be high-minded !
And truly they do say Alkmene's child once
Bore being sold, slaves' barley-bread his living.
If, then, necessity of this lot o'erbalance,
Much is the favor of old-wealthy masters :
For those who, never hoping, made fine harvest
Are harsh to slaves in all things, beyond measure.
Thou hast — with us — such usage as law warrants.

CHOROS.

To thee it was, she paused plain speech from speaking.
Being inside the fatal nets — obeying,
Thou may'st obey : but thou may'st disobey too !

KLUTAIMNESTRA.

Why, if she is not, in the swallow's fashion,
An unknown and barbaric voice possessed of,
I, with speech — speaking in mind's scope — per-
    suade her.

CHOROS.

Follow!   The best — as things now stand — she
    speaks of.
Obey thou, leaving this thy car-enthronement !

KLUTAIMNESTRA.

Well, with this thing at door, for me no leisure
To waste time : as concerns the hearth mid-naveled,
Already stand the sheep for fireside slaying
By those who never hoped to have such favor.
If thou, then, aught of this wilt do, delay not !
But if thou, being witless, tak'st no word in,
Speak thou, instead of voice, with hand as Kars do !

CHOROS.

She seems a plain interpreter in need of,
The stranger ! and her way — a beast's new-captured !

KLUTAIMNESTRA.

Why, she is mad, sure, — hears her own bad senses, —
Who, while she comes, leaving a town new-captured,
Yet knows not how to bear the bit o' the bridle
Before she has out-frothed her bloody fierceness.
Not I — throwing away more words — will shamed
    be!

CHOROS.

But I, — for I compassionate, — will chafe not.
Come, O unhappy one, this car vacating,
Yielding to this necessity, prove yoke's use!

KASSANDRA.

Otototoi, Gods, Earth —
Apollon, Apollon!

CHOROS.

Why didst thou " ototoi " concerning Loxias?
Since he is none such as to suit a mourner.

KASSANDRA.

Otototoi, Gods, Earth, —
Apollon, Apollon!

CHOROS.

Ill-boding here again the god invokes she
— Nowise empowered in woes to stand by helpful.

5

KASSANDRA.

Apollon, Apollon,
Guard of the ways, my destroyer!
For thou hast quite, this second time, destroyed me.

CHOROS.

To prophesy she seems of her own evils:
Remains the god-gift to the slave-soul present.

KASSANDRA.

Apollon, Apollon,
Guard of the ways, my destroyer!
Ha, whither hast thou led me? to what roof now?

CHOROS.

To the Atreidai's roof: if this thou know'st not,
I tell it thee, nor this wilt thou call falsehood.

KASSANDRA.

How! How!
God-hated, then! Of many a crime it knew —
Self-slaying evils, halters too:
Man's-shambles, blood-besprinkler of the ground!

CHOROS.

She seems to be good-nosed, the stranger: dog-like,
She snuffs indeed the victims she will find there.

KASSANDRA.

How! How!
By the witnesses here I am certain now!
These children bewailing their slaughters — flesh
dressed in the fire
And devoured by their sire!

CHOROS.

Ay, we have heard of thy soothsaying glory,
Doubtless: but prophets none are we in scent of!

KASSANDRA.

Ah, gods, what ever does she meditate?
What this new anguish great?
Great in the house here she meditates ill
Such as friends cannot bear, cannot cure it: and still
Off stands all Resistance
Afar in the distance!

CHOROS.

Of these I witless am — these prophesyings.
But those I knew: for the whole city bruits them.

KASSANDRA.

Ah, unhappy one, this thou consummatest?
Thy husband, thy bed's common guest,

In the bath having brightened. . . . How shall I de-
clare
Consummation? It soon will be there :
For hand after hand she outstretches,
At life as she reaches!

CHOROS.

Nor yet I 've gone with thee ! for — after riddles —
Now, in blind oracles, I feel resourceless.

KASSANDRA.

Eh, eh, papai, papai,
What this, I espy?
Some net of Hades undoubtedly!
Nay, rather, the snare
Is she who has share
In his bed, who takes part in the murder there !
But may a revolt —
Unceasing assault —
On the Race, raise a shout
Sacrificial, about
A victim — by stoning —
For murder atoning!

CHOROS.

What this Erinus which i' the house thou callest

To raise her cry? Not me thy word enlightens!
To my heart has run
A drop of the crocus-dye :
Which makes for those
On earth by the spear that lie,
A common close
With life's descending sun.
Swift is the curse begun !

KASSANDRA.

How! How!
See — see quick!
Keep the bull from the cow !
In the vesture she catching him, strikes him now
With the black-horned trick,
And he falls in the watery vase !
Of the craft-killing cauldron I tell thee the case !

CHOROS.

I would not boast to be a topping critic
Of oracles : but to some sort of evil
I liken these. From oracles, what good speech
To mortals, beside, is sent?
It comes of their evils : these arts word-abounding
        that sing the event
Bring the fear 't is their office to teach.

KASSANDRA.

Ah me, ah me —
Of me unhappy, evil-destined fortunes !
For I bewail my proper woe
As, mine with his, all into one I throw.
Why hast thou hither me unhappy brought ?
— Unless that I should die with him — for nought !
What else was sought ?

CHOROS.

Thou art some mind-mazed creature, god-possessed :
And all about thyself dost wail
A lay — no lay !
Like some brown nightingale
Insatiable of noise, who — well away ! —
From her unhappy breast
Keeps moaning Itus, Itus, and his life
With evils, flourishing on each side, rife.

KASSANDRA.

Ah me, ah me,
The fate o' the nightingale, the clear resounder !
For a body wing-borne have the gods cast round her,
And sweet existence, from misfortunes free :
But for myself remains a sundering
With spear, the two-edged thing !

CHOROS.

Whence hast thou this on-rushing god-involving pain
And spasms in vain ?
For, things that terrify,
With changing unintelligible cry
Thou strikest up in tune, yet all the while
After that Orthian style !
Whence hast thou limits to the oracular road,
That evils bode ?

KASSANDRA.

Ah me, the nuptials, the nuptials of Paris, the deadly
    to friends !
Ah me, of Skamandros the draught
Paternal !   There once, to these ends,
On thy banks was I brought,
The unhappy !   And now, by Kokutos and Acheron's
    shore
I shall soon be, it seems,· these my oracles singing
    once more !

CHOROS.

Why this word, plain too much,
Hast thou uttered ?   A babe might learn of such !
I am struck with a bloody bite — here under —
At the fate woe-wreaking

Of thee shrill-shrieking :
To me who hear — a wonder !

KASSANDRA.

Ah me, the toils — the toils of the city
The wholly destroyed : ah, pity,
Of the sacrificings my father made
In the ramparts' aid —
Much slaughter of grass-fed flocks — that afforded no
    cure
That the city should not, as it does now, the burthen
    endure !
But I, with the soul on fire,
Soon to the earth shall cast me and expire !

CHOROS.

To things, on the former consequent,
Again hast thou given vent :
And 't is some evil-meaning fiend doth move thee,
Heavily falling from above thee,
To melodize thy sorrows — else, in singing,
Calamitous, death-bringing !
And of all this the end
I am without resource to apprehend.

KASSANDRA.

Well then, the oracle from veils no longer

Shall be outlooking, like a bride new-married :
But bright it seems, against the sun's uprisings
Breathing, to penetrate thee : so as, wave-like,
To wash against the rays a woe much greater
Than this.   I will no longer teach by riddles.
And witness, running with me, that of evils
Done long ago, I nosing track the footstep !
For, this same roof here — never quits a Choros
One-voiced, not well-tuned since no " well " it utters :
And truly having drunk, to get more courage,
Man's blood — the Komos keeps within the household
— Hard to be sent outside — of sister Furies :
They hymn their hymn — within the house close sit-
    ting —
The first beginning curse : in turn spit forth at
The Brother's bed, to him who spurned it hostile.
Have I missed aught, or hit I like a bowman ?
False prophet am I, — knock at doors, a babbler ?
Henceforward witness, swearing now, I know not
By other's word the old sins of this household !

CHOROS.

And how should oath, bond honorably binding,
Become thy cure ?   No less I wonder at thee
— That thou, beyond sea reared, a strange-tongued
    city
Should'st hit in speaking, just as if thou stood'st by !

KASSANDRA.

Prophet Apollon put me in this office.

CHOROS.

What, even though a god, with longing smitten?

KASSANDRA.

At first, indeed, shame was to me to say this.

CHOROS.

For, more relaxed grows everyone who fares well.

KASSANDRA.

But he was athlete to me — huge grace breathing!

CHOROS.

Well, to the work of children, went ye law's way?

KASSANDRA.

Having consented, Loxias I played false to.

CHOROS.

Already when the wits inspired possessed of?

KASSANDRA.

Already townsmen all their woes I foretold.

CHOROS.

How wast thou then unhurt by Loxias' anger ?

KASSANDRA.

I no one aught persuaded, when I sinned thus.

CHOROS.

To us, at least, now sooth to say thou seemest.

KASSANDRA.

Halloo, Halloo, ah, evils !
Again. straightforward foresight's fearful labor
Whirls me. distracting with prelusive last-lays !
Behold ye those there, in the household seated, —
Young ones, — of dreams approaching to the figures ?
Children, as if they died by their beloveds —
Hands they have filled with flesh, the meal domestic —
Entrails and vitals both. most piteous burthen,
Plain they are holding ! — which their father tasted !
For this, I say. plans punishment a certain
Lion ignoble, on the bed that wallows,
House-guard (ah, me !) to the returning master
— Mine, since to bear the slavish yoke behoves me !
The ships' commander. Ilion's desolator,
Knows not what things the tongue of the lewd she-dog
Speaking, outspreading, shiny-souled, in fashion

Of Até hid, will reach to, by ill fortune !
Such things she dares — the female, the male's slayer!
She is . . . how calling her the hateful bite-beast
May I hit the mark ?   Some amphisbaina — Skulla
Housing in rocks, of mariners the mischief,
Revelling Hades' mother, — curse, no truce with,.
Breathing at friends !   How piously she shouted,
The all-courageous, as at turn of battle !
She seems to joy at the back-bringing safety !
Of this, too, if I nought persuade, all 's one !   Why ?
What is to be will come !   And soon thou, present,
" True prophet all too much " wilt pitying style me !

CHOROS.

Thuestes' feast, indeed, on flesh of children,
I went with, and I shuddered.   Fear too holds me
Listing what 's true as life, nowise out-imaged !

KASSANDRA.

I say, thou Agamemnon's fate shalt look on !

CHOROS.

Speak good words, O unhappy !   Set mouth sleeping

KASSANDRA.

But Paian stands in no stead to the speech here.

CHOROS.

Nay, if the thing be near : but never be it !

KASSANDRA.

Thou, indeed, prayest : they to kill are busy !

CHOROS.

Of what man is it ministered, this sorrow ?

KASSANDRA.

There again, wide thou look'st of my foretellings.

CHOROS.

For, the fulfiller's scheme I have not gone with.

KASSANDRA.

And yet too well I know the speech Hellenic.

CHOROS.

For Puthian oracles, thy speech, and hard too !

KASSANDRA.

Papai : what fire this ! and it comes upon me !
Ototoi, Lukeion Apollon, ah me — me !
She, the two-footed lioness that sleeps with
The wolf, in absence of the generous lion,

Kills me the unhappy one : and as a poison
Brewing, to put my price too in the anger,
She vows, against her mate this weapon whetting
To pay him back the bringing me, with slaughter.
Why keep I then these things to make me laughed at,
Both wands and, round my neck, oracular fillets ?
Thee, at least, ere my own fate will I ruin :
Go, to perdition falling ! Boons exchange we —
Some other Até in my stead make wealthy !
See there — himself, Apollon stripping from me
The oracular garment ! having looked upon me
— Even in these adornments, laughed by friends at,
As good as foes, i' the balance weighed : and vainly —
For, called crazed stroller, — as I had been gipsy,
Beggar, unhappy, starved to death, — I bore it.
And now the Prophet — prophet me undoing,
Has led away to these so deadly fortunes !
Instead of my sire's altar, waits the hack-block
She struck with first warm bloody sacrificing !
Yet nowise unavenged of gods will death be :
For there shall come another, our avenger,
The mother-slaying scion, father's doomsman :
Fugitive, wanderer, from this land an exile,
Back shall he come, — for friends, copestone these
          curses !
For there is sworn a great oath from the gods that
Him shall bring hither his fallen sire's prostration.

Why make I then, like an indweller, moaning?
Since at the first I foresaw Ilion's city
Suffering as it has suffered: and who took it,
Thus by the judgment of the gods are faring.
I go, will suffer, will submit to dying!
But, Hades' gates — these same I call, I speak to,
And pray that on an opportune blow chancing,
Without a struggle, — blood the calm death bringing
In easy outflow, — I this eye may close up!

CHOROS.

O much unhappy, but, again, much learned ʼ
Woman, long hast thou outstretched! But if truly
Thou knowest thine own fate, how comes that, like to
A god-led steer, to altar bold thou treadest?

KASSANDRA.

There's no avoidance, — strangers, no! Some time
    more!
CHOROS.

He last is, anyhow, by time advantaged.

KASSANDRA.

It comes, the day: I shall by flight gain little.

CHOROS.

But know thou patient art from thy brave spirit!

KASSANDRA.

Such things hears no one of the happy-fortuned.

CHOROS.

But gloriously to die — for man is grace, sure !

KASSANDRA.

Ah, sire, for thee and for thy noble children !

CHOROS.

But what thing is it ? What fear turns thee back-
wards ?

KASSANDRA.

Alas, alas !

CHOROS.

Why this " Alas ? " if 't is no spirit's loathing. . . .

KASSANDRA.

Slaughter blood-dripping does the household smell of !

CHOROS.

How else ? This scent is of hearth-sacrifices.

KASSANDRA.

Such kind of steam as from a tomb is proper !

CHOROS.

No Surian honor to the House thou speak'st of !

KASSANDRA.

But I will go, — even in the household wailing
My fate and Agamemnon's.   Life suffice me !
Ah, strangers !
I cry not "ah" — as bird at bush — through terror
Idly ! to me, the dead, bear witness this much :
When, for me — woman, there shall die a woman,
And, for a man ill-wived, a man shall perish !
This hospitality I ask as dying.

CHOROS.

O sufferer, thee — thy foretold fate I pity.

KASSANDRA.

Yet once for all, to speak a speech, I fain am :
No dirge, mine for myself !   The sun I pray to,
Fronting his last light ! — to my own avengers —
That from my hateful slayers they exact too
Pay for the dead slave — easy-managed hand's work !

CHOROS.

Alas for mortal matters !   Happy-fortuned, —
Why, any shade would turn them : if unhappy,

6

By throws the wetting sponge has spoiled the picture !
And more by much in mortals this I pity.
The being well-to-do —
Insatiate a desire of this
Born with all mortals is,
Nor any is there who
Well-being forces off, aroints
From roofs whereat a finger points,
" No more come in !" exclaiming.   This man, too,
To take the city of Priamos did the celestials give,
And, honored by the god, he homeward comes ;
But now if, of the former, he shall pay
The blood back, and, for those who ceased to live,
Dying, for deaths in turn new punishment he dooms —
Who, being mortal, would not pray
With an unmischievous
Daimon to have been born — who would not, hearing
        thus ?

AGAMEMNON.

Ah me ! I am struck — a right-aimed stroke within me !

CHOROS.

Silence ! Who is it shouts "stroke " — " right-aimed-
ly " a wounded one ?

AGAMEMNON.

Ah me ! indeed again, — a second, struck by !

CHOROS.

This work seems to me completed by this "Ah me"
    of the king's ;
But we somehow may together share in solid counsel-
    ings.

CHOROS 1.

I, in the first place, my opinion tell you :
— To cite the townsmen, by help-cry, to house here.

CHOROS 2.

To me, it seems we ought to fall upon them
At quickest — prove the fact by sword fresh-flowing !

CHOROS 3.

And I, of such opinion the partaker,
Vote — to do something : not to wait — the main
    point !

CHOROS 4.

'T is plain to see : for they prelude as though of
A tyranny the signs they gave the city.

CHOROS 5.

For we waste time ; while they, — this waiting's glory
Treading to ground, — allow the hand no slumber.

CHOROS 6.

I know not — chancing on some plan — to tell
       it :
'T is for the doer to plan of the deed also.

CHOROS 7.

And I am such another: since I 'm schemeless
How to raise up again by words — a dead man !

CHOROS 8.

What, and, protracting life, shall we give way
       thus
To the disgracers of our home, these rulers ?

CHOROS 9.

Why, 't is unbearable : but to die is better :
For death than tyranny is the riper finish !

CHOROS 10.

What, by the testifying "Ah me" of him,
Shall we prognosticate the man as perished ?

CHOROS 11.

We must quite know ere speak these things concern-
       ing :
For to conjecture and " quite know " are two things.

CHOROS 12.

This same to praise I from all sides abound in —
Clearly to know — Atreides, what he 's doing !

KLUTAIMNESTRA.

Much having been before to purpose spoken,
The opposite to say I shall not shamed be :
For how should one, to enemies, — in semblance,
Friends, — enmity proposing, — sorrow's net-frame
Enclose, a height superior to outleaping?
To me, indeed, this struggle of old — not mindless
Of an old victory — came : with time, I grant you !
I stand where I have struck, things once accom-
      plished :
And so have done, — and this deny I shall not, —
As that his fate was nor to fly nor ward off.
A wrap-round with no outlet, as for fishes,
I fence about him — the rich woe of the garment :
I strike him twice, and in a double " Ah-me ! "
He let his limbs go — *there !* And to him, fallen,
The third blow add I, giving — of Below-ground
Zeus, guardian of the dead — the votive favor.
Thus in the mind of him he rages, falling,
And blowing forth a brisk blood-spatter, strikes me
With the dark drop of slaughterous dew — rejoicing
No less than, at the god-given dewy-comfort,

The sown-stuff in its birth-throes from the calyx.
Since so these things are, — Argives, my revered
    here, —
Ye may rejoice — if ye rejoice : but I — boast !
If it were fit on corpse to pour libation,
That would be right — right over and above, too !
The cup of evils in the house he, having
Filled with such curses, himself coming drinks of.

CHOROS.

We wonder at thy tongue : since bold-mouthed truly
Is she who in such speech boasts o'er her husband !

KLUTAIMNESTRA.

Ye test me as I were a witless woman :
But I — with heart intrepid — to you knowers
Say (and thou — if thou wilt or praise or blame me,
Comes to the same) — this man is Agamemnon,
My husband, dead, the work of the right hand here,
Ay, of a just artificer : so things are.

CHOROS.

What evil, O woman, food or drink, earth-bred
Or sent from the flowing sea,
Of such having fed
Didst thou set on thee
This sacrifice

And popular cries
Of a curse on thy head?
Off thou hast thrown him, off hast cut
The man from the city : but —
Off from the city thyself shalt be
Cut — to the citizens
A hate immense !

KLUTAIMNESTRA.

Now, indeed, thou adjudgest exile to me,
And citizens' hate, and to have popular curses :
Nothing of this against the man here bringing,
Who, no more awe-checked than as 't were a beast's
     fate, —
With sheep abundant in the well-fleeced graze-
     flocks, —
Sacrificed *his* child, — dearest fruit of travail
To me, — as song-spell against Threkian blowings.
Not *him* did it behove thee hence to banish
— Pollution's penalty?   But hearing *my* deeds
Justicer rough thou art !   Now, this I tell thee :
To threaten thus — me, one prepared to have thee
(On like conditions, thy hand conquering) o'er me
Rule : but if God the opposite ordain us,
Thou shalt learn — late taught, certes — to be mod-
     est.

Greatly-intending thou art :
Much-mindful, too, hast thou cried
(Since thy mind, with its slaughter-outpouring part,
Is frantic) that over the eyes, a patch
Of blood — with blood to match —
Is plain for a pride !
Yet still, bereft of friends, thy fate
Is — blow with blow to expiate !

And this thou hearest — of my oaths, just warrant !
By who fulfilled things for my daughter, Justice,
Até, Erinus, — by whose help I slew him, —
Not mine the fancy — Fear will tread my palace
So long as on my hearth there burns a fire,
Aigisthos as before well-caring for me ;
Since he to me is shield, no small, of boldness.
Here does he lie — outrager of this female,
Dainty of all the Chruseids under Ilion ;
And she — the captive, the soothsayer also
And couchmate of this man, oracle-speaker,
Faithful bed-fellow, — ay, the sailors' benches
They wore in common, nor unpunished did so,
Since he is — thus !   While, as for her, — swan-
      fashion,

Her latest having chanted, — dying wailing
She lies, — to him, a sweetheart : me she brought to
My bed's by-nicety, the whet of dalliance.

CHOROS.

Alas, that some
Fate would come
Upon us in quickness —
Neither much sickness
Neither bed-keeping —
And bear unended sleeping,
Now that subdued
Is our keeper, the kindest of mood !
Having borne, for a woman's sake, much **strife** —
By a woman he withered from life !
Ah me !
Law-breaking Helena who, one,
Hast many, so many souls undone
'Neath Troia ! and now the consummated
Much-memorable curse
Hast thou made flower-forth, red
With the blood no rains disperse,
That which was then in the House —
Strife all-subduing, the woe of a spouse.

KLUTAIMNESTRA.

Nowise, of death the fate —

Burdened by these things — supplicate !
Nor on Helena turn thy wrath
As the man-destroyer, as " she who hath,
Being but one,
Many and many a soul undone
Of the men, the Danaoi " —
And wrought immense annoy !

CHOROS.

Daimon, who fallest
Upon this household and the double-raced
Tantalidai, a rule, minded like theirs displaced,
Thou rulest me with, now,
Whose heart thou gallest !
And on the body, like a hateful crow,
Stationed, all out of tune, his chant to chant
Doth something vaunt !

KLUTAIMNESTRA.

Now, of a truth, hast thou set upright
Thy mouth's opinion, —
Naming the Sprite,
The triply-gross,
O'er the race that has dominion :
For through him it is that Eros
The carnage-licker
In the belly is bred : ere ended quite
Is the elder throe — new ichor !

CHOROS.

Certainly, great of might
And heavy of wrath, the Sprite
Thou tellest of, in the palace
(Woe, woe!)
— An evil tale of a fate
By Até's malice
Rendered insatiate!
Oh, oh, —
King, king, how shall I beweep thee?
From friendly soul what ever say?
Thou liest where webs of the spider o'ersweep thee;
In impious death, life breathing away.
O me — me!
This couch, not free!
By a slavish death subdued thou art,
From the hand, by the two-edged dart.

KLUTAIMNESTRA.

Thou boastest this deed to be mine:
But leave off styling me
" The Agamemnonian wife!"
For, showing himself in sign
Of the spouse of the corpse thou dost see,
Did the ancient bitter avenging-ghost
Of Atreus, savage host,

Pay the man here as price —
A full-grown for the young one's sacrifice.

CHOROS.

That no cause, indeed, of this killing art thou,
Who shall be witness-bearer?
How shall he bear it — how?
But the sire's avenging-ghost might be in the deed a
    sharer.
He is forced on and on
By the kin born flowing of blood,
—Black Ares: to where, having gone,
He shall leave off, flowing done,
At the frozen-child's-flesh food.
King, king, how shall I beweep thee!
From friendly soul what ever say?
Thou liest where webs of the spider o'ersweep thee,
In impious death, life breathing away.
Oh, me — me!
This couch not free!
By a slavish death subdued thou art,
From the hand, by the two-edged dart.

KLUTAIMNESTRA.

No death "unfit for the free"
Do I think this man's to be:
For did not himself a slavish curse

To his household decree ?
But the scion of him, myself did nurse —
That much-bewailed Iphigeneia, he
Having done well by, —and as well, nor worse,
Been done to, — let him not in Hades loudly
Bear himself proudly !
Being by sword-destroying death amerced
For that sword's punishment himself inflicted first.

CHOROS.

I at a loss am left —
Of a feasible scheme of mind bereft —
Where I may turn : for the house is falling :
I fear the bloody crash of the rain
That ruins the roof as it bursts amain :
The warning-drop
Has come to a stop.
Destiny doth Justice whet
For other deed of hurt, on other whetstones yet.
Woe, earth, earth — would thou hadst taken *me*
Ere I saw the man I see,
On the pallet-bed
Of the silver-sided bath-vase, dead !
Who is it shall bury him, who
Sing his dirge ?   Can it be true
That *thou* wilt dare this same to do —
Having slain thy husband, thine own,

To make his funeral moan :
And for the soul of him, in place
Of his mighty deeds, a graceless grace
To wickedly institute ?   By whom
Shall the tale of praise o'er the tomb
At the god-like man be sent —
From the truth of his mind as he toils intent?

KLUTAIMNESTRA.

It belongs not to thee to declare
This object of care !
By us did he fall — down there !
Did he die — down there ! and down, no less,
We will bury him there, and not beneath
The wails of the household over his death :
But Iphigeneia, — with kindliness, —
His daughter, — as the case requires,
Facing him full, at the rapid-flowing
Passage of Groans shall — both hands throwing
Around him — kiss that kindest of sires !

CHOROS.

This blame comes in the place of blame :
Hard battle it is to judge each claim.
" He is borne away who bears away :
And the killer has all to pay."
And this remains while Zeus is remaining,

"The doer shall suffer in time" — for, such his or-
    daining.
Who may cast out of the House its cursed brood?
The race is to Até glued !

KLUTAIMNESTRA.

Thou hast gone into this oracle
With a true result.   For me, then, — I will
— To the Daimon of the Pleisthenidai
Making an oath — with all these things comply
Hard as they are to bear.   For the rest —
Going from out this House, a guest,
May he wear some other family
To nought, with the deaths of kin by kin !
And, — keeping a little part of my goods, —
Wholly am I contented in
Having expelled from the royal House
These frenzied moods
The mutually-murderous.

AIGISTHOS.

O light propitious of day justice-bringing !
I may say truly, now, that men's avengers,
The gods from high, of earth behold the sorrows —
Seeing, as I have, i' the spun robes of the Erinues,
This man here lying, — sight to me how pleasant ! —
His father's hands' contrivances repaying.

For Atreus, this land's lord, of this man father,
Thuestes, my own father — to speak clearly —
His brother too, — being i' the rule contested, —
Drove forth to exile from both town and household :
And, coming back, to the hearth turned, a suppliant,
Wretched Thuestes found the fate assured him
— Not to die, bloodying his paternal threshold
Just there : but host-wise this man's impious father
Atreus, soul-keenly more than kindly, — seeming
To joyous hold a flesh-day, — to my father
Served up a meal, the flesh of his own children.
The feet indeed and the hands' top divisions
He hid, high up and isolated sitting :
But, their unshowing parts in ignorance taking,
He forthwith eats food — as thou seest — perdition
To the race : and then, 'ware of the deed ill-omened,
He shrieked O ! — falls back, vomiting, from the car-
　　　nage,
And fate on the Pelopidai past bearing
He prays down — putting in his curse together
The kicking down o' the feast — that so might perish
The race of Pleisthenes entire : and thence is
That it is given thee to see this man prostrate.
And I was rightly of this slaughter stitch-man :
Since me, — being third from ten, — with my poor
　　　father
He drives out — being then a babe in swathe-bands :

But, grown up, back again has justice brought me :
And of this man I got hold — being without-doors —
Fitting together the whole scheme of ill-will,
So, sweet, in fine, even to die were to me,
Seeing, as I have, this man i' the toils of justice !

CHOROS.

Aigisthos, arrogance in ills I love not.
Dost thou say — willing, thou didst kill the man
 here,
And, alone, plot this lamentable slaughter ?
I say — thy head in justice will escape not
The people's throwing — know that ! — stones and
 curses !

AIGISTHOS.

Thou such things soundest — seated at the lower
Oarage to those who rule at the ship's mid-bench ?
Thou shalt know, being old, how heavy is teaching
To one of the like age — bidden be modest !
But chains and old age and the pangs of fasting
Stand out before all else in teaching, — prophets
At souls'-cure ! Dost not, seeing aught, see this too ?
Against goads kick not, lest tript-up thou suffer !

CHOROS.

Woman, thou, — of him coming new from battle

7

Houseguard — thy husband's bed the while disgrac-
  ing, —
For the Army-leader didst thou plan this fate too?

AIGISTHOS.

These words too are of groans the prime-begetters !
Truly a tongue opposed to Orpheus hast thou :
For he led all things by his voice's grace-charm,
But thou, upstirring them by these wild yelpings,
Wilt lead them !   Forced, thou wilt appear the tamer!

CHOROS.

So — thou shalt be my king then of the Argeians —
Who, not when for this man his fate thou plannedst,
Daredst to do this deed — thyself the slayer !

AIGISTHOS.

For, to deceive him was the wife's part, certes :
I was looked after — foe, ay, old-begotten !
But out of this man's wealth will I endeavor
To rule the citizens : and the no-man-minder
— Him will I heavily yoke — by no means trace-horse,
A corned-up colt ! but that bad friend in darkness,
Famine its housemate, shall behold him gentle.

CHOROS.

Why then, this man here, from a coward spirit,

Didst not thou slay thyself? But, — helped, — a
  woman,
The country's pest, and that of gods o' the country,
Killed him! Orestes, where may he see light now?
That coming hither back, with gracious fortune,
Of both these he may be the all-conquering slayer?

AIGISTHOS.

But since this to do thou thinkest — and not talk —
  thou soon shalt know!
Up then, comrades dear! the proper thing to do —
  not distant this!

CHOROS.

Up then! hilt in hold, his sword let everyone aright
  dispose!

AIGISTHOS.

Ay, but I myself too, hilt in hold, do not refuse to die!

CHOROS.

Thou wilt die, thou say'st, to who accept it. We the
  chance demand!

KLUTAIMNESTRA.

Nowise, O belovedest of men, may we do other ills!
To have reaped away these, even, is a harvest much
  to me!

Go, both thou and these the old men, to the homes
    appointed each,
Ere ye suffer!   It behoved one do these things just
    as we did :
And if of these troubles, there should be enough —
    we may assent
— By the Daimon's heavy heel unfortunately stricken
    ones !
So a woman's counsel hath it — if one judge it learn-
    ing-worth.

AIGISTHOS.

But to think that these at me the idle tongue should
    thus o'er-bloom,
And throw out such words — the Daimon's power ex-
    perimenting on —
And, of modest knowledge missing, — me, the
    ruler, . . .

CHOROS.

Ne'er may this befall Argeians — wicked man to fawn
    before !

AIGISTHOS.

Anyhow, in after days, will I, yes, I, be at thee yet !

CHOROS.

Not if hither should the Daimon make Orestes
    straightway come !

AIGISTHOS.

O, I know, myself, that fugitives on hopes are pasture-fed !

CHOROS.

Do thy deed, get fat, defiling justice, since the power is thine !

AIGISTHOS.

Know that thou shalt give me satisfaction for this folly's sake !

CHOROS.

Boast on, bearing thee audacious, like a cock his females by !

KLUTAIMNESTRA.

Have not thou respect for these same idle yelpings ! I and thou
Will arrange it, ruling o'er this household excellently well.

LA SAISIAZ.

DEDICATED

TO

MRS. SUTHERLAND ORR.

1.

Good, to forgive ;
  Best, to forget !
  Living, we fret ;
Dying, we live.
Fretless and free,
  Soul, clap thy pinion !
  Earth have dominion,
Body, o'er thee !

2.

Wander at will,
  Day after day, —
  Wander away,
Wandering still —
Soul that canst soar !
  Body may slumber :
  Body shall cumber
Soul-flight no more.

3.

Waft of soul's wing !
  What lies above ?

Sunshine and Love,
Skyblue and Spring!
Body hides — where?
Ferns of all feather,
Mosses and heather,
Yours be the care!

LA SAISIAZ.

A. E. S. September 14, 1877.

Dared and done : at last I stand upon the summit,
    Dear and True !
Singly dared and done ; the climbing both of us were
    bound to do.
Petty feat and yet prodigious : every side my glance
    was bent
O'er the grandeur and the beauty lavished through
    the whole ascent.
Ledge by ledge, out broke new marvels, now minute
    and now immense :
Earth's most exquisite disclosure, heaven's own God
    in evidence !
And no berry in its hiding, no blue space in its out-
    spread,
Pleaded to escape my footstep, challenged my emerg-
    ing head,

(As I climbed or paused from climbing, now o'er-
    branched by shrub and tree,
Now built round by rock and boulder, now at just a
    turn set free,
Stationed face to face with — Nature? rather with
    Infinitude)
— No revealment of them all, as singly I my path
    pursued,
But a bitter touched its sweetness, for the thought
    stung " Even so
Both of us had loved and wondered just the same,
    five days ago ! "
Five short days, sufficient hardly to entice, from out its
    den
Splintered in the slab, this pink perfection of the
    cyclamen ;
Scarce enough to heal and coat with amber gum the
    sloe-tree's gash,
Bronze the clustered wilding apple, redden ripe the
    mountain-ash :
Yet of might to place between us — Oh the barrier !
    You Profound
Shrinks beside it, proves a pin-point : barrier this,
    without a bound !
Boundless though it be, I reach you : somehow seem
    to have you here
— Who are there. Yes, there you dwell now, plain
    the four low walls appear ;

Those are vineyards, they enclose from ; and the little
    spire which points
— That's Collonge, henceforth your dwelling! All
    the same, howe'er disjoints
Past from present, no less certain you are here, not
    there : have dared,
Done the feat of mountain-climbing, — five days since,
    we both prepared
Daring, doing, arm in arm, if other help should haply
    fail.
For you asked, as forth we sallied to see sunset from
    the vale,
"Why not try for once the mountain, — take a fore-
    taste, snatch by stealth
Sight and sound, some unconsidered fragment of the
    hoarded wealth ?
Six weeks at its base, yet never once have we together
    won
Sight or sound by honest climbing : let us two have
    dared and done
Just so much of twilight journey as may prove to-mor-
    row's jaunt
Not the only mode of wayfare — wheeled to reach the
    eagle's haunt ! "
So, we turned from the low grass-path you were pleased
    to call "your own,"
Set our faces to the rose-bloom o'er the summit's front
    of stone

Where Salève obtains, from Jura and the sunken sun
    she hides,
Due return of blushing " Good Night," rosy as a borne-
    off bride's,
For his masculine " Good Morrow " when, with sun-
    rise still in hold,
Gay he hails her, and, magnific, thrilled her black
    length burns to gold.
Up and up we went, how careless — nay, how joy
    ous! All was new,
All was strange. " Call progress toilsome ? that we re
    just insulting you !
How the trees must temper noontide ! Ah, the thick-
    et's sudden break !
What will be the morning glory, when at dusk thus
    gleams the lake ?
Light by light puts forth Geneva : what a land — and,
    of the land,
Can there be a lovelier station than this spot where
    now we stand ?
Is it late, and wrong to linger? True, to-morrow
    makes amends.
Toilsome progress? child's play, call it — specially
    when one descends !
There, the dread descent is over — hardly our adven-
    ture, though !
Take the vale where late we left it, pace the grass-
    path, 'mine,' you know !

Proud completion of achievement ! " And we paced
    it, praising still
That soft tread on velvet verdure as it wound through
    hill and hill ;
And at very end there met us, coming from Collonge,
    the pair
— All our people of the Chalet — two, enough and
    none to spare.
So, we made for home together, and we reached it as
    the stars
One by one came lamping — chiefly that prepotency
    of Mars —
And your last word was " I owe you this enjoyment ! "
    — met with " Nay :
With yourself it rests to have a month of morrows
    like to-day ! "
Then the meal, with talk and laughter, and the news
    of that rare nook
Yet untroubled by the tourist, touched on by no travel-
    book,
All the same — though latent — patent, hybrid birth
    of land and sea,
And (our travelled friend assured you) — if such mir-
    acle might be —
Comparable for completeness of both blessings — all
    around
Nature, and, inside her circle, safety from world's sight
    and sound —

Comparable to our Saisiaz. "Hold it fast and guard
it well!
Go and see and vouch for certain, then come back
and never tell
Living soul but us; and haply, prove our sky from
cloud as clear,
There may we four meet, praise fortune just as now,
another year!"
Thus you charged him on departure : not without the
final charge
"Mind to-morrow's early meeting! We must leave
our journey marge
Ample for the wayside wonders : there's the stoppage
at the inn
Three-parts up the mountain, where the hardships of
the track begin ;
There's the convent worth a visit; but, the triumph
crowning all —
There's Salève's own platform facing glory which
strikes greatness small,
— Blanc, supreme above his earth-brood, needles red
and white and green,
Horns of silver, fangs of crystal set on edge in his
demense.
So, some three weeks since, we saw them : so, to-
morrow we intend
You shall see them likewise ; therefore Good Night
till to-morrow, friend!"

Last, the nothings that extinguish embers of a vivid
    day:
"What might be the Marshal's next move, what Gam-
    betta's counter-play,"
Till the landing on the staircase saw escape the latest
    spark :
"Sleep you well!" "Sleep but as well, you!" —
    lazy love quenched, all was dark.

Nothing dark next day at sundawn! Up I rose and
    forth I fared :
Took my plunge within the bath-pool, pacified the
    watch-dog scared,
Saw proceed the transmutation — Jura's black to one
    gold glow,
Trod your level path that let me drink the morning
    deep and slow,
Reached the little quarry — ravage recompensed by
    shrub and fern —
Till the overflowing ardors told me time was for
    return.
So, return I did, and gayly. But, for once, from no far
    mound
Waved salute a tall white figure. "Has her sleep
    been so profound ?
Foresight, rather, prudent saving strength for day's
    expenditure !

8

Ay, the chamber-window's open : out and on the terrace, sure ! "
No, the terrace showed no figure, tall, white, leaning
 through the wreaths,
Tangle-twine of leaf and bloom that intercept the air
 one breathes,
Interpose between one's love and Nature's loving, hill
 and dale
Down to where the blue lake's wrinkle marks the
 river's inrush pale
— Mazy Arve : whereon no vessel but goes sliding
 white and plain,
Not a steam-boat pants from harbor but one hears
 pulsate amain,
Past the city's congregated peace of homes and pomp
 of spires
— Man's mild protest that there's something more
 than Nature, man requires,
And that, useful as is Nature to attract the tourist's
 foot,
Quiet slow sure money-making proves the matter's
 very root, —
Need for body, — while the spirit also needs a com-
 fort reached
By no help of lake or mountain, but the texts whence
 Calvin preached.

" Here 's the veil withdrawn from landscape : up to
Jura and beyond,

All awaits us ranged and ready ; yet she violates the
bond,

Neither leans nor looks nor listens : why is this ? "
A turn of eye

Took the whole sole answer, gave the undisputed reason " why ! "

This dread way you had your summons ! No pre-
monitory touch,

As you talked and laughed ('t is told me) scarce a
minute ere the clutch

Captured you in cold forever. Cold ? nay, warm you
were as life

When I raised you, while the others used, in passionate poor strife,

All the means that seemed to promise any aid, and all
in vain.

Gone you were, and I shall never see that earnest
face again

Grow transparent, grow transfigured with the sudden
light that leapt,

At the first word's provocation, from the heart-deeps
where it slept.

Therefore, paying piteous duty, what seemed you have
we consigned

Peacefully to — what I think were, of all earth-beds,
to your mind

Most the choice for quiet, yonder : low walls stop the
    vines' approach,
Lovingly Salève protects you ; village-sports will ne'er
    encroach
On the stranger lady's silence, whom friends bore so
    kind and well
Thither "just for love's sake,"—such their own word
    was: and who can tell?
You supposed that few or none had known and loved
    you in the world :
May be ! flower that 's full-blown tempts the butterfly,
    not flower that 's furled.
But more learned sense unlocked you, loosed the
    sheath and let expand
Bud to bell and outspread flower-shape at the least
    warm touch of hand
— May be, throb of heart, beneath which,— quicken-
    ing farther than it knew,—
Treasure oft was disembosomed, scent all strange and
    unguessed hue.
Disembosomed, reëmbosomed,—must one memory
    suffice,
Prove I knew an Alpine-rose which all beside named
    Edelweiss?

Rare thing, red or white, you rest now: two days
    slumbered through ; and since

One day more will see me rid of this same scene
    whereat I wince,
Tetchy at all sights and sounds and pettish at each
    idle charm
Proffered me who pace now singly where we two went
    arm in arm, —
I have turned upon my weakness : asked "And what,
    forsooth, prevents
That, this latest day allowed me, I fulfil of her intents
One she had the most at heart — that we should thus
    again survey
From Salève Mont Blanc together?"   Therefore, —
    dared and done to-day
Climbing, — here I stand : but you — where ?

                                    If a spirit of the place
Broke the silence, bade me question, promised an-
    swer, — what disgrace
Did I stipulate "Provided answer suit my hopes, not
    fears !"
Would I shrink to learn my life-time's limit — days,
    weeks, months or years ?
Would I shirk assurance on each point whereat I can
    but guess —
"Does the soul survive the body ?   Is there God's
    self, no or yes ?"

If I know my mood, 't were constant — come in what-
so'er uncouth
Shape it should, nay, formidable — so the answer were
but truth.

Well, and wherefore shall it daunt me, when 't is I
myself am tasked,
When, by weakness weakness questioned, weakly
answers — weakly asked ?
Weakness never needs be falseness : truth is truth in
each degree
— Thunderpealed by God to Nature, whispered by
my soul to me.
Nay, the weakness turns to strength and triumphs in
a truth beyond :
"Mine is but man's truest answer — how were it did
God respond ? "
I shall no more dare to mimic such response in futile
speech,
Pass off human lisp as echo of the sphere-song out of
reach,
Than, — because it well may happen yonder, where
the far snows blanch
Mute Mont Blanc, that who stands near them sees
and hears an avalanche, —
I shall pick a clod and throw, — cry " Such the sight
and such the sound !

What though I nor see nor hear them? Others do,
    the proofs abound!"
Can I make my eye an eagle's, sharpen ear to recog-
    nize
Sound o'er league and league of silence? Can I
    know, who but surmise?
If I dared no self-deception when, a week since, I and
    you
Walked and talked along the grass-path, passing light-
    ly in review
What seemed hits and what seemed misses in a cer-
    tain fence-play, — strife
Sundry minds of mark engaged in "On the Soul and
    Future Life," —
If I ventured estimating what was come of parried
    thrust,
Subtle stroke, and, rightly, wrongly, estimating could
    be just
— Just, though life so seemed abundant in the form
    which moved by mine,
I might well have played at feigning, fooling, —
    laughed "What need opine
Pleasure must succeed to pleasure else past pleasure
    turns to pain,
And this first life claims a second, else I count its
    good no gain?" —
Much less have I heart to palter when the matter to
    decide

Now becomes "Was ending ending once and always,
    when you died?"
Did the face, the form I lifted as it lay, reveal the
    loss
Not alone of life but soul? A tribute to yon flowers
    and moss,
What of you remains beside? A memory! Easy to
    attest
"Certainly from out the world that one believes who
    knew her best
Such was good in her, such fair, which fair and good
    were great perchance
Had but fortune favored, bidden each shy faculty
    advance;
After all — who knows another? Only as I know, I
    speak."
So much of you lives within me while I live my year
    or week.
Then my fellow takes the tale up, not unwilling to
    aver
Duly in his turn "I knew him best of all, as he knew
    her:
Such he was, and such he was not, and such other
    might have been
But that somehow every actor, somewhere in this
    earthly scene,
Fails." And so both memories dwindle, yours and
    mine together linked,

Till there is but left for comfort, when the last spark
 proves extinct,
This — that somewhere new existence led by men and
 women new
Possibly attains perfection coveted by me and you ;
While ourselves, the only witness to what work our
 life evolved,
Only to ourselves proposing problems proper to be
 solved
By ourselves alone, — who working ne'er shall know
 if work bear fruit
Others reap and garner, heedless how produced by
 stalk and root, —
We who, darkling, timed the day's birth, — struggling,
 testified to peace, —
Earned, by dint of failure, triumph, — we, creative
 thought, must cease
In created word, thought's echo, due to impulse long
 since sped !
Why repine ? There's ever some one lives although
 ourselves be dead !
Well, what signifies repugnance ? Truth is truth how-
 e'er it strike.
Fair or foul the lot apportioned life on earth, we bear
 alike.
Stalwart body idly yoked to stunted spirit, powers,
 that fain

Else would soar, condemned to grovel, groundlings
    through the fleshly chain, —
Help that hinders, hindrance proved but help dis-
    guised when all too late, —
Hindrance is the fact acknowledged, howso'er ex-
    plained as Fate,
Fortune, Providence : we bear, own life a burthen
    more or less.
Life thus owned unhappy, is there supplemental hap-
    piness
Possible and probable in life to come ? or must we
    count
Life a curse and not a blessing, summed-up in its
    whole amount,
Help and hindrance, joy and sorrow ?
                    Why should I want courage here ?
I will ask and have an answer, — with no favor, with
    no fear, —
From myself. How much, how little, do I inwardly
    believe
True that controverted doctrine ? Is it fact to which
    I cleave,
Is it fancy I but cherish, when I take upon my lips
Phrase the solemn Tuscan fashioned, and declare the
    soul's eclipse
Not the soul's extinction ? take his " I believe and I
    declare —

Certain am I — from this life I pass into a better,
    there
Where that lady lives of whom enamored was my
    soul " — where this
Other lady, my companion ˙dear and true, she also is ?

I have questioned and am answered. Question, an-
    swer presuppose
Two points : that the thing itself which questions, an-
    swers, — is, it knows ;
As it also knows the thing perceived outside itself, —
    a force
Actual ere its own beginning, operative through its
    course,
Unaffected by its end, — that this thing likewise
    needs must be ;
Call this — God, then, call that — soul, and both —
    the only facts for me.
Prove them facts ? that they o'erpass my power of
    proving, proves them such :
Fact it is I know I know not something which is fact
    as much.
What before caused all the causes, what effect of all
    effects
Haply follows, — these are fancy. Ask the rush if it
    suspects
Whence and how the stream which floats it had a rise,
    and where and how

Falls or flows on still ! What answer makes the rush
    except that now
Certainly it floats and is, and, no less certain than
    itself,
Is the everyway external stream that now through
    shoal and shelf
Floats it onward, leaves it — may be — wrecked at
    last, or lands on shore
There to root again and grow and flourish stable
    evermore.
— May be ! mere surmise not knowledge : much con-
    jecture styled belief,
What the rush conceives the stream means through
    the voyage blind and brief.
Why, because I doubtless am, shall I as doubtless be?
    " Because
God seems good and wise." Yet under this our life's
    apparent laws
Reigns a wrong which, righted once, would give quite
    other laws to life.
" He seems potent." Potent here, then : why are
    right and wrong at strife ?
Has in life the wrong the better? Happily life ends
    so soon !
Right predominates in life ? Then why two lives and
    double boon ?
" Anyhow, we want it : wherefore want ? " Because,
    without the want,

Life, now human, would be brutish : just that hope,
    however scant,
Makes the actual life worth leading ; take the hope
    therein away,
All we have to do is surely not endure another day.
This life has its hopes for this life, hopes that promise
    joy : life done —
Out of all the hopes, how many had complete fulfil-
    ment ? none.
" But the soul is not the body : " and the breath is
    not the flute ;
Both together make the music : either marred and all
    is mute.
Truce to such old sad contention whence, according
    as we shape
Most of hope or most of fear, we issue in a half-
    escape :
" We believe " is sighed. I take the cup of comfort
    proffered thus,
Taste and try each soft ingredient, sweet infusion, and
    discuss
What their blending may accomplish for the cure of
    doubt, till — slow,
Sorrowful, but how decided ! needs must I o'erturn it
    — so !
Cause before, effect behind me — blanks ! The mid-
    way point I am,

Caused, itself — itself efficient: in that narrow space
    must cram
All experience — out of which there crowds conjecture
    manifold,
But, as knowledge, this comes only — things may be
    as I behold,
Or may not be, but, without me and above me, things
    there are ;
I myself am what I know not — ignorance which
    proves no bar
To the knowledge that I am, and, since I am, can
    recognize
What to me is pain and pleasure : this is sure, the rest
    — surmise.
If my fellows are or are not, what may please them
    and what pain, —
Mere surmise : my own experience — that is knowl-
    edge, once again !

I have lived, then, done and suffered, loved and
    hated, learnt and taught
This — there is no reconciling wisdom with a world
    distraught,
Goodness with triumphant evil, power with failure in
    the aim,
If — (to my own sense, remember ! though none other
    feel the same !) —

If you bar me from assuming earth to be a pupil's
place,
And life, time, — with all their chances, changes, —
just probation-space,
Mine, for me.   But those apparent other mortals —
theirs, for them?
Knowledge stands on my experience: all outside its
narrow hem,
Free surmise may sport and welcome!   Pleasures,
pains affect mankind
Just as they affect myself?   Why, here's my neighbor
color-blind,
Eyes like mine to all appearance: "green as grass"
do I affirm?
"Red as grass" he contradicts me — which employs
the proper term?
Were we two the earth's sole tenants, with no third
for referee,
How should I distinguish?   Just so, God must judge
'twixt man and me.
To each mortal peradventure earth becomes a new
machine,
Pain and pleasure no more tally in our sense than red
and green;
Still, without what seems such mortal's pleasure, pain,
my life were lost
— Life, my whole sole chance to prove — although at
man's apparent cost —

What is beauteous and what ugly, right to strive for,
    right to shun,
Fit to help and fit to hinder, — prove my forces every-
    one,
Good and evil, — learn life's lesson, hate of evil, love
    of good,
As 't is set me, understand so much as may be under-
    stood —
Solve the problem : " From thine apprehended scheme
    of things, deduce
Praise or blame of its contriver, shown a niggard or
    profuse
In each good or evil issue! nor miscalculate alike
Counting one the other in the final balance, which to
    strike,
Soul was born and life allotted : ay, the show of things
    unfurled
For thy summing-up and judgment, — thine, no other
    mortal's world ! "
What though fancy scarce may grapple with the com-
    plex and immense
— "His own world for every mortal ? " Postulate
    omnipotence !
Limit power, and simple grows the complex : shrunk
    to atom size,
That which loomed immense to fancy low before my
    reason lies, —

I survey it and pronounce it work like other work :
    success

Here and there, the workman's glory, — here and
    there, his shame no less,

Failure as conspicuous. Taunt not "Human work
    ape work divine ? "

As the power, expect performance ! God's be God's
    as mine is mine !

God whose power made man and made man's wants,
    and made, to meet those wants,

Heaven and earth which, through the body, prove the
    spirit's ministrants,

Excellently all, — did he lack power or was the will
    in fault

When he let blue heaven be shrouded o'er by vapors
    of the vault,

Gay earth drop her garlands shrivelled at the first in-
    fecting breath

Of the serpent pains which herald, swarming in, the
    dragon death ?

What, no way but this that man may learn and lay to
    heart how rife

Life were with delights would only death allow their
    taste to life ?

Must the rose sigh " Pluck — I perish !" must the
    eve weep "Gaze — I fade ! "

9

— Every sweet warn "'Ware my bitter!" every shine
    bid "Wait my shade?"

Can we love but on condition, that the thing we love
    must die?

Needs there groan a world in anguish just to teach us
    sympathy —

Multitudinously wretched that we, wretched too, may
    guess

What a preferable state were universal happiness?

Hardly do I so conceive the outcome of that power
    which went

To the making of the worm there in yon clod its ten-
    ement,

Any more than I distinguish aught of that which, wise
    and good,

Framed the leaf, its plain of pasture, dropped the
    dew, its fineless food.

Nay, were fancy fact, were earth and all it holds illu-
    sion mere,

Only a machine for teaching love and hate and hope
    and fear

To myself, the sole existence, single truth mid false-
    hood, — well!

If the harsh throes of the prelude die not off into the
    swell

Of that perfect piece they sting me to become a-strain
    for, — if

Roughness of the long rock-clamber lead not to the
 last of cliff,

First of level country where is sward my pilgrim-foot
 can prize, —

Plainlier! if this life's conception new life fail to real-
 ize, —

Though earth burst and proved a bubble glassing hues
 of hell, one huge

Reflex of the devil's doings — God's work by no subterfuge —

(So death's kindly touch informed me as it broke the
 glamour, gave

Soul and body both release from life's long nightmare
 in the grave)

Still, — with no more Nature, no more Man as riddle
 to be read,

Only my own joys and sorrows now to reckon real
 instead, —

I must say — or choke in silence — " Howsoever came
 my fate,

Sorrow did and joy did nowise, — life well weighed, —
 preponderate."

By necessity ordained thus? I shall bear as best I
 can ;

By a cause all-good, all-wise, all-potent? No, as I
 am man !

Such were God : and was it goodness that the good
 within my range

Or had evil in admixture or grew evil's self by
    change ?
Wisdom — that becoming wise meant making slow
    and sure advance
From a knowledge proved in error to acknowledged
    ignorance ?
Power? 't is just the main assumption reason most
    revolts at ! power
Unavailing for bestowment on its creature of an hour,
Man, of so much proper action rightly aimed and
    reaching aim,
So much passion, — no defect there, no excess, but
    still the same, —
As what constitutes existence, pure perfection bright
    as brief
For yon worm, man's fellow-creature, on yon happier
    world — its leaf !
No, as I am man, I mourn the poverty I must
    impute :
Goodness, wisdom, power, all bounded, each a
    human attribute !

But, O world outspread beneath me ! only for myself
    I speak,
Nowise dare to play the spokesman for my brothers
    strong and weak,
Full and empty, wise and foolish, good and bad, in
    every age,

Every clime, I turn my eyes from, as in one or other
    stage
Of a torture writhe they, Job-like couched on dung
    and crazed with blains
— Wherefore? whereto? ask the whirlwind what the
    dread voice thence explains !
I shall "vindicate no way of God's to man," nor stand
    apart,
"Laugh, be candid," while I watch it traversing the
    human heart !
Traversed heart must tell its story uncommented on :
    no less
Mine results in "Only grant a second life, I acqui-
    esce
In this present life as failure, count misfortune's
    worst assaults
Triumph, not defeat, assured that loss so much the
    more exalts
Gain about to be. For at what moment did I so
    advance
Near to knowledge as when frustrate of escape from
    ignorance ?
Did not beauty prove most precious when its oppo-
    site obtained
Rule, and truth seem more than ever potent because
    falsehood reigned ?
While for love — Oh how but, losing love, does whoso
    loves succeed

By the death-pang to the birth-throe — learning what
    is love indeed ?
Only grant my soul may carry high through death her
    cup unspilled,
Brimming though it be with knowledge, life's loss
    drop by drop distilled,
I shall boast it mine — the balsam, bless each kindly
    wrench that wrung
From life's tree its inmost virtue, tapped the root
    whence pleasure sprung,
Barked the bole, and broke the bough, and bruised
    the berry, left all grace
Ashes in death's stern alembic, loosed elixir in its
    place !

Witness, Dear and True, how little I was 'ware of —
    not your worth
— That I knew, my heart assures me — but of what a
    shade on earth
Would the passage from my presence of the tall white
    figure throw
O'er the ways we walked together!   Somewhat nar-
    row, somewhat slow,
Used to seem the ways, the walking : narrow ways are
    well to tread
When there's moss beneath the footstep, honeysuckle
    overhead :

Walking slow to beating bosom surest solace soonest
 gives,

Liberates the brain o'er-loaded — best of all restora-
 tives.

Nay, do I forget the open vast where soon or late con-
 verged

Ways though winding? — world-wide heaven-high sea
 where music slept or surged

As the angel had ascendant, and Beethoven's Titan
 mace

Smote the immense to storm, Mozart would by a finger's lifting chase?

Yes, I knew — but not with knowledge such as thrills
 me while I view

Yonder precinct which henceforward holds and hides
 the Dear and True.

Grant me (once again) assurance we shall each meet
 each some day,

Walk — but with how bold a footstep ! on a way —
 but what a way !

— Worst were best, defeat were triumph, utter loss
 were utmost gain.

Can it be, and must, and will it?

      Silence ! Out of fact's domain,

Just surmise prepared to mutter hope, and also fear —
 dispute

Fact's inexorable ruling "Outside fact, surmise be
 mute ! "

Well !

> Ay, well and best, if fact's self I may force
> the answer from !

'T is surmise I stop the mouth of ! Not above in
yonder dome

All a rapture with its rose-glow, — not around, where
pile and peak

Strainingly await the sun's fall, — not beneath, where
crickets creak,

Birds assemble for their bed-time, soft the tree-top
swell subsides, —

No, nor yet within my deepest sentient self the knowledge hides !

Aspiration, reminiscence, plausibilities of trust

— Now the ready " Man were wronged else," now the
rash " and God unjust " —

None of these I need ! Take thou, my soul, thy solitary stand,

Umpire to the champions Fancy, Reason, as on either
hand

Amicable war they wage and play the foe in thy be-
hoof !

Fancy thrust and Reason parry ! Thine the prize
who stand aloof !

FANCY.

I concede the thing refused : henceforth no certainty
more plain

Than this mere surmise that after body dies soul lives
   again.

Two, the only facts acknowledged late, are now increased to three —

God is, and the soul is, and, as certain, after death
   shall be.

Put this third to use in life, the time for using fact !

REASON.

I do

Find it promises advantage, coupled with the other
   two.

Life to come will be improvement on the life that 's
   now ; destroy

Body's thwartings, there 's no longer screen betwixt
   soul and soul's joy.

Why should we expect new hindrance, novel tether ?
   In this first

Life, I see the good of evil, why our world began at
   worst :

Since time means amelioration, tardily enough displayed,

Yet a mainly onward moving, never wholly retro-
   grade.

We know more though we know little, we grow
   stronger though still weak,

Partly see though all too purblind, stammer though
   we cannot speak.

There is no such grudge in God as scared the ancient
    Greek, no fresh
. Substitute of trap for dragnet, once a breakage in the
    mesh.
Dragons were, and serpents are, and blindworms will
    be : ne'er emerged
Any new-created Python for man's plague since earth
    was purged.
Failing proof, then, of invented trouble to replace the
    old,
O'er this life the next presents advantage much and
    manifold :
Which advantage — in the absence of a fourth and
    farther fact
Now conceivably surmised, of harm to follow from the
    act —
I pronounce for man's obtaining at this moment.
    Why delay ?
Is he happy? happiness will change : anticipate the
    day !
Is he sad? there 's ready refuge : of all sadness
    death's prompt cure !
Is he both, in mingled measure ? cease a burthen to
    endure !
Pains with sorry compensations, pleasures stinted in
    the dole,
Power that sinks and pettiness that soars, all halved
    and nothing whole,

Idle hopes that lure man onward, forced back by as
    idle fears —

What a load he stumbles under through his glad sad
    seventy years,

When a touch sets right the turmoil, lifts his spirit
    where, flesh-freed,

Knowledge shall be rightly named so, all that seems
    be truth indeed !

Grant his forces no accession, nay, no faculty's in-
    crease,

Only let what now exists continue, let him prove in
    peace

Power whereof the interrupted unperfected play en-
    ticed

Man through darkness, which to lighten any spark of
    hope sufficed, —

What shall then deter his dying out of darkness into
    light ?

Death itself perchance, brief pain that 's pang, con-
    densed and infinite ?

But at worst, he needs must brave it one day, while,
    at best he laughs —

Drops a drop within his chalice, sleep not death his
    science quaffs !

Any moment claims more courage when, by crossing
    cold and gloom,

Manfully man quits discomfort, makes for the pro-
    vided room

Where the old friends want their fellow, where the
   new acquaintance wait,
Probably for talk assembled, possibly to sup in state!
I affirm and reaffirm it therefore : only make as plain
As that man now lives, that after dying man will live
   again, —
Make as plain the absence, also, of a law to contra-
   vene
Voluntary passage from this life to that by change of
   scene, —
And I bid him — at suspicion of first cloud athwart
   his sky,
Flower's departure, frost's arrival — never hesitate,
   but die!

FANCY.

Then I double my concession : grant, along with new
   life sure,
This same law found lacking now : ordain that,
   whether rich or poor
Present life is judged in aught man counts advantage
   — be it hope,
Be it fear that brightens, blackens most or least his
   horoscope, —
He, by absolute compulsion such as made him live
   at all,
Go on living to the fated end of life whate'er befall.

What though, as on earth he darkling grovels, man
    descry the sphere,
Next life's — call it, heaven of freedom, close above
    and crystal-clear?
He shall find — say, hell to punish who in aught cur-
    tails the term,
Fain would act the butterfly before he has played out
    the worm!
God, soul, earth, heaven, hell, — five facts now: what
    is to desiderate?

REASON.

Nothing!. Henceforth man's existence bows to the
    monition "Wait!
Take the joys and bear the sorrows — neither with
    extreme concern!
Living here means nescience simply: 't is next life
    that helps to learn.
Shut those eyes, next life will open, — stop those ears,
    next life will teach
Hearing's office, — close those lips, next life will give
    the power of speech!
Or, if action more amuse thee than the passive atti-
    tude,
Bravely bustle through thy being, busy thee for ill or
    good,

Reap this life's success or failure! Soon shall things
    be unperplexed
And the right and wrong, now tangled, lie unravelled
    in the next."

FANCY.

Not so fast! Still more concession! not alone do I
    declare
Life must needs be borne, — I also will that man be-
    come aware
Life has worth incalculable, every moment that he
    spends
So much gain or loss for that next life which on this
    life depends.
Good, done here, be there rewarded, — evil, worked
    here, there amerced!
Six facts now, and all established, plain to man the
    last as first.

REASON.

There was good and evil, then, defined to man by this
    decree?
Was — for at its promulgation both alike have ceased
    to be.
Prior to this last announcement "Certainly as God
    exists,
As he made man's soul, as soul is quenchless by the
    deathly mists,

Yet is, all the same, forbidden premature escape from
    time
To eternity's provided purer air and brighter clime, —
Just so certainly depends it on the use to which man
    turns
Earth, the good or evil done there, whether after death
    he earns
Life eternal, — heaven, the phrase be, or eternal death,
    — say, hell.
As his deeds, so proves his portion, doing ill or doing
    well ! "
— Prior to this last announcement, earth was man's
    probation-place :
Liberty of doing evil gave his doing good a grace ;
Once lay down the law, with Nature's simple " Such
    effects succeed
Causes such, and heaven or hell depends upon man's
    earthly deed
Just as surely as depends the straight or else the
    crooked line
On his making point meet point or with or else with-
    out incline," —
Thenceforth neither good nor evil does man, doing
    what he must.
Lay but down that law as stringent " Would'st thou
    live again, be just ! "
As this other " Would'st thou live now, regularly draw
    thy breath !

For, suspend the operation, straight law's breach re-
    sults in death " —
And (provided always, man, addressed this mode, be
    sound and sane)
Prompt and absolute obedience, never doubt, will law
    obtain !
Tell not me " Look round us ! nothing each side but
    acknowledged law,
Now styled God's — now, Nature's edict ! "   Where 's
    obedience without flaw
Paid to either?   What 's the adage rife in man's
    mouth ?   Why, " The best
I both see and praise, the worst I follow " — which,
    despite professed
Seeing, praising, all the same he follows, since he dis-
    believes
In the heart of him that edict which for truth his head
    receives.
There 's evading and persuading and much making
    law amends
Somehow, there 's the nice distinction 'twixt fast foes
    and faulty friends,
— Any consequence except inevitable death when
    " Die,
Whoso breaks our law ! " they publish, God and Nat-
    ure equally.
Law that 's kept or broken — subject to man's will
    and pleasure !   Whence ?

How comes law to bear eluding? Not because of im-
    potence :
Certain laws exist already which to hear means to
    obey ;
Therefore not without a purpose these man must,
    while those man may
Keep and, for the keeping, haply gain approval and
    reward.
Break through this last superstructure, all is empty air
    — no sward
Firm like my first fact to stand on " God there is, and
    soul there is,"
And soul's earthly life-allotment : wherein, by hypoth-
    esis,
Soul is bound to pass probation, prove its powers, and
    exercise
Sense and thought on fact, and then, from fact educ-
    ing fit surmise,
Ask itself, and of itself have solely answer, " Does
    the scope
Earth affords of fact to judge by warrant future fear
    or hope ?"

Thus have we come back full circle : fancy's footsteps
    one by one
Go their round conducting reason to the point where
    they begun,

Left where we were left so lately, Dear and True!
　　When, half a week
Since, we walked and talked and thus I told you, how
　　suffused a cheek
You had turned me had I sudden brought the blush
　　into the smile
By some word like "Idly argued! you know better all
　　the while!"
Now, from me — Oh not a blush but, how much more,
　　a joyous glow,
Laugh triumphant, would it strike did your "Yes, bet-
　　ter I do know"
Break, my warrant for assurance! which assurance
　　may not be
If, supplanting hope, assurance needs must change
　　this life to me.
So, I hope — no more than hope, but hope — no less
　　than hope, because
I can fathom, by no plumb-line sunk in life's apparent
　　laws,
How I may in any instance fix where change should
　　meetly fall
Nor involve, by one revisal, abrogation of them all
— Which again involves as utter change in life thus
　　law-released,
Whence the good of goodness vanished when the ill
　　of evil ceased.

Whereas, life and laws apparent re-instated, — all we
    know,
All we know not, — o'er our heaven again cloud
    closes, until, lo —
Hope the arrowy, just as constant, comes to pierce its
    gloom, compelled
By a power and by a purpose which, if no one else
    beheld,
I behold in life, so — hope !

                Sad summing-up of all to say!
Athanasius contra mundum, why should he hope more
    than they ?
So are men made notwithstanding, such magnetic vir-
    tue darts
From each head their fancy haloes to their unresist-
    ing hearts !

Here I stand, methinks a stone's throw from yon vil-
    lage I this morn
Traversed for the sake of looking one last look at its
    forlorn
Tenement's ignoble fortune : through a crevice, plain
    its floor
Piled with provender for cattle, while a dung-heap
    blocked the door.
In that squalid Bossex, under that obscene red roof,
    arose,

Like a fiery flying serpent from its egg, a soul —
    Rousseau's.
Turn thence!   Is it Diodati joins the glimmer of the
    lake?
There I plucked a leaf, one week since, — ivy, plucked
    for Byron's sake.
Famed unfortunates!   And yet, because of that phos-
    phoric fame
Swathing blackness' self with brightness till putridity
    looked flame,
All the world was witched: and wherefore? what
    could lie beneath, allure
Heart of man to let corruption serve man's head as
    cynosure?
Was the magic in the dictum "All that's good is gone
    and past ;
Bad and worse still grows the present, and the worst
    of all comes last :
Which believe — for I believe it?"   So preached one
    his gospel-news ;
While melodious moaned the other " Dying day with
    dolphin-hues !
Storm, for loveliness and darkness like a woman's eye !
    Ye mounts
Where I climb to 'scape my fellow, and thou sea
    wherein he counts
Not one inch of vile dominion ! What were your
    especial worth

Failed ye to enforce the maxim 'Of all objects found
    on earth
Man is meanest, much too honored when compared
    with — what by odds
Beats him — any dog : so, let him go a-howling to his
    gods !'
Which believe — for I believe it !" such the comfort
    man received
Sadly since perforce he must : for why? the famous
    bard believed !

Fame ! Then, give me fame, a moment ! As I gather
    at a glance
Human glory after glory vivifying yon expanse,
Let me grasp them altogether, hold on high and
    brandish well
Beacon-like above the rapt world ready, whether
    heaven or hell
Send the dazzling summons downward, to submit itself
    the same,
Take on trust the hope or else despair flashed full on
    face by — Fame !
Thanks, thou pine-tree of Makistos, wide thy giant
    torch I wave !
Know ye whence I plucked the pillar, late with sky
    for architrave ?
This the trunk, the central solid Knowledge, kindled
    core, began

Tugging earth-deeps, trying heaven-heights, rooted
  yonder at Lausanne.
This which flits and spits, the aspic, — sparkles in and
  out the boughs
Now, and now condensed, the python, coiling round
  and round allows
Scarce the bole its due effulgence, dulled by flake on
  flake of Wit —
Laughter so bejewels Learning, — what but Ferney
  nourished it ?
Nay, nor fear — since every resin feeds the flame —
  that I dispense
With yon Bossex terebinth-tree's all-explosive Elo-
  quence :
No, be sure! nor, any more than thy resplendency,
  Jean-Jacques,
Dare I want thine, Diodati ! What though monkeys
  and macaques
Gibber " Byron ? " Byron's ivy rears a branch beyond
  the crew,
Green forever, no deciduous trash macaques and mon-
  keys chew !
As Rousseau, then, eloquent, as Byron prime in poet's
  power, —
Detonations, fulgurations, smiles — the rainbow, tears
  — the shower, —
Lo, I lift the coruscating marvel — Fame ! and,
  famed, declare

— Learned for the nonce as Gibbon, witty as wit's self
    Voltaire . . .
O the sorriest of conclusions to whatever man of
    sense
Mid the millions stands the unit, takes no flare for
    evidence !
Yet the millions have their portion, live their calm or
    troublous day,
Find significance in fireworks : so, by help of mine,
    they may
Confidently lay to heart and lock in head their life
    long — this :
" He there with the brand flamboyant, broad o'er
    night's forlorn abyss,
Crowned by prose and verse ; and wielding, with Wit's
    bauble, Learning's rod . . .
Well ? Why, he at least believed in Soul, was very
    sure of God !

So the poor smile played, that evening : pallid smile
    long since extinct
Here in London's mid-November ! Not so loosely
    thoughts were linked,
Six weeks since as I, descending in the sunset from
    Salève,
Found the chain, I seemed to forge there, flawless till
    it reached your grave. —

Not so filmy was the texture, but I bore it in my
    breast
Safe thus far. And since I found a something in me
    would not rest
Till I, link by link, unravelled any tangle of the chain,
— Here it lies, for much or little ! I have lived all
    o'er again
That last pregnant hour : I saved it, just as I could
    save a root
Disinterred for re-interment when the time best helps
    to shoot.
Life is stocked with germs of torpid life ; but may I
    never wake
Those of mine whose resurrection could not be with-
    out earthquake !
Rest all such, unraised forever ! Be this, sad yet
    sweet, the sole
Memory evoked from slumber ! Least part this · then
    what the whole ?
November 9, 1877.

THE TWO POETS OF CROISIC.

1.

Such a starved bank of moss
  Till, that May-morn,
Blue ran the flash across :
  Violets were born !

2.

Sky — what a scowl of cloud
  Till, near and far,
Ray on ray split the shroud :
  Splendid, a star !

3.

World — how it walled about
  Life with disgrace
Till God's own smile came out :
  That was thy face !

THE TWO POETS OF CROISIC.

I.

"FAME!" Yes, I said it and you read it. First,
   Praise the good log-fire! Winter howls without.
Crowd closer, let us! Ha, the secret nursed
   Inside yon hollow, crusted roundabout
With copper where the clamp was, — how the burst
   Vindicates flame the stealthy feeder! Spout
Thy splendidest — a minute and no more?
So soon again all sobered as before?

2.

Nay, for I need to see your face! One stroke
   Adroitly dealt, and lo, the pomp revealed!
Fire in his pandemonium, heart of oak
   Palatial, where he wrought the works concealed
Beneath the solid seeming roof I broke,
   As redly up and out and off they reeled
Like disconcerted imps, those thousand sparks
From fire's slow tunnelling of vaults and arcs!

8.

Up with thee, mouldering ash men never knew,
   But I know ! flash thou forth, and figure bold,
Calm and columnar as yon flame I view !
   Oh and I bid thee, — to whom fortune doled
Scantly all other gifts out — bicker blue,
   Beauty for all to see, zinc's uncontrolled
Flake-brilliance ! Not my fault if these were shown,
Grandeur and beauty both, to me alone.

9.

No ! as the first was boy's play, this proves mere
   Stripling's amusement : manhood's sport be grave !
Choose rather sparkles quenched in mid career,
   True boldness and true brightness could not save
(In some old night of time on some lone drear
   Sea-coast, monopolized by crag or cave)
— Save from ignoble exit into smoke,
Silence, oblivion, all death-damps that choke !

10.

Launched by our ship-wood, float we, once adrift,
   In fancy to that land-strip waters wash,
We both know well ! Where uncouth tribes made
     shift
   Long since to keep the life in billows dash

Right over ; still they shudder at each lift
  Of the old tyrant tempest's whirlwind-lash
Though they have built the serviceable town
Tempests but tease now, billows drench, not drown.

11.

Croisic, the spit of sandy rock which juts
  Spitefully northward, bears nor tree nor shrub
To tempt the ocean, show what Guérande shuts
  Behind her, past wild Batz whose Saxons grub
The ground for crystals grown where ocean gluts
  Their promontory's breadth with salt : all stub
Of rock and stretch of sand, the land's last strife
To rescue just a remnant for dear life.

12.

And what life !   Here was, from the world to
    choose,
  The Druids' chosen chief of homes : they reared
— Only their women, — mid the slush and ooze
  Of yon low islet, — to their sun, revered
In strange stone guise, — a temple.   May-dawn
    dews
  Saw the old structure levelled ; when there peered
May's earliest eve-star, high and wide once more
Up towered the new pile perfect as before :

11

13.

Seeing that priestesses — and all were such —
    Unbuilt and then rebuilt it every May,
Each alike helping — well, if not too much !
    For, mid their eagerness to outstrip day
And get work done, if any loosed her clutch
    And let a single stone drop, straight a prey
Herself fell, torn to pieces, limb from limb,
By sisters in full chorus glad and grim.

14.

And still so much remains of that gray cult,
    That even now, of nights, do women steal
To the sole Menhir standing, and insult
    The antagonistic church-spire by appeal
To power discrowned in vain, since each adult
    Believes the gruesome thing she clasps may heal
Whatever plague no priestly help can cure :
Kiss but the cold stone, the event is sure !

15.

Nay more : on May-morns, that primeval rite
    Of temple-building, with its punishment
For rash precipitation, lingers, spite
    Of all remonstrance ; vainly are they shent,
Those girls who form a ring and, dressed in white,

Dance round it, till some sister's strength be spent :
Touch but the Menhir, straight the rest turn roughs
From gentles, fall on her with fisticuffs.

16.

Oh and, for their part, boys from door to door
　　Sing unintelligible words to tunes
As obsolete : "scraps of Druidic lore,"
　　Sigh scholars, as each pale man importunes
Vainly the mumbling to speak plain once more.
　　Enough of this old worship, rounds and runes !
They serve my purpose, which is just to show
Croisic to-day and Croisic long ago.

17.

What have we sailed to see, then, wafted there
　　By fancy from the log that ends its days
Of much adventure 'neath skies foul or fair,
　　On waters rough or smooth, in this good blaze
We two crouch round so closely, bidding care
　　Keep outside with the snow-storm? Something says
"Fit time for story-telling !" I begin —
Why not at Croisic, port we first put in ?

18.

Anywhere serves : for point me out the place
　　Wherever man has made himself a home,

And there I find the story of our race
   In little, just at Croisic as at Rome.
What matters the degree? the kind I trace.
   Druids their temple, Christians have their dome :
So with mankind ; and Croisic, I 'll engage,
With Rome yields sort for sort, in age for age.

19.

No doubt, men vastly differ: and we need
   Some strange exceptional benevolence
Of nature's sunshine to develop seed
   So well, in the less-favored clime, that thence
We may discern how shrub means tree indeed
   Though dwarfed till scarcely shrub in evidence.
Man in the ice-house and the hot-house ranks
With beasts or gods : stove-forced, give warmth the
      thanks !

20.

While, is there any ice-checked? Such shall learn
   I am thankworthy, who propose to slake
His thirst for tasting how it feels to turn
   Cedar from hyssop-on-the-wall. I wake
No memories of what is harsh and stern
   In ancient Croisic-nature, much less rake
The ashes of her last warmth till out leaps
Live Hervé Riel, the single spark she keeps.

21.

Take these two, see, each outbreak, — spirt and spirt
  Of fire from our brave billet's either edge
Which call maternal Croisic ocean-girt ! —
  These two shall thoroughly redeem my pledge.
One flames fierce gules, its feebler rival — vert,
  Heralds would tell you : heroes, I allege,
They both were : soldiers, sailors, statesmen, priests,
Lawyers, physicians — guess what gods or beasts !

22.

None of them all, but — poets, if you please !
  "What, even there, endowed with knack of rhyme,
Did two among the aborigines
  Of that rough region pass the ungracious time
Suiting, to rumble-tumble of the sea's,
  The songs forbidden a serener clime ?
Or had they universal audience — that 's
To say, the folk of Croisic, ay and Batz ? "

23.

Open your ears ! Each poet in his day
  Had such a mighty moment of success
As pinnacled him straight, in full display,
  For the whole world to worship — nothing less !
Was not the whole polite world Paris, pray ?
  And did not Paris, for one moment — yes,

Worship these poet-flames, our red and green,
One at a time, a century between?

24.

And yet you never heard their names!   Assist,
   Clio, Historic Muse, while I record
Great deeds!   Let fact, not fancy, break the mist
   And bid each sun emerge, in turn play lord
Of day, one moment!   Hear the annalist
   Tell a strange story, true to the least word!
At Croisic, sixteen hundred years and ten
Since Christ, forth flamed yon liquid ruby, then.

25.

Know him henceforth as René Gentilhomme
   — Appropriate appellation! noble birth
And knightly blazon, the device wherefrom
   Was " Better do than say " !   In Croisic's dearth
Why prison his career while Christendom
   Lay open to reward acknowledged worth?
He therefore left it at the proper age
And got to be the Prince of Condé's page.

26.

Which Prince of Condé, whom men called " The
   Duke,"
   — Failing the king, his cousin, of an heir,

(As one might hold would hap, without rebuke,
  Since Anne of Austria, all the world was 'ware,
Twenty-three years long sterile, scarce could look
  For issue) — failing Louis of so rare
A godsend, it was natural the Prince
Should hear men call him "Next King" too, nor
    wince.

27.

Now, as this reasonable hope, by growth
  Of years, nay, tens of years, looked plump almost
To bursting, — would the brothers, childless both,
  Louis and Gaston, give but up the ghost —
Condé, called "Duke" and "Next King," nothing
    loth
  Awaited his appointment to the post,
And wiled away the time, as best he might,
Till providence should settle things aright.

28.

So, at a certain pleasure-house, withdrawn
  From cities where a whisper breeds offence,
He sat him down to watch the streak of dawn
  Testify to first stir of providence;
And, since dull country life makes courtiers yawn,
  There wanted not a poet to dispense
Song's remedy for spleen-fits all and some,
Which poet was Page René Gentilhomme.

29.

A poet born and bred, his very sire
  A poet also, author of a piece
Printed and published, " Ladies — their attire " :
  Therefore the son, just born at his decease,   ,
Was bound to keep alive the sacred fire,
  And kept it, yielding moderate increase
Of songs and sonnets, madrigals, and much
Rhyming thought poetry and praised as such.

30.

Rubbish unutterable (bear in mind !)
  Rubbish not wholly without value, though,
Being to compliment the Duke designed
  And bring the complimenter credit so, —
Pleasure with profit happily combined.
  Thus René Gentilhomme rhymed, rhymed till — lo,
This happened, as he sat in an alcove
Elaborating rhyme for " love " — *not* " dove."

31.

He was alone : silence and solitude
  Befit the votary of the Muse.   Around,
Nature — not our new picturesque and rude,
  But trim tree-cinctured stately garden-ground —
Breathed polish and politeness.   All-imbued

With these, he sat absorbed in one profound
Excogitation "Were it best to hint
Or boldly boast 'She loves me, — Araminte?'"

32.

When suddenly flashed lightning, searing sight
    Almost, so close his eyes ; then, quick on flash,
Followed the thunder, splitting earth downright
    Where René sat a-rhyming : with huge crash
Of marble into atoms infinite —
    Marble which, stately, dared the world to dash
The stone-thing proud, high-pillared, from its place :
One flash, and dust was all that lay at base.

33.

So, when the horrible confusion loosed
    Its wrappage round his senses, and, with breath,
Seeing and hearing by degrees induced
    Conviction what he felt was life, not death —
His fluttered faculties came back to roost
    One after one, as fowls do : ay, beneath,
About his very feet there, lay in dust
Earthly presumption paid by heaven's disgust.

34.

For, what might be the thunder-smitten thing
    But, pillared high and proud, in marble guise,

A ducal crown — which meant "Now Duke : Next,
    King ? "
Since such the Prince was, not in his own eyes
Alone, but all the world's.   Pebble from sling
    Prostrates a giant ; so can pulverize
Marble pretension — how much more make moult
His plume, a peacock-prince — God's thunderbolt !

35.

That was enough for René, that first fact
    Thus flashed into him.   Up he looked : all blue
And bright the sky above ; earth firm, compact
    Beneath his footing, lay apparent too ;
Opposite stood the pillar : nothing lacked
    There, but the Duke's crown : see, its fragments
    strew
The earth, — about his feet lie atoms fine
Where he sat nursing late his fourteenth line !

36.

So, for the moment, all the universe
    Being abolished, all 'twixt God and him, —
Earth's praise or blame, its blessing or its curse,
    Of one and the same value, — to the brim
Flooded with truth for better or for worse, —
    He pounces on the writing-paper, prim
Keeping its place on table : not a dint
Nor speck had damaged "Ode to Araminte."

37.

And over the neat crowquill calligraph
  His pen goes blotting, blurring, as an ox
Tramples a flower-bed in a garden, — laugh
  You may! — so does not he, whose quick heart
    knocks
Audibly at his breast : an epitaph
  On earth's break-up, amid the falling rocks,
He might be penning in a wild dismay,
Caught with his work half-done on Judgment Day.

38.

And what is it so terribly he pens,
  Ruining " Cupid, Venus, wile and smile,
Hearts, darts," and all his day's *divinior mens*
  Judged necessary to a perfect style ?
Little recks René, with a breast to cleanse,
  Of Rhadamanthine law that reigned erewhile :
Brimful of truth, truth's outburst will convince
(Style or no style) who bears truth's brunt — the
    Prince.

39.

" Condé, called ' Duke,' be called just ' Duke,' not
    more,
  To life's end ! ' Next King ' thou forsooth wilt
    be ?

Ay, when this bauble, as it decked before
  Thy pillar, shall again, for France to see,
Take its proud station there !   Let France adore
  No longer an illusive mock-sun — thee —
But keep her homage for Sol's self, about
To rise and put pretenders to the rout !

40.

"What ?   France so God-abandoned that her root
  Regal, though many a Spring it gave no sign,
Lacks power to make the bole, now branchless, shoot
  Greenly as ever?   Nature, though benign,
Confuses the ambitious and astute.
  In store for such is punishment condign :
Sure as thy Duke's crown to the earth was hurled,
So sure, next year, a Dauphin glads the world !"

41.

Which penned — some forty lines to this effect —
  Our René folds his paper, marches brave
Back to the mansion, luminous, erect,
  Triumphant, an emancipated slave.
There stands the Prince.   "How now?   My Duke's
    crown wrecked ?
  What may this mean ? "   The answer René gave
Was — handing him the verses, with the due
Incline of body : " Sir, God's word to you !"

42.

The Prince read, paled, was silent ; all around,
　The courtier-company, to whom he passed
The paper, read, in equal silence bound.
　By degrees René also grew aghast
At his own fit of courage — palely found
　Way of retreat from that pale presence : classed
Once more among the cony-kind. "Oh, son,
It is a feeble folk !" saith Solomon.

43.

Vainly he apprehended evil : since,
　When, at the year's end, even as foretold,
Forth came the Dauphin who discrowned the Prince
　Of that long-craved mere visionary gold,
'T was no fit time for envy to evince
　Malice, be sure ! The timidest grew bold :
Of all that courtier-company not one
But left the semblance for the actual sun.

44.

And all sorts and conditions that stood by
　At René's burning moment, bright escape
Of soul, bore witness to the prophecy.
　Which witness took the customary shape
Of verse ; a score of poets in full cry

Hailed the inspired one. Nantes and Tours agape,
Soon Paris caught the infection ; gaining strength,
How could it fail to reach the Court at length ?

45.

"O poet!" smiled King Louis, "and besides,
    O prophet ! Sure, by miracle announced,
My babe will prove a prodigy. Who chides
    Henceforth the unchilded monarch shall be trounced
For irreligion : since the fool derides
    Plain miracle by which this prophet pounced
Exactly on the moment I should lift
Like Simeon, in my arms, a babe, 'God's gift !'

46.

" So call the boy ! and call this bard and seer
    By a new title ! him I raise to rank
Of ' Royal Poet : ' poet without peer !
    Whose fellows only have themselves to thank
If humbly they must follow in the rear
    My René. He 's the master : they must clank
Their chains of song, confessed his slaves ; for why?
They poetize, while he can prophesy ! "

47.

So said, so done ; our René rose august,
    " The Royal Poet ; " straightway put in type

His poem-prophecy, and (fair and just
  Procedure) added, — now that time was ripe
For proving friends did well his word to trust, —
  Those attestations, tuned to lyre or pipe,
Which friends broke out with when he dared foretell
The Dauphin's birth : friends trusted, and did well !

48.

Moreover he got painted by Du Pré,
  Engraved by Daret also ; and prefixed
The portrait to his book : a crown of bay
  Circled his brows, with rose and myrtle mixed ;
And Latin verses, lovely in their way,
  Described him as " the biforked hill betwixt :
Since he hath scaled Parnassus at one jump,
Joining the Delphic quill and Getic trump."

49.

Whereof came . . . What, it lasts, our spirt, thus
      long
  — The red fire ?   That 's the reason must excuse
My letting flicker René's prophet-song
  No longer ; for its pertinacious hues
Must fade before its fellow joins the throng
  Of sparks departed up the chimney, dues
To dark oblivion.   At the word, it winks,
Rallies, relapses, dwindles, dwindles, sinks !

50.

So does our poet.   All this burst of fame,
  Fury of favor, Royal Poetship,
Prophetship, book, verse, picture — thereof came
  — Nothing!   That 's why I would not let outstrip
Red his green rival flamelet : just the same
  Ending in smoke waits both !   In vain we rip
The past, no further faintest trace remains
Of René to reward our pious pains.

51.

Somebody saw a portrait framed and glazed
  At Croisic.   "Who may be this glorified
Mortal unheard-of hitherto?" amazed
  That person asked the owner by his side,
Who proved as ignorant.   The question raised
  Provoked inquiry ; key by key was tried
On Croisic's portrait-puzzle, till back flew
The wards at one key's touch, which key was — Who

52.

The other famous poet !   Wait thy turn,
  Thou green, our red's competitor !   Enough
Just now to note 't was he that itched to learn
  (A hundred years ago) how fate could puff
Heaven-high (a hundred years before) then spurn

To suds so big a bubble in some huff :
Since green too found red's portrait, — having heard
Hitherto of red's rare self not one word.

53.

And he with zeal addressed him to the task
  Of hunting out, by all and any means,
— Who might the brilliant bard be, born to bask
  Butterfly-like in shine which kings and queens
And baby-dauphins shed ? Much need to ask !
  Is fame so fickle that what perks and preens
The eyed wing, one imperial minute, dips
Next sudden moment into blind eclipse ?

54.

After a vast expenditure of pains,
  Our second poet found the prize he sought :
Urged in his search by something that restrains
  From undue triumph famed ones who have fought,
Or simply, poetizing, taxed their brains :
  Something that tells such — dear is triumph bought
If it means only basking in the midst
Of fame's brief sunshine, as thou, René, didst !

55.

For, what did searching find at last but this ?
  Quoth somebody, " I somehow somewhere seem

12

To think I heard one old De Chevaye is
  Or was possessed of René's works !" which gleam
Of light from out the dark proved not amiss
  To track, by correspondence on the theme ;
And soon the twilight broadened into day,
For thus to question answered De Chevaye.

56.

"True it is, I did once possess the works
  You want account of — works — to call them
    so, —
Comprised in one small book : the volume lurks
  (Some fifty leaves *in duodecimo*)
'Neath certain ashes which my soul it irks
  Still to remember, because long ago
That and my other rare shelf-occupants
Perished by burning of my house at Nantes.

57.

" Yet of that book one strange particular
  Still stays in mind with me " — and thereupon
Followed the story. " Few the poems are ;
  The book was two thirds filled up with this one,
And sundry witnesses from near and far
  That here at least was prophesying done
By prophet, so as to preclude all doubt,
Before the thing he prophesied about."

58.

That's all he knew, and all the poet learned,
  And all that you and I are like to hear
Of René ; since not only book is burned
  But memory extinguished, — nay, I fear,
Portrait is gone too : nowhere I discerned
  A trace of it at Croisic. "Must a tear
Needs fall for that?" you smile. "How fortune fares
With such a mediocrity, who cares?"

59.

Well, I care — intimately care to have
  Experience how a human creature felt
In after-life, who bore the burden grave
  Of certainly believing God had dealt
For once directly with him : did not rave
  — A maniac, did not find his reason melt
— An idiot, but went on, in peace or strife,
The world's way, lived an ordinary life.

60.

How many problems that one fact would solve!
  An ordinary soul, no more, no less,
About whose life earth's common sights revolve,
  On whom is brought to bear, by thunder-stress,
This fact — God tasks him, and will not absolve

Task's negligent performer! Can you guess
How such a soul, — the task performed to point, —
Goes back to life nor finds things out of joint?

61.

Does he stand stock-like henceforth? or proceed
   Dizzily, yet with course straight-forward still,
Down-trampling vulgar hindrance? — as the reed
   Is crushed beneath its tramp when that blind will
Hatched in some old-world beast's brain bids it speed
   Where the sun wants brute presence to fulfil
Life's purpose in a new far zone, ere ice
Enwomb the pasture-tract its fortalice.

62.

I think no such direct plain truth consists
   With actual sense and thought and what they take
To be the solid walls of life: mere mists —
   How such would, at that truth's first piercing, break
Into the nullity they are! — slight lists
   Wherein the puppet-champions wage, for sake
Of some mock-mistress, mimic war: laid low
At trumpet-blast, there 's shown the world, one foe!

63.

No, we must play the pageant out, observe
   The tourney-regulations, and regard

Success — to meet the blunted spear nor swerve,
    Failure — to break no bones yet fall on sward ;
Must prove we have — not courage ? well then, —
        nerve ?
    And, at the day's end, boast the crown's award —
Be warranted as promising to wield
Weapons, no sham, in a true battle-field.

64.

Meantime, our simulated thunderclaps
    Which tell us counterfeited truths — these same
Are — sound, when music storms the soul, perhaps ?
    — Sight, beauty, every dart of every aim
That touches just, then seems, by strange relapse,
    To fall effectless from the soul it came
As if to fix its own, but simply smote
And startled to vague beauty more remote ?

65.

So do we gain enough — yet not too much —
    Acquaintance with that outer element
Wherein there 's operation (call it such !)
    Quite of another kind than we the pent
On earth are proper to receive.   Our hutch
    Lights up at the least chink : let roof be rent —
How inmates huddle, blinded at first spasm,
Cognizant of the sun's self through the chasm !

66.

Therefore, who knows if this our René's quick
  Subsidence from as sudden noise and glare
Into oblivion was impolitic ?
  No doubt his soul became at once aware
That, after prophecy, the rhyming-trick
  Is poor employment : human praises scare
Rather than soothe ears all a-tingle yet
With tones few hear and live, but none forget.

67.

There 's our first famous poet ! Step thou forth
  Second consummate songster ! See, the tongue
Of fire that typifies thee, owns thy worth
  In yellow, purple mixed its green among,
No pure and simple resin from the North,
  But composite with virtues that belong
To Southern culture ! Love not more than hate
Helped to a blaze . . . but I anticipate.

68.

Prepare to witness a combustion rich
  And riotously splendid, far beyond
Poor René's lambent little streamer which
  Only played candle to a Court grown fond
By baby-birth : this soared to such a pitch,

Alternately such colors doffed and donned,
That when I say it dazzled Paris — please
Know that it brought Voltaire upon his knees !

69.

Who did it, was a dapper gentleman,
   Paul Desforges Maillard, Croisickese by birth,
Whose birth that century ended which began
   By similar bestowment on our earth
Of the aforesaid René. Cease to scan
   The ways of Providence ! See Croisic's dearth —
Not Paris in its plenitude — suffice
To furnish France with her best poet twice !

70.

Till he was thirty years of age, the vein
   Poetic yielded rhyme by drops and spirts :
In verses of society had lain
   His talent chiefly ; but the Muse asserts
Privilege most by treating with disdain
   Epics the bard mouths out, or odes he blurts
Spasmodically forth. Have people time
And patience nowadays for thought in rhyme ?

71.

So, his achievements were the quatrain's inch
   Of homage, or at most the sonnet's ell

Of admiration : welded lines with clinch
  Of ending word and word, to every belle
In Croisic's bounds ; these, brisk as any finch,
  He twittered till his fame had reached as well
Guérande as Batz ; but there fame stopped, for —
    curse
On fortune — outside lay the universe !

72.

That 's Paris.   Well, — why not break bounds, and
    send
  Song onward till it echo at the gates
Of Paris whither all ambitions tend,
  And end too, seeing that success there sates
The soul which hungers most for fame ?   Why spend
  A minute in deciding, while, by Fate's
Decree, there happens to be just the prize
Proposed there, suiting souls that poetize ?

73.

A prize indeed, the Academy's own self
  Proposes to what bard shall best indite
A piece describing how, through shoal and shelf,
  The Art of Navigation, steered aright,
Has, in our last king's reign, — the lucky elf, —
  Reached, one may say, Perfection's haven quite,
And there cast anchor.   At a glance one sees
The subject's crowd of capabilities !

74.

Neptune and Amphitrité! Thetis, who
   Is either Tethys or as good — both tag!
Triton can shove along a vessel too :
   It 's Virgil! Then the winds that blow or lag, —
De Maille, Vendôme, Vermandois! Toulouse blew
   Longest, we reckon : he must puff the flag
To fullest outflare : while our lacking nymph
Be Anne of Austria, Regent o'er the lymph!

75.

Promised, performed! Since *irritabilis gens*
   Holds of the feverish impotence that strives
To stay an itch by prompt resource to pen's
   Scratching itself on paper : placid lives,
Leisurely works mark the *divinior mens :*
   Bees brood above the honey in their hives ;
Gnats are the busy bustlers. Splash and scrawl, —
Completed lay thy piece, swift penman Paul!

76.

To Paris with the product! This despatched,
   One had to wait the Forty's slow and sure
Verdict, as best one might. Our penman scratched
   Away perforce the itch that knows no cure
But daily paper-friction : more than matched

His first feat by a second — tribute pure
And heartfelt to the Forty when their voice
Should peal with one accord, " Be Paul our choice ! "

77.

Scratch, scratch went much laudation of that sane
   And sound Tribunal, delegates august
Of Phœbus and the Muses' sacred train —
   Whom every poetaster tries to thrust
From where, high-throned, they dominate the Seine :
   Fruitless endeavor, — fail it shall and must !
Whereof in witness have not one and all
The Forty voices pealed, " Our choice be Paul ? "

78.

Thus Paul discounted his applause.   Alack
   For human expectation !   Scarcely ink
Was dry when, lo, the perfect piece came back
   Rejected, shamed !   Some other poet's clink
" Thetis and Tethys " had seduced the pack
   Of pedants to declare perfection's pink
A singularly poor production.   " Whew !
The Forty are stark fools, I always knew ! "

79.

First fury over (for Paul's race — to-wit,
   Brain vibrios — wriggle clear of protoplasm

Into minute life that's one fury-fit),
"These fools shall find a bard's enthusiasm
Comports with what should counterbalance it —
   Some knowledge of the world! No doubt, or-
     gasm
Effects the birth of verse which, born, demands
Prosaic ministration, swaddling-bands!

80.

"Verse must be cared for at this early stage,
   Handled, nay dandled even. I should play
Their game indeed if, till it grew of age,
   I meekly let these dotards frown away
My bantling from the rightful heritage
   Of smiles and kisses! Let the public say
If it be worthy praises or rebukes,
My poem, from these Forty old perukes!"

81.

So, by a friend, who boasts himself in grace
   With no less than the Chevalier La Roque, —
Eminent in those days for pride of place
   Seeing he had it in his power to block
The way or smooth the road to all the race
   Of literators trudging up to knock
At Fame's exalted temple-door — for why?
He edited the Paris "Mercury:" —

82.

By this friend's help the Chevalier receives
  Paul's poem, prefaced by the due appeal
To Cæsar from the Jews.   As duly heaves
  A sigh the Chevalier, about to deal
With case so customary — turns the leaves,
  Finds nothing there to borrow, beg or steal —
Then brightens up the critic's brow deep-lined.
" The thing may be so cleverly declined ! "

83.

Down to desk, out with paper, up with quill,
  Dip and indite !   " Sir, gratitude immense
For this true draught from the Pierian rill !
  Our Academic clodpoles must be dense
Indeed to stand unirrigated still.
  No less, we critics dare not give offence
To grandees like the Forty : while we mock,
We grin and bear.   So, here 's your piece ! La
    Roque."

84.

" There now ! " cries Paul : " the fellow can't avoid
  Confessing that my piece deserves the palm ;
And yet he dares not grant me space enjoyed
  By every scribbler he permits embalm

His crambo in the Journal's corner ! Cloyed
  With stuff like theirs, no wonder if a qualm
Be caused by verse like mine : though that's no
    cause
For his defrauding me of just applause.

85.

" Aha, he fears the Forty, this poltroon ?
  First let him fear *me!* Change smooth speech to
    rough !
I 'll speak my mind out, show the fellow soon
  Who is the foe to dread : insist enough
On my own merits till, as clear as noon,
  He sees I am no man to take rebuff
As patiently as scribblers may and must !
Quick to the onslaught, out sword, cut and thrust ! "

86.

And thereupon a fierce epistle flings
  Its challenge in the critic's face. Alack !
Our bard mistakes his man ! The gauntlet rings
  On brazen visor proof against attack.
Prompt from his editorial throne up springs
  The insulted magnate, and his mace falls, thwack,
On Paul's devoted brainpan, — quite away
From common courtesies of fencing-play !

87.

"Sir, will you have the truth ?   This piece of yours
    Is simply execrable past belief.
I shrank from saying so ; but, since nought cures
    Conceit but truth, truth 's at your service !   Brief,
Just so long as 'The Mercury' endures,
    So long are you excluded by its Chief
From corner, nay, from cranny !   Play the cock
O' the roost, henceforth, at Croisic !" wrote La
    Roque.

88.

Paul yellowed, whitened, as his wrath from red
    Waxed incandescent.   Now, this man of rhyme
Was merely foolish, faulty in the head
    Not heart of him : conceit 's a venial crime.
"Oh by no means malicious !" cousins said :
    Fussily feeble, — harmless all the time,
Piddling at so-called satire — well-advised
He held in most awe whom he satirized.

89.

Accordingly his kith and kin — removed
    From emulation of the poet's gift
By power and will — these rather liked, nay, loved
    The man who gave his family a lift
Out of the Croisic level ; disapproved

Satire so trenchant, — still our poet sniffed
Home-incense, — though too churlish to unlock
"The Mercury's" box of ointment proved La Roque.

90.

But when Paul's visage grew from red to white,
  And from his lips a sort of mumbling fell
Of who was to be kicked, — "And serve him right!"
  A soft voice interposed, "Did kicking well
Answer the purpose! Only — if I might
  Suggest as much — a far more potent spell
Lies in another kind of treatment. Oh,
Women are ready at resource, you know!

91.

"Talent should minister to genius! good :
  The proper and superior smile returns.
Hear me with patience! Have you understood
  The only method whereby genius earns
His guerdon nowadays? In knightly mood
  You entered lists with visor up; one learns
Too late that, had you mounted Roland's crest,
'Room!' they had roared — La Roque with all the
    rest!

92.

"Why did you first of all transmit your piece
  To those same priggish Forty unprepared

Whether to rank you with the swans or geese
    By friendly intervention? If they dared
Count you a cackler, — wonders never cease!
    I think it still more wondrous that you bared
Your brow (my earlier image) as if praise
Were gained by simple fighting nowadays!

93.

"Your next step showed a touch of the true means
    Whereby desert is crowned : not force but wile
Came to the rescue. 'Get behind the scenes!'
    Your friend advised : he writes, sets forth your
        style
And title, to such purpose intervenes
    That you get velvet-compliment three-pile ;
And, though 'The Mercury' said 'nay,' nor stock
Nor stone did his refusal prove La Roque.

94.

"Why must you needs revert to the high hand,
    Imperative procedure — what you call
'Taking on merit your exclusive stand?'
    Stand, with a vengeance ! Soon you went to wall,
You and your merit ! Only fools command
    When folks are free to disobey them, Paul !
You 've learnt your lesson, found out what 's o'clock,
By this uncivil answer of La Roque.

95.

"Now let me counsel! Lay this piece on shelf
   — Masterpiece though it be! From out your desk
Hand me some lighter sample, verse the elf
   Cupid inspired you with, no god grotesque
Presiding o'er the Navy! I myself
   Hand-write what 's legible yet picturesque ;
I 'll copy fair and femininely frock
Your poem masculine that courts La Roque!

96.

"Deïdamia he — Achilles thou!
   Ha, ha, these ancient stories come so apt !
My sex, my youth, my rank I next avow
   In a neat prayer for kind perusal. Sapped
I see the walls which stand so stoutly now !
   I see the toils about the game entrapped
By honest cunning! Chains of lady's-smock,
Not thorn and thistle, tether fast La Roque !"

97.

Now, who might be the speaker sweet and arch
   That laughed above Paul's shoulder as it heaved
With the indignant heart ? — bade steal a march
   And not continue charging ? Who conceived
This plan which set our Paul, like pea you parch

13

On fire-shovel, skipping, of a load relieved,
From arm-chair moodiness to escritoire
Sacred to Phœbus and the tuneful choir?

98.

Who but Paul's sister! named of course like him
  "Desforges"; but, mark you, in those days a queer
Custom obtained, — who knows whence grew the
    whim? —
That people could not read their title clear
To reverence till their own true names, made dim
  By daily mouthing, pleased to disappear,
Replaced by brand-new bright ones : Arouet,
For instance, grew Voltaire, Desforges — Malcrais.

99.

"Demoiselle Malcrais de la Vigne" — because
  The family possessed at Brederac
A vineyard, — few grapes, many hips and haws, —
  Still a nice Breton name. As breast and back
Of this vivacious beauty gleamed through gauze,
  So did her sprightly nature nowise lack
Lustre when draped, the fashionable way,
In "Malcrais de la Vigne" — more short, "Malcrais."

100.

Out from Paul's escritoire behold escape
  The hoarded treasure! verse falls thick and fast,

Sonnets and songs of every size and shape.
  The lady ponders on her prize ; at last
Selects one which — Oh angel and yet ape ! —
  Her malice thinks is probably surpassed
In badness by no fellow of the flock,
Copies it fair, and " Now for my La Roque ! "

101.

So, to him goes, with the neat manuscript,
  The soft petitionary letter. " Grant
A fledgeling novice that with wing unclipt
  She soar her little circuit, habitant
Of an old manor ; buried in which crypt,
  How can the youthful châtelaine but pant
For disemprisonment by one *ad hoc*
Appointed ' Mercury 's ' Editor, La Roque ? "

102.

'T was an epistle that might move the Turk !
  More certainly it moved our middle-aged
Pen-driver drudging at his weary work,
  Raked the old ashes up and disengaged
The sparks of gallantry which always lurk
  Somehow in literary breasts, assuaged
In no degree by compliments on style ;
Are Forty wagging beards worth one girl's smile ?

103.

In trips the lady's poem, takes its place
  Of honor in the gratified Gazette,
With due acknowledgment of power and grace ;
  Prognostication, too, that higher yet
The Breton Muse will soar : fresh youth, high race,
  Beauty and wealth have amicably met
That Demoiselle Malcrais may fill the chair
Left vacant by the loss of Deshoulières.

104.

" There ! " cried the lively lady, " Who was right —
  You in the dumps, or I the merry maid
Who know a trick or two can baffle spite
  Tenfold the force of this old fool's ?   Afraid
Of Editor La Roque ?   But come ! next flight
  Shall outsoar — Deshoulières alone ?   My blade,
Sappho herself shall you confess outstript !
Quick, Paul, another dose of manuscript ! "

105.

And so, once well a-foot, advanced the game :
  More and more verses, corresponding gush
On gush of praise, till everywhere acclaim
  Rose to the pitch of uproar.   " Sappho ?   Tush !
Sure ' Malcrais on her Parrot ' puts to shame

Deshoulières' pastorals, clay not worth a rush
Beside this find of treasure, gold in crock,
Unearthed in Brittany, — nay, ask La Roque!"

106.

Such was the Paris tribute.   "Yes," you sneer,
  "Ninnies stock Noodledom, but folks more sage
Resist contagious folly, never fear!"
  Do they?   Permit me to detach one page
From the huge Album which from far and near
  Poetic praises blackened in a rage
Of rapture! and that page shall be — who stares
Confounded now, I ask you? — just Voltaire's!

107.

Ay, sharpest shrewdest steel that ever stabbed
  To death Imposture through the armor-joints!
How did it happen that gross Humbug grabbed
  Thy weapons, gouged thine eyes out?   Fate ap-
      points
That pride shall have a fall, or I had blabbed
  Hardly that Humbug, whom thy soul aroints,
Could thus cross-buttock thee caught unawares,
And dismalest of tumbles proved — Voltaire's!

108.

See his epistle extant yet, wherewith
  "Henri" in verse and "Charles" in prose he sent

To do her suit and service !   Here 's the pith
  Of half a dozen stanzas — stones which went
To build that simulated monolith —
  Sham love in due degree with homage blent
As sham — which in the vast of volumes scares
The traveller still : " That stucco-heap — Voltaire's ? "

109.

" Oh thou, whose clarion-voice has overflown
  The wilds to startle Paris that 's one ear !
Thou who such strange capacity hast shown
  For joining all that 's grand with all that 's dear,
Knowledge with power to please — Deshoulières
    grown
  Learned as Dacier in thy person ! mere
Weak fruit of idle hours, these crabs of mine
I dare lay at thy feet, O Muse divine !

110.

" Charles was my task-work only ; Henri trod
  My hero forth, and now, my heroine — she
Shall be thyself !   True — is it true, great God ?
  Certainly love henceforward must not be !
Yet all the crowd of Fine Arts fail — how odd ! —
  Tried turn by turn, to fill a void in me !
There 's no replacing love with these, alas !
Yet all I can I do to prove no ass.

III.

"I labor to amuse my freedom ; but
  Should any sweet young creature slavery preach,
And — borrowing thy vivacious charm, the slut ! —
  Make me, in thy engaging words, a speech,
Soon should I see myself in prison shut
  With all imaginable pleasure." Reach
The washhand-basin for admirers ! There 's
A stomach-moving tribute — and Voltaire's !

112.

Suppose it a fantastic billet-doux,
  Adulatory flourish, not worth frown !
What say you to the Fathers of Trévoux ?
  These in their Dictionary have her down
Under the heading " Author " : " Malcrais, too,
  Is 'Author' of much verse that claims renown."
While Jean-Baptiste Rousseau . . . but why proceed ?
Enough of this — something too much, indeed !

113.

At last La Roque, unwilling to be left
  Behindhand in the rivalry, broke bounds
Of figurative passion ; hilt and heft,
  Plunged his huge downright love through what sur
    rounds

The literary female bosom ; reft
  Away its veil of coy reserve with " Zounds !
I love thee, Breton Beauty ! All 's no use !
Body and soul I love, — the big word 's loose ! "

114.

He 's greatest now and to de-struc-ti-on
  Nearest. Attend the solemn word I quote,
Oh Paul ! *There 's no pause at per-fec-ti-on.*
  Thy   knell   thus   knolls   the   Doctor's   **bronzed**
    throat !
Greatness a period hath, no sta-ti-on !
  Better and truer verse none ever wrote
(Despite the antique outstretched *a-i-on*)
Than thou, revered and magisterial Donne !

115.

Flat   on   his   face,   La   Roque,   and, — pressed   to
    heart
  His dexter hand, — Voltaire with bended knee !
Paul sat and sucked-in triumph ; just apart
  Leaned   over   him   his   sister.   " Well ? "   smirks
    he,
And " Well ? " she answers, smiling — woman's art
  To let a man's own mouth, not her's, decree
What shall be next move which decides the game :
Success ? She said so. Failure ? His the blame.

116.

" Well ! " this time forth affirmatively comes
  With smack of lip, and long-drawn sigh through
    teeth
Close clenched o'er satisfaction, as the gums
  `Were tickled by a sweetmeat teazed beneath
Palate by lubricating tongue : " Well ! crums
  Of comfort these, undoubtedly ! no death
Likely from famine at Fame's feast ! 't is clear
I may put claim in for my pittance, Dear !

117.

" La Roque, Voltaire, my lovers ?   Then disguise
  Has served its turn, grows idle ; let it drop !
I shall to Paris, flaunt there in men's eyes
  My proper manly garb and mount a-top
The pedestal that waits me, take the prize
  Awarded Hercules !   He threw a sop
To Cerberus who let him pass, you know,
Then, following, licked his heels : exactly so !

118.

" I like the prospect — their astonishment,
  Confusion : wounded vanity, no doubt,
Mixed motives ; how I see the brows quick bent !
  ' What, sir, yourself, none other, brought about

This change of estimation ?   Phœbus sent
  His shafts as from Diana ?   Critic pout
Turns courtier smile : 'Lo, him we took for her !
Pleasant mistake !   You bear no malice, sir ? '

119.

" Eh, my Diana ? "   But Diana kept
  Smilingly silent with fixed needle-sharp
Much-meaning eyes that seemed to intercept
  Paul's very thoughts ere they had time to warp
From earnest into sport the words they leapt
    To life with — changed as when maltreated
      harp
Renders in tinkle what some player-prig
Means for a grave tune though it proves a jig.

120.

"What, Paul, and are my pains thus thrown
    away,
  My lessons perfect loss ? " at length fall slow
The pitying syllables, her lips allay
  The satire of by keeping in full flow,
Above their coral reef, bright smiles at play :
  " Can it be, Paul thus fails to rightly know
And altogether estimate applause
As just so many asinine he haws ?

121.

"I thought to show you" . . . "Show me," Paul in-
    broke
  "My poetry is rubbish, and the world
That rings with my renown a sorry joke !
  What fairer test of worth than that, form furled,
I entered the arena ? Yet you croak
  Just as if Phœbé and not Phœbus hurled
The dart and struck the Python ! What, he crawls
Humbly in dust before your feet, not Paul's ?

122.

"Nay, 't is no laughing matter though absurd
  If there 's an end of honesty on earth !
La Roque sends letters, lying every word !
  Voltaire makes verse, and of himself makes mirth
To the remotest age ! Rousseau 's the third
  Who, driven to despair amid such dearth
Of people that want praising, finds no one
More fit to praise than Paul the simpleton !

123.

"Somebody says — if a man writes at all
  It is to show the writer's kith and kin
He was unjustly thought a natural ;
  And truly, sister, I have yet to win

Your favorable word, it seems, for Paul
  Whose poetry you count not worth a pin
Though well enough esteemed by these Voltaires,
Rousseaus and suchlike : let them quack, who
    cares ? "

124.

"— To Paris with you, Paul ! Not one word's
    waste
  Further : my scrupulosity was vain !
Go triumph ! Be my foolish fears effaced
  From memory's record ! Go, to come again
With glory crowned, — by sister reëmbraced,
  Cured of that strange delusion of her brain
Which led her to suspect that Paris gloats
On male limbs mostly when in petticoats ! "

125.

So laughed her last word, with the little touch
  Of malice proper to the outraged pride
Of any artist in a work too much
  Shorn of its merits. " By all means, be tried
The opposite procedure ! Cast your crutch
  Away, no longer crippled, nor divide
The credit of your march to the World's Fair
With sister Cherry-cheeks who helped you there ! "

126.

Crippled, forsooth ! what courser sprightlier pranced
  Paris-ward than did Paul ? Nay, dreams lent wings :
He flew, or seemed to fly, by dreams entranced.
  Dreams ? wide-awake realities : no things
Dreamed merely were the missives that advanced
  The claim of Malcrais to consort with kings
Crowned by Apollo — not to say with queens
Cinctured by Venus for Idalian scenes.

127.

Soon he arrives, forthwith is found before
  The outer gate of glory. Bold tic-toc
Announces there's a giant at the door.
  " Ay, sir, here dwells the Chevalier La Roque."
" Lackey ! Malcrais, — mind, no word less nor
    more ! —
  Desires his presence. I've unearthed the brock :
Now, to transfix him ! " There stands Paul erect,
Inched out his uttermost, for more effect.

128.

A bustling entrance : " Idol of my flame !
  Can it be that my heart attains at last
Its longing ? that you stand, the very same
  As in my visions ? . . . Ha ! hey, how ? " aghast

Stops short the rapture.   "Oh, my boy's to blame!
   You merely are the messenger!   Too fast
My fancy rushed to a conclusion.   Pooh!
Well, sir, the lady's substitute is — who?"

129.

Then Paul's smirk grows inordinate.   "Shake hands!
   Friendship not love awaits you, master mine,
Though nor Malcrais nor any mistress stands
   To meet your ardor!   So, you don't divine
Who wrote the verses wherewith ring the land's
   Whole length and breadth?   Just he whereof no line
Had ever leave to blot your Journal — eh?
Paul Desforges Maillard — otherwise Malcrais!"

130.

And there the two stood, stare confronting smirk,
   Awhile uncertain which should yield the *pas.*
In vain the Chevalier beat brain for quirk
   To help in this conjuncture ; at length " Bah!
Boh!   Since I've made myself a fool, why shirk
   The punishment of folly?   Ha, ha, ha,
Let me return your handshake!"   Comic sock
For tragic buskin prompt thus changed La Roque.

131.

" I'm nobody — a wren-like journalist ;
   You've flown at higher game and winged your bird,

The golden eagle ! That 's the grand acquist !
  Voltaire's sly Muse, the tiger-cat, has purred
Prettily round your feet ; but if she missed
  Priority of stroking, soon were stirred
The dormant spit-fire. To Voltaire ! away,
Paul Desforges Maillard, otherwise Malcrais ! "

132.

Whereupon, arm in arm, and head in air,
  The two begin their journey. Need I say,
La Roque had felt the talon of Voltaire,
  Had a long-standing little debt to pay,
And pounced, you may depend, on such a rare
  Occasion for its due discharge ? So, gay
And grenadier-like, marching to assault,
They reach the enemy's abode, there halt.

133.

" I 'll be announcer ! " quoth La Roque : " I know,
  Better than you, perhaps, my Breton bard,
How to procure an audience ! He 's not slow
  To smell a rat, this scamp Voltaire ! Discard
The petticoats too soon, — you 'll never show
  Your *haut-de-chausses* and all they 've made or
    marred
In your true person. Here 's his servant. Pray,
Will the great man see Demoiselle Malcrais ? "

134.

Now, the great man was also, no whit less,
　The man of self-respect, — more great man he !
And bowed to social usage, dressed the dress,
　And decorated to the fit degree
His person ; 't was enough to bear the stress
　Of battle in the field, without, when free
From outside foes, inviting friends' attack
By — sword in hand ?   No, ill-made coat on back.

135.

And, since the announcement of his visitor
　Surprised him at his toilet, — never glass
Had such solicitation !   " Black, now — or
　Brown be the killing wig to wear ?   Alas,
Where 's the rouge gone, this cheek were better for
　A tender touch of ?   Melted to a mass,
All my pomatum !   There 's at all events
A devil — for he 's got among my scents ! "

136.

So, " barbered ten times o'er," as Antony
　Paced to his Cleopatra, did at last
Voltaire proceed to the fair presence : high
　In color, proud in port, as if a blast
Of trumpet bade the world " Take note ! draws nigh

To Beauty, Power! Behold the Iconoclast,
The Poet, the Philosopher, the Rod
Of iron for imposture! Ah my God!"

137.

For there stands smirking Paul, and — what lights
    fierce
The situation as with sulphur flash —
There grinning stands La Roque! No carte-and-
    tierce
Observes the grinning fencer, but, full dash
From breast to shoulderblade, the thrusts trans-
    pierce
That armor against which so idly clash
The swords of priests and pedants! Victors there,
Two smirk and grin who have befooled — Voltaire!

138.

A moment's horror ; then quick turn-about
    On high-heeled shoe, — flurry of ruffles, flounce
Of wig-ties and of coat-tails, — and so out
    Of door banged wrathfully behind, goes — bounce —
Voltaire in tragic exit! vows, no doubt,
    Vengeance upon the couple. Did he trounce
Either, in point of fact? His anger's flash
Subsided if a culprit craved his cash.

14

139.

As for La Roque, he having laughed his laugh
    To heart's content, — the joke defunct at once,
Dead in the birth, you see, — its epitaph
    Was sober earnest.   " Well, sir, for the nonce,
You 've gained the laurel ; never hope to graff
    A second sprig of triumph there !   Ensconce
Yourself again at Croisic : let it be
Enough you mastered both Voltaire and — me !

140.

" Don't linger here in Paris to parade
    Your victory, and have the very boys
Point at you !   ' There 's the little mouse which made
    Believe those two big lions that its noise,
Nibbling away behind the hedge, conveyed
    Intelligence that — portent which destroys
All courage in the lion's heart, with horn
That 's fable — there lay couched the unicorn ! '

141.

" Beware us, now we 've found who fooled us !   Quick
    To cover !   ' In proportion to men's fright,
Expect their fright's revenge ! ' quoth politic
    Old Macchiavelli.   As for me, — all 's right :
I 'm but a journalist.   But no pin's prick

The tooth leaves when Voltaire is roused to bite !
So, keep your counsel, I advise !   Adieu !
Good journey !   Ha, ha, ha, Malcrais was — you !"

142.

" — Yes, I 'm Malcrais, and somebody beside,
    You snickering monkey !" thus winds up the tale
Our hero, safe at home, to that black-eyed
    Cherry-cheeked sister, as she soothes the pale
Mortified poet.   "Let their worst be tried,
    I 'm their match henceforth — very man and male !
Don't talk to me of knocking-under ! man
And male must end what petticoats began !

143.

" How woman-like it is to apprehend
    The world will eat its words ! why, words transfixed
To stone, they stare at you in print, — at end,
    Each writer's style and title !   Choose betwixt
Fool and knave for his name, who should intend
    To perpetrate a baseness so unmixed
With prospect of advantage !   What is writ
Is writ : they 've praised me, there 's an end of it !

144.

" No, Dear, allow me !   I shall print these same
    Pieces, with no omitted line, as Paul's.

Malcrais no longer, let me see folks blame
    What they — praised simply? — placed on pedestals,
Each piece a statue in the House of Fame!
    Fast will they stand there, though their presence
        galls
The envious crew: such show their teeth, perhaps,
And snarl, but never bite! I know the chaps!"

145.

Oh Paul, oh piteously deluded! Pace
    Thy sad sterility of Croisic flats,
Watch, from their southern edge, the foamy race
    Of high-tide as it heaves the drowning mats
Of yellow-berried web-growth from their place,
    The rock-ridge, when, rolling as far as Batz,
One broadside crashes on it, and the crags,
That needle under, stream with weedy rags!

146.

Or, if thou wilt, at inland Bergerac,
    Rude heritage but recognized domain,
Do as two here are doing: make hearth crack
    With logs until thy chimney roar again
Jolly with fire-glow! Let its angle lack
    No grace of Cherry-cheeks thy sister, fain
To do a sister's office and laugh smooth
Thy corrugated brow — that scowls forsooth!

147.

Wherefore? Who does not know how these La Roques,
  Voltaires, can say and unsay, praise and blame,
Prove black white, white black, play at paradox
  And, when they seem to lose it, win the game?
Care not thou what this badger, and that fox,
  His fellow in rascality, call "fame!"
Fiddlepin's end! Thou hadst it, — quack, quack,
    quack!
Have quietude from geese at Bergerac!

148.

Quietude! For, be very sure of this!
  A twelvemonth hence, and men shall know or care
As much for what to-day they clap or hiss
  As for the fashion of the wigs they wear,
Then wonder at. There's fame which, bale or bliss, —
  Got by no gracious word of great Voltaire
Or not-so-great La Roque, — is taken back
By neither, any more than Bergerac

149.

Too true! or rather, true as ought to be!
  No more of Paul the man, Malcrais the maid,
Thenceforth forever! One or two, I see,
  Stuck by their poet: who the longest stayed

Was Jean-Baptiste Rousseau, and even he
   Seemingly saddened as perforce he paid
A rhyming tribute "After death, survive —
He hoped he should : and died while yet alive !"

150.

No, he hoped nothing of the kind, or held
   His peace and died in silent good old age.
Him it was, curiosity impelled
   To seek if there were extant still some page
Of his great predecessor, rat who belled
   The cat once, and would never deign engage
In after-combat with mere mice, — saved from
More sonnetteering, — René Gentilhomme.

151.

Paul's story furnished forth that famous play
   Of Piron's "Métromanie" : there you 'll find
He 's Francaleu, while Demoiselle Malcrais
   Is Demoiselle No-end-of-names-behind !
As for Voltaire, he 's Damis.   Good and gay
   The plot and dialogue, and all 's designed
To spite Voltaire : at " Something" such the laugh
Of simply " Nothing !" (see his epitaph.)

152.

But truth, truth, that 's the gold ! and all the good
   I find in fancy is, it serves to set

Gold's inmost glint free, gold which comes up rude
  And rayless from the mine. All fume and fret
Of artistry beyond this point pursued
  Brings out another sort of burnish : yet
Always the ingot has its very own
Value, a sparkle struck from truth alone.

153.

Now, take this sparkle and the other spirt
  Of fitful flame, — twin births of our grey brand
That 's sinking fast to ashes ! I assert,
  As sparkles want but fuel to expand
Into a conflagration no mere squirt
  Will quench too quickly, so might Croisic strand,
Had Fortune pleased posterity to chowse,
Boast of her brace of beacons luminous.

154.

Did earlier Agamemnons lack their bard ?
  But later bards lacked Agamemnons too !
How often frustrate they of fame's award
  Just because Fortune, as she listed, blew
Some slight bark's sails to bellying, mauled and
        marred
  And forced to put about the First-rate ! True,
Such tacks but for a time: still — small-craft ride
At anchor, rot while Beddoes breasts the tide !

155.

Dear, shall I tell you ?   There 's a simple test
  Would serve, when people take on them to weigh
The worth of poets, "Who was better, best,
  This, that, the other bard ?" (bards none gainsay
As good, observe ! no matter for the rest)
  "What quality preponderating may
Turn the scale as it trembles ?"   End the strife
By asking, "Which one led a happy life? "

156.

If one did, over his antagonist
  That yelled or shrieked or sobbed or wept or wailed
Or simply had the dumps, — dispute who list, —
  I count him victor.   Where his fellow failed,
Mastered by his own means of might, — acquist
  Of necessary sorrows, — he prevailed,
A strong since joyful man who stood distinct
Above slave-sorrows to his chariot linked.

157.

Was not his lot to feel more ?   What meant "feel "
  Unless to suffer !   Not, to see more ?   Sight —
What helped it but to watch the drunken reel
  Of vice and folly round him, left and right,
One dance of imps and idiots !   Not, to deal

More with things lovely? What provoked the spite
Of filth incarnate, like the poet's need
Of other nutriment than strife and greed !

158.

Who knows most, doubts most ; entertaining hope,
    Means recognizing fear ; the keener sense
Of all comprised within our actual scope
    Recoils from aught beyond earth's dim and dense.
Who, grown familiar with the sky, will grope
    Henceforward among groundlings? That 's offence
Just as indubitably: stars abound
O'erhead, but then — what flowers make glad the
      ground !

159.

So, force is sorrow, and each sorrow, force :
    What then ? since Swiftness gives the charioteer
The palm, his hope be in the vivid horse
    Whose neck God clothed with thunder, not the
      steer
Sluggish and safe ! Yoke Hatred, Crime, Remorse,
    Despair : but ever mid the whirling fear,
Let, through the tumult, break the poet's face
Radiant, assured his wild slaves win the race !

160.

Therefore I say . . . no, shall not say, but think,
    And save my breath for better purpose. White

From grey our log has burned to : just one blink
   That quivers, loth to leave it, as a sprite
The outworn body.   Ere your eyelids' wink
   Punish who sealed so deep into the night
Your mouth up, for two poets dead so long, —
Here pleads a live pretender : right your wrong !

1.

What a pretty tale you told me
  Once upon a time
— Said you found it somewhere (scold me !)
  Was it prose or was it rhyme,
Greek or Latin ?   Greek, you said,
While your shoulder propped my head.

2.

Anyhow there 's no forgetting
  This much if no more,
That a poet (pray, no petting !)
  Yes, a bard, sir, famed of yore,
Went where suchlike used to go,
Singing for a prize, you know.

3.

Well, he had to sing, nor merely
  Sing but play the lyre ;
Playing was important clearly
  Quite as singing : I desire,
Sir, you keep the fact in mind
For a purpose that 's behind.

4.

There stood he, while deep attention.
  Held the judges round,
— Judges able, I should mention,
  To detect the slightest sound
Sung or played amiss : such ears
Had old judges, it appears !

5.

None the less he sang out boldly,
  Played in time and tune,
Till the judges, weighing coldly
  Each note's worth, seemed, late or soon,
Sure to smile : " In vain one tries
Picking faults out : take the prize ! "

6.

When, a mischief ! Were they seven
  Strings the lyre possessed ?
Oh, and afterwards eleven,
  Thank you ! Well, sir, — who had guessed
Such ill luck in store ? — it happed
One of those same seven strings snapped.

7.

All was lost, then ! No ! a cricket
  (What " cicada " ? Pooh !)

— Some mad thing that left its thicket
   For mere love of music — flew
With its little heart on fire,
Lighted on the crippled lyre.

8.

So that when (Ah joy !) our singer
   For his truant string
Feels with disconcerted finger,
   What does cricket else but fling
Fiery heart forth, sound the note
Wanted by the throbbing throat ?

9.

Ay and, ever to the ending,
   Cricket chirps at need,
Executes the hand's intending,
   Promptly, perfectly, — indeed
Saves the singer from defeat
With her chirrup low and sweet.

10.

Till, at ending, all the judges
   Cry with one assent
" Take the prize — a prize who grudges
   Such a voice and instrument ?
Why, we took your lyre for harp,
So it shrilled us forth F sharp ! "

11.

Did the conqueror spurn the creature,
   Once its service done ?
That 's no such uncommon feature
   In the case when Music's son
Finds his Lotte's power too spent
For aiding soul-development.

12.

No !   This other, on returning
   Homeward, prize in hand,
Satisfied his bosom's yearning :
   (Sir, I hope you understand !)
— Said " Some record there must be
Of this cricket's help to me ! "

13.

So, he made himself a statue :
   Marble stood, life-size ;
On the lyre, he pointed at you,
   Perched his partner in the prize ;
Never more apart you found
Her, he throned, from him, she crowned.

14.

That 's the tale : its application ?
   Somebody I know

Hopes one day for reputation
   Through his poetry that's — Oh,
All so learned and so wise
And deserving of a prize !

15.

If he gains one, will some ticket,
   When his statue's built,
Tell the gazer " 'T was a cricket
   Helped my crippled lyre, whose lilt
Sweet and low, when strength usurped
Softness' place i' the scale, she chirped ?

16.

" For as victory was nighest,
   While I sang and played, —
With my lyre at lowest, highest,
   Right alike, — one string that made
' Love ' sound soft was snapped in twain,
Never to be heard again, —

17.

" Had not a kind cricket fluttered,
   Perched upon the place
Vacant left, and duly uttered
   ' Love, Love, Love,' whene'er the bass
Asked the treble to atone
For its somewhat sombre drone."

18.

But you don't know music !   Wherefore
Keep on casting pearls
To a — poet ?   All I care for
Is — to tell him that a girl's
" Love " comes aptly in when gruff
Grows his singing.   (There, enough !)

January 15, 1878.

PAULINE:

A FRAGMENT OF A CONFESSION.

15

Non dubito, quin titulus libri nostri raritate suâ quamplurimos alliciat ad legendum : inter quos nonnulli obliquæ opinionis, mente languidi, multi etiam maligni, et in ingenium nostrum ingrati accedent, qui temerariâ suâ ignorantiâ, vix conspecto titulo clamabunt : Nos vetita docere, hæresium semina jacere : piis auribus offendiculo, præclaris ingeniis scandalo esse : . . . adeò conscientiæ suæ consulentes, ut nec Apollo, nec Musæ omnes, neque Angelus de cœlo me ab illorum execratione vindicare queant : quibus et ego nunc consulo, ne scripta nostra legant, nec intelligant, nec meminerint : nam noxia sunt, venenosa sunt : Acherontis ostium est in hoc libro, lapides loquitur, caveant, ne cerebrum illis excutiat. Vos autem, qui æquâ mente ad legendum venitis, si tantam prudentiæ discretionem adhibueritis, quantam in melle legendo apes, jam securi legite. Puto namque vos et utilitatis haud parùm et voluptatis plurimùm accepturos. Quod si qua repereritis, quæ vobis non placeant, mittite illa, nec utimini. NAM ET EGO VOBIS ILLA NON PROBO, SED NARRO. Cætera tamen propterea non respuite. . . . Ideo, si quid liberius dictum sit, ignoscite adolescentiæ nostræ, qui minor quam adolescens hoc opus composui. — HEN. CORN. AGRIPPA, *De Occult. Philosoph. in Prefat.*

LONDON, *January*, 1833.

PAULINE.

PAULINE, mine own, bend o'er me — thy soft breast
Shall pant to mine — bend o'er me — thy sweet eyes
And loosened hair and breathing lips, and arms
Drawing me to thee — these build up a screen
To shut me in with thee, and from all fear;
So that I might unlock the sleepless brood
Of fancies from my soul, their lurking place,
Nor doubt that each would pass, ne'er to return
To one so watched, so loved and so secured.
But what can guard thee but thy naked love?
Ah dearest, whoso sucks a poisoned wound
Envenoms his own veins! Thou art so good,
So calm — if thou shouldst wear a brow less light
For some wild thought which, but for me, were kept
From out thy soul as from a sacred star!
Yet till I have unlocked them it were vain
To hope to sing; some woe would light on me;
Nature would point at one whose quivering lip

Was bathed in her enchantments, whose brow burned
Beneath the crown, to which her secrets knelt,
Who learned the spell which can call up the dead,
And then departed smiling like a fiend
Who has deceived God, — if such one should seek
Again her altars, and stand robed and crowned
Amid the faithful : sad confession first,
Remorse and pardon and old claims renewed,
Ere I can be — as I shall be no more.

I had been spared this shame if I had sat
By thee forever from the first, in place
Of my wild dreams of beauty and of good,
Or with them, as an earnest of their truth :
No thought nor hope having been shut from thee,
No vague wish unexplained, no wandering aim
Sent back to bind on fancy's wings and seek
Some strange fair world where it might be a law ;
But doubting nothing, had been led by thee,
Thro' youth, and saved, as one at length awaked
Who has slept through a peril.   Ah vain, vain !

Thou lovest me ; the past is in its grave
Tho' its ghost haunts us ; still this much is ours,
To cast away restraint, lest a worse thing
Wait for us in the darkness.   Thou lovest me ;
And thou art to receive not love, but faith,

For which thou wilt be mine, and smile and take
All shapes and shames, and veil without a fear
That form which music follows like a slave :
And I look to thee and I trust in thee,
As in a Northern night one looks alway
Unto the East for morn and spring and joy.
Thou seest then my aimless, hopeless state,
And, resting on some few old feelings won
Back by thy beauty, wouldst that I essay
The task which was to me what now thou art :
And why should I conceal one weakness more?

Thou wilt remember one warm morn when winter
Crept aged from the earth, and spring's first breath
Blew soft from the moist hills ; the black-thorn
      boughs,
So dark in the bare wood, when glistening
In the sunshine were white with coming buds,
Like the bright side of a sorrow, and the banks
Had violets opening from sleep like eyes.
I walked with thee, who knew not a deep shame
Lurked beneath smiles and careless words which
      sought
To hide it till they wandered and were mute,
As we stood listening on a sunny mound
To the wind murmuring in the damp copse,
Like heavy breathings of some hidden thing

Betrayed by sleep; until the feeling rushed
That I was low indeed, yet not so low
As to endure the calmness of thine eyes;
And so I told thee all, while the cool breast
I leaned on altered not its quiet beating,
And long ere words like a hurt bird's complaint
Bade me look up and be what I had been,
I felt despair could never live by thee:
Thou wilt remember. Thou art not more dear
Than song was once to me; and I ne'er sung
But as one entering bright halls where all
Will rise and shout for him: sure I must own
That I am fallen, having chosen gifts
Distinct from theirs — that I am sad and fain
Would give up all to be but where I was,
Not high as I had been if faithful found,
But low and weak yet full of hope, and sure
Of goodness as of life — that I would lose
All this gay mastery of mind, to sit
Once more with them, trusting in truth and love,
And with an aim — not being what I am.
Oh Pauline, I am ruined who believed
That though my soul had floated from its sphere
Of wild dominion into the dim orb
Of self — that it was strong and free as ever!
It has conformed itself to that dim orb,
Reflecting all its shades and shapes, and now

Must stay where it alone can be adored.
I have felt this in dreams — in dreams in which
I seemed the fate from which I fled ; I felt
A strange delight in causing my decay ;
I was a fiend in darkness chained forever
Within some ocean-cave ; and ages rolled,
Till through the cleft rock, like a moonbeam, came
A white swan to remain with me ; and ages
Rolled, yet I tired not of my first joy
In gazing on the peace of its pure wings :
And then I said "It is most fair to me,
Yet its soft wings must sure have suffered change
From the thick darkness, sure its eyes are dim,
Its silver pinions must be cramped and numbed
With sleeping ages here ; it cannot leave me,
For it would seem, in light beside its kind,
Withered, tho' here to me most beautiful."
And then I was a young witch whose blue eyes,
As she stood naked by the river springs,
Drew down a god ; I watched his radiant form
Growing less radiant and it gladdened me ;
Till one morn, as he sat in the sunshine
Upon my knees, singing to me of heaven,
He turned to look at me, ere I could lose
The grin with which I viewed his perishing :
And he shrieked and departed and sat long
By his deserted throne, but sank at last

Murmuring, as I kissed his lips and curled
Around him, "I am still a god — to thee."
Still I can lay my soul bare in its fall,
For all the wandering and all the weakness
Will be a saddest comment on the song :
And if, that done, I can be young again,
I will give up all gained, as willingly
As one gives up a charm which shuts him out
From hope or part or care in human kind.
As life wanes, all its cares and strife and toil
Seem strangely valueless, while the old trees
Which grew by our youth's home, the waving mass
Of climbing plants heavy with bloom and dew,
The morning swallows with their songs like words,
All these seem clear and only worth our thoughts :
So, aught connected with my early life,
My rude songs or my wild imaginings,
How I look on them — most distinct amid
The fever and the stir of after years !

I ne'er had ventured e'en to hope for this ;
Had not the glow I felt at His award,
Assured me all was not extinct within :
His whom all honor, whose renown springs up
Like sunlight which will visit all the world,
So that e'en they who sneered at him at first,
Come out to it, as some dark spider crawls

From his foul nets which some lit torch invades,
Yet spinning still new films for his retreat.
Thou didst smile, poet, but can we forgive ?
Sun-treader, life and light be thine forever !
Thou art gone from us ; years go by and spring
Gladdens and the young earth is beautiful
Yet thy songs come not, other bards arise,
But none like thee : they stand, thy majesties,
Like mighty works which tell some spirit there
Hath sat regardless of neglect and scorn,
Till, its long task completed, it hath risen
And left us, never to return, and all
Rush in to peer and praise when all in vain.
The air seems bright with thy past presence yet,
But thou art still for me as thou hast been
When I have stood with thee as on a throne
With all thy dim creations gathered round
Like mountains, and I felt of mould like them,
And creatures of my own were mixed with them,
Like things half-lived, catching and giving life.
But thou art still for me, who have adored,
Tho' single, panting but to hear thy name
Which I believed a spell to me alone,
Scarce deeming thou wast as a star to men !
As one should worship long a sacred spring
Scarce worth a moth's flitting, which long grasses
    cross,

And one small tree embowers droopingly,
Joying to see some wandering insect won
To live in its few rushes, or some locust
To pasture on its boughs, or some wild bird
Stoop for its freshness from the trackless air :
And then should find it but the fountain-head,
Long lost, of some great river washing towns
And towers, and seeing old woods which will live
But by its banks untrod of human foot,
Which, when the great sun sinks, lie quivering
In light as something lieth half of life
Before God's foot, waiting a wondrous change ;
Then girt with rocks which seek to turn or stay
Its course in vain, for it does ever spread
Like a sea's arm as it goes rolling on,
Being the pulse of some great country — so
Wast thou to me, and art thou to the world !
And I, perchance, half feel a strange regret,
That I am not what I have been to thee :
Like a girl one has loved long silently
In her first loveliness in some retreat,
When, first emerged, all gaze and glow to view
Her fresh eyes and soft hair and lips which bleed
Like a mountain berry : doubtless it is sweet
To see her thus adored, but there have been
Moments when all the world was in his praise,
Sweeter than all the pride of after hours.

Yet, sun-treader, all hail! From my heart's heart
I bid thee hail! E'en in my wildest dreams,
I am proud to feel I would have thrown up all
The wreaths of fame which seemed o'erhanging me,
To have seen thee for a moment as thou art.
And if thou livest, if thou lovest, spirit!
Remember me who set this final seal
To wandering thought — that one so pure as thou
Could never die. Remember me who flung
All honor from my soul yet paused and said,
" There is one spark of love remaining yet,
For I have nought in common with him, shapes
Which followed him avoid me, and foul forms
Seek me, which ne'er could fasten on his mind;
And though I feel how low I am to him,
Yet I aim not even to catch a tone
Of all the harmonies which he called up;
So, one gleam still remains, although the last."
Remember me who praise thee e'en with tears,
For never more shall I walk calm with thee;
Thy sweet imaginings are as an air,
A melody some wondrous singer sings,
Which, though it haunt men oft in the still eve,
They dream not to essay; yet it no less
But more is honored. I was thine in shame,
And now when all thy proud renown is out,
I am a watcher whose eyes have grown dim

With looking for some star which breaks on him
Altered and worn and weak and full of tears.

Autumn has come like spring returned to us,
Won from her girlishness ; like one returned
A friend that was a lover nor forgets
The first warm love, but full of sober thoughts
Of fading years ; whose soft mouth quivers yet
With the old smile but yet so changed and still !
And here am I the scoffer, who have probed
Life's vanity, won by a word again
Into my old life — for one little word
Of this sweet friend who lives in loving me,
Lives strangely on my thoughts and looks and words,
As fathoms down some nameless ocean thing
Its silent course of quietness and joy.
O dearest, if indeed I tell the past,
May'st thou forget it as a sad sick dream !
Or if it linger — my lost soul too soon
Sinks to itself and whispers, we shall be
But closer linked, two creatures whom the earth
Bears singly, with strange feelings unrevealed
But to each other ; or two lonely things
Created by some power whose reign is done,
Having no part in God or his bright world.
I am to sing whilst ebbing day dies soft,
As a lean scholar dies worn o'er his book,

And in the heaven stars steal out one by one
As hunted men steal to their mountain watch.
I must not think, lest this new impulse die
In which I trust ; I have no confidence :
So, I will sing on fast as fancies come ;
Rudely, the verse being as the mood it paints.

I strip my mind bare, whose first elements
I shall unveil — not as they struggled forth
In infancy, nor as they now exist,
That I am grown above them and can rule —
But in that middle stage when they were full
Yet ere I had disposed them to my will ;
And then I shall show how these elements
Produced my present state, and what it is.

I am made up of an intensest life,
Of a most clear idea of consciousness
Of self, distinct from all its qualities,
From all affections, passions, feelings, powers ;
And thus far it exists, if tracked in all :
But linked, in me, to self-supremacy,
Existing as a centre to all things,
Most patent to create and rule and call
Upon all things to minister to it ;
And to a principle of restlessness
Which would be all, have, see, know, taste, feel, all —

This is myself ; and I should thus have been
Though gifted lower than the meanest soul.

And of my powers, one springs up to save
From utter death a soul with such desire
Confined to clay — which is the only one
Which marks me — an imagination which
Has been an angel to me, coming not
In fitful visions but beside me ever
And never failing me ; so, though my mind
Forgets not, not a shred of life forgets,
Yet I can take a secret pride in calling
The dark past up to quell it regally.

A mind like this must dissipate itself,
But I have always had one lode-star ; now,
As I look back, I see that I have wasted
Or progressed as I look towards that star —
A need, a trust, a yearning after God :
A feeling I have analyzed but late,
But it existed, and was reconciled
With a neglect of all I deemed his laws,
Which yet, when seen in others, I abhorred.
I felt as one beloved, and so shut in
From fear : and thence I date my trust in signs
And omens, for I saw God everywhere ;
And I can only lay it to the fruit

Of a sad after-time that I could doubt
Even his being — having always felt
His presence, never acting from myself,
Still trusting in a hand that leads me through
All danger; and this feeling still has fought
Against my weakest reason and resolve.

And I can love nothing — and this dull truth
Has come the last : but sense supplies a love
Encircling me and mingling with my life.

These make myself : for I have sought in vain
To trace how they were formed by circumstance,
For I still find them turning my wild youth
Where they alone displayed themselves, converting
All objects to their use : now see their course.

They came to me in my first dawn of life
Which passed alone with wisest ancient books
All halo-girt with fancies of my own ;
And I myself went with the tale — a god
Wandering after beauty, or a giant
Standing vast in the sunset — an old hunter
Talking with gods, or a high-crested chief,
Sailing with troops of friends to Tenedos.
I tell you, nought has ever been so clear
As the place, the time, the fashion of those lives :

I had not seen a work of lofty art,
Nor woman's beauty nor sweet nature's face,
Yet, I say, never morn broke clear as those
On the dim clustered isles in the blue sea,
The deep groves and white temples and wet caves :
And nothing ever will surprise me now —
Who stood beside the naked Swift-footed,
Who bound my forehead with Proserpine's hair.

And strange it is that I who could so dream
Should e'er have stooped to aim at aught beneath —
Aught low, or painful ; but I never doubted,
So, as I grew, I rudely shaped my life
To my immediate wants ; yet strong beneath
Was a vague sense of powers folded up —
A sense that though those shadowy times were past
Their spirit dwelt in me, and I should rule.

Then came a pause, and long restraint chained down
My soul, till it was changed.   I lost myself,
And were it not that I so loathe that time,
I could recall how first I learned to turn
My mind against itself ; and the effects
In deeds for which remorse were vain as for
The wanderings of delirious dream ; yet thence
Came cunning, envy, falsehood, which so long
Have spotted me : at length I was restored.

Yet long the influence remained ; and nought
But the still life I led, apart from all,
Which left my soul to seek its old delights,
Could e'er have brought me thus far back to peace.
As peace returned, I sought out some pursuit ;
And song rose, no new impulse, but the one
With which all others best could be combined.
My life has not been that of those whose heaven
Was lampless save where poesy shone out ;
But as a clime where glittering mountain-tops
And glancing sea and forests steeped in light
Give back reflected the far-flashing sun ;
For music (which is earnest of a heaven,
Seeing we know emotions strange by it,
Not else to be revealed) is as a voice,
A low voice calling fancy, as a friend,
To the green woods in the gay summer time :
And she fills all the way with dancing shapes
Which have made painters pale, and they go on
While stars look at them and winds call to them
As they leave life's path for the twilight world
Where the dead gather.   This was not at first,
For I scarce knew what I would do.   I had
No wish to paint, no yearning ; but I sang.

And first I sang as I in dream have seen
Music wait on a lyrist for some thought,

Yet singing to herself until it came.
I turned to those old times and scenes where all
That's beautiful had birth for me, and made
Rude verses on them all ; and then I paused —
I had done nothing, so I sought to know
What mind had yet achieved.   No fear was mine
As I gazed on the works of mighty bards,
In the first joy of finding my own thoughts
Recorded and my powers exemplified,
And feeling their aspirings were my own.
And then I first explored passion and mind ;
And I began afresh ; I rather sought
To rival what I wondered at, than form
Creations of my own ; so, much was light
Lent back by others, yet much was my own.

I paused again, a change was coming on,
I was no more a boy, the past was breaking
Before the coming and like fever worked.
I first thought on myself, and here my powers
Burst out : I dreamed not of restraint but gazed
On all things : schemes and systems went and came,
And I was proud (being vainest of the weak)
In wandering o'er them to seek out some one
To be my own, as one should wander o're
The white way for a star.

And my choice fell

Not so much on a system as a man —
On one, whom praise of mine would not offend,
Who was as calm as beauty, being such
Unto mankind as thou to me, Pauline, —
Believing in them and devoting all
His soul's strength to their winning back to peace ;
Who sent forth hopes and longings for their sake,
Clothed in all passion's melodies, which first
Caught me and set me, as to a sweet task,
To gather every breathing of his songs :
And woven with them there were words which seemed
A key to a new world, the muttering
Of angels of some thing unguessed by man.
How my heart beat as I went on, and found
Much there, I felt my own mind had conceived,
But there living and burning !   Soon the whole
Of his conceptions dawned on me ; their praise
Is in the tongues of men, men's brows are high
When his name means a triumph and a pride,
So, my weak hands may well forbear to dim
What then seemed my bright fate : I threw myself
To meet it, I was vowed to liberty,
Men were to be as gods and earth as heaven,
And I — ah, what a life was mine to be !
My whole soul rose to meet it.   Now, Pauline,
I shall go mad, if I recall that time !

Oh let me look back cre I leave forever
The time which was an hour that one waits
For a fair girl that comes a withered hag !
And I was lonely, far from woods and fields,
And amid dullest sights, who should be loose
As a stag ; yet I was full of joy, who lived
With Plato and who had the key to life ;
And I had dimly shaped my first attempt,
And many a thought did I build up on thought,
As the wild bee hangs cell to cell ; in vain,
For I must still go on, my mind rests not.

'T was in my plan to look on real life
Which was all new to me ; my theories
Were firm, so I left them, to look upon
Men and their cares and hopes and fears and joys ;
And as I pondered on them all I sought
How best life's end might be attained — an end
Comprising every joy.   I deeply mused.

And suddenly without heart-wreck I awoke
As from a dream : I said " 'T was beautiful
Yet but a dream, and so adieu to it ! "
As some world-wanderer sees in a far meadow
Strange towers and walled gardens thick with trees,
Where singing goes on and delicious mirth,
And laughing fairy creatures peeping over,

And on the morrow when he comes to live
Forever by those springs and trees fruit-flushed
And fairy bowers, all his search is vain.
First went my hopes of perfecting mankind,
And faith in them, then freedom in itself
And virtue in itself, and then my motives, ends
And powers and loves, and human love went last.
I felt this no decay, because new powers
Rose as old feelings left — wit, mockery
And happiness ; for I had oft been sad,
Mistrusting my resolves, but now I cast
Hope joyously away : I laughed and said
" No more of this ! " I must not think : at length
I looked again to see how all went on.

My powers were greater : as some temple seemed
My soul, where nought is changed and incense rolls
Around the altar, only God is gone
And some dark spirit sitteth in his seat.
So, I passed through the temple and to me
Knelt troops of shadows, and they cried " Hail king !
We serve thee now and thou shalt serve no more !
Call on us, prove us, let us worship thee ! "
And I said " Are ye strong ? Let fancy bear me
Far from the past ! " And I was borne away,
As Arab birds float sleeping in the wind,
O'er deserts, towers and forests, I being calm ;

And I said "I have nursed up energies,
They will prey on me " And a band knelt low
And cried " Lord, we are here and we will make
A way for thee in thine appointed life !
O look on us ! " And I said "Ye will worship
Me ; but my heart must worship too." They shouted
" Thyself, thou art our king ! " So, I stood there
Smiling . . .

And buoyant and rejoicing was the spirit
With which I looked out how to end my days :
I felt once more myself, my powers were mine ;
I found that youth or health so lifted me
That, spite of all life's vanity, no grief
Came nigh me, I must ever be light-hearted ;
And that this feeling was the only veil
Betwixt me and despair: so, if age came,
I should be as a wreck linked to a soul
Yet fluttering, or mind-broken, and aware
Of my decay. So a long summer morn
Found me ; and ere noon came, I had resolved
No age should come on me ere youth's hope went,
For I would wear myself out, like that morn
Which wasted not a sunbeam ; every joy
I would make mine, and die. And thus I sought
To chain my spirit down which I had fed
With thoughts of fame : I said " The troubled life

Of genius, seen so bright when working forth
Some trusted end, seems sad, when all in vain —
Most sad when men have parted with all joy
For their wild fancy's sake, which waited first
As an obedient spirit when delight
Came not with her alone ; but alters soon,
Comes darkened, seldom, hastening to depart,
Leaving a heavy darkness and warm tears.
But I shall never lose her ; she will live
Brighter for such seclusion.   I but catch
A hue, a glance of what I sing, so, pain
Is linked with pleasure, for I ne'er may tell
The radiant sights which dazzle me ; but now
They shall be all my own ; and let them fade
Untold — others shall rise as fair, as fast !
And when all 's done, the few dim gleams trans-
    ferred," —
(For a new thought sprang up that it were well
To leave all shadowy hope, and weave such lays
As would encircle me with praise and love,
So, I should not die utterly, I should bring
One branch from the gold forest, like the knight
Of old tales, witnessing I had been there) —
"And when all 's done, how vain seems e'en suc-
    cess
And all the influence poets have o'er men !
'T is a fine thing that one weak as myself

Should sit in his lone room, knowing the words
He utters in his solitude shall move
Men like a swift wind — that tho' he be forgotten,
Fair eyes shall glisten when his beauteous dreams
Of love come true in happier frames than his.
Ay, the still night brought thoughts like these, but
     morn
Came and the mockery again laughed out
At hollow praises, and smiles almost sneers ;
And my soul's idol seemed to whisper me
To dwell with him and his unhonored name :
And I well knew my spirit, that would be
First in the struggle, and again would make
All bow to it, and I should sink again.

"And then know that this curse will come on us,
To see our idols perish ; we may wither,
Nor marvel, we are clay, but our low fate
Should not extend to them, whom trustingly
We sent before into time's yawning gulf
To face whate'er might lurk in darkness there.
To see the painters' glory pass, and feel
Sweet music move us not as once, or, worst,
To see decaying wits ere the frail body
Decays !   Nought makes me trust in love so really,
As the delight of the contented lowness
With which I gaze on souls I 'd keep forever

In beauty ; I 'd be sad to equal them ;
I 'd feed their fame e'en from my heart's best blood,
Withering unseen that they might flourish still."

Pauline, my sweet friend, thou dost not forget
How this mood swayed me when thou first wast mine,
When I had set myself to live this life,
Defying all opinion.   Ere thou camest
I was most happy, sweet, for old delights
Had come like birds again ; music, my life,
I nourished more than ever, and old lore
Loved for itself and all it shows — the king
Treading the purple calmly to his death,
While round him, like the clouds of eve, all dusk,
The giant shades of fate, silently flitting,
Pile the dim outline of the coming doom ;
And him sitting alone in blood while friends
Are hunting far in the sunshine ; and the boy
With his white breast and brow and clustering curls
Streaked with his mother's blood, and striving hard
To tell his story ere his reason goes.
And when I loved thee as I 've loved so oft,
Thou lovedst me, and I wondered and looked in
My heart to find some feeling like such love,
Believing I was still what I had been ;
And soon I found all faith had gone from me,
And the late glow of life, changing like clouds,

'T was not the morn-blush widening into day,
But evening colored by the dying sun
While darkness is quick hastening.   I will tell
My state as though 't were none of mine — despair
Cannot come near me — thus it is with me.
Souls alter not, and mine must progress still :
And this I knew not when I flung away
My youth's chief aims.   I ne'er supposed the loss
Of what few I retained, for no resource
Awaits me : now behold the change of all.
I cannot chain my soul, it will not rest
In its clay prison, this most narrow sphere :
It has strange powers and feelings and desires,
Which I cannot account for nor explain,
But which I stifle not, being bound to trust
All feelings equally, to hear all sides :
Yet I cannot indulge them, and they live,
Referring to some state or life unknown.

My selfishness is satiated not,
It wears me like a flame ; my hunger
For all pleasure, howsoe'er minute, is pain ;
I envy — how I envy him whose mind
Turns with its energies to some one end,
To elevate a sect or a pursuit
However mean !   So, my still baffled hopes
Seek out abstractions ; I would have but one

Delight on earth, so it were wholly mine,
One rapture all my soul could fill : and this
Wild feeling places me in dream afar
In some wild country where the eye can see
No end to the far hills and dales bestrewn
With shining towers and dwellings : I grow mad
Well-nigh, to know not one abode but holds
Some pleasure, for my soul could grasp them all
But must remain with this vile form.   I look
With hope to age at last, which quenching much,
May let me concentrate the sparks it spares.

This restlessness of passion meets in me
A craving after knowledge : the sole proof
Of a commanding will is in that power
Repressed ; for I beheld it in its dawn,
That sleepless harpy with its budding wings,
And I considered whether I should yield
All hopes and fears, to live alone with it,
Finding a recompense in its wild eyes ;
And when I found that I should perish so,
I bade its wild eyes close from me forever,
And I am left alone with my delights ;
So, it lies in me a chained thing, still ready
To serve me, if I loose its slightest bond :
I cannot but be proud of my bright slave.

And thus I know this earth is not my sphere,
For I cannot so narrow me but that
I still exceed it : in their elements
My love would pass my reason ; but since here
Love must receive its objects from this earth
While reason will be chainless, the few truths
Caught from its wanderings have sufficed to quell
All love below ; then what must be that love
Which, with the object it demands, would quell
Reason tho' it soared with the seraphim ?
No, what I feel may pass all human love
Yet fall far short of what my love should be.
And yet I seem more warped in this than aught,
For here myself stands out more hideously :
I can forget myself in friendship, fame,
Or liberty, or love of mighty souls ;
But I begin to know what thing hate is —
To sicken and to quiver and grow white —
And I myself have furnished its first prey.
All my sad weaknesses, this wavering will,
This selfishness, this still decaying frame. . . .
But I must never grieve while I can pass
Far from such thoughts — as now, Andromeda !
And she is with me : years roll, I shall change,
But change can touch her not — so beautiful
With her dark eyes, earnest and still, and hair
Lifted and spread by the salt-sweeping breeze,

And one red beam, all the storm leaves in heaven,
Resting upon her eyes and face and hair
As she awaits the snake on the wet beach
By the dark rock and the white wave just breaking
At her feet; quite naked and alone; a thing
You doubt not, nor fear for, secure that God
Will come in thunder from the stars to save her.
Let it pass! I will call another change.
I will be gifted with a wondrous soul,
Yet sunk by error to men's sympathy,
And in the wane of life, yet only so
As to call up their fears; and there shall come
A time requiring youth's best energies;
And straight I fling age, sorrow, sickness off,
And I rise triumphing over my decay.

And thus it is that I supply the chasm
'Twixt what I am and all that I would be:
But then to know nothing, to hope for nothing,
To seize on life's dull joys from a strange fear
Lest, losing them, all 's lost and nought remains!

There's some vile juggle with my reason here;
I feel I but explain to my own loss
These impulses; they live no less the same.
Liberty! what though I despair? my blood
Rose not at a slave's name proudlier than now,

And sympathy, obscured by sophistries !
Why have not I sought refuge in myself,
But for the woes I saw and could not stay ?
And love ! do not I love thee, my Pauline ?
I cherish prejudice, lest I be left
Utterly loveless — witness this belief
In poets, though sad change has come there too ;
No more I leave myself to follow them —
Unconsciously I measure me by them —
Let me forget it : and I cherish most
My love of England — how her name, a word
Of hers in a strange tongue makes my heart beat !

Pauline, I could do anything — not now —
All 's fever — but when calm shall come again,
I am prepared : I have made life my own.
I would not be content with all the change
One frame should feel, but I have gone in thought
Thro' all conjuncture, I have lived all life
When it is most alive, where strangest fate
Now shapes it past surmise — the tales of men
Bit by some curse or in the grasps of doom
Half-visible and still increasing round,
Or crowning their wide being's general aim.

These are wild fancies, but I feel, sweet friend,
As one breathing his weakness to the ear

Of pitying angel — dear as a winter flower,
A slight flower growing alone, and offering
Its frail cup of three leaves to the cold sun,
Yet joyous and confiding like the triumph
Of a child : and why am I not worthy thee ?
I can live all the life of plants, and gaze
Drowsily on the bees that flit and play,
Or bare my breast for sunbeams which will kill,
Or open in the night of sounds, to look
For the dim stars ; I can mount with the bird
Leaping airily his pyramid of leaves
And twisted boughs of some tall mountain tree,
Or rise cheerfully springing to the heavens ;
Or like a fish breathe in the morning air
In the misty sun-warm water ; or with flowers
And trees can smile in light at the sinking sun
Just as the storm comes, as a girl would look
On a departing lover — most serene.

Pauline, come with me, see how I could build
A home for us, out of the world, in thought !
I am inspired : come with me, Pauline !

Night, and one single ridge of narrow path
Between the sullen river and the woods
Waving and muttering, for the moonless night
Has shaped them into images of life,

Like the upraising of the giant-ghosts,
Looking on earth to know how their sons fare :
Thou art so close by me, the roughest swell
Of wind in the tree-tops hides not the panting
Of thy soft breasts.   No, we will pass to morning —
Morning, the rocks and valleys, and old woods.
How the sun brightens in the mist, and here,
Half in the air, like creatures of the place,
Trusting the element, living on high boughs
That swing in the wind — look at the golden spray
Flung from the foam-sheet of the cataract
Amid the broken rocks !   Shall we stay here
With the wild hawks ?   No, ere the hot noon come,
Dive we down — safe ?   See this our new retreat
Walled in with a sloped mound of matted shrubs,
Dark, tangled, old and green, still sloping down
To a small pool whose waters lie asleep
Amid the trailing boughs turned water-plants :
And tall trees over-arch to keep us in,
Breaking the sunbeams into emerald shafts,
And in the dreamy water one small group
Of two or three strange trees are got together
Wondering at all around, as strange beasts herd
Together far from their own land : all wildness,
No turf nor moss, for boughs and plants pave all,
And tongues of bank go shelving in the waters,
Where the pale-throated snake reclines his head,

And old grey stones lie making eddies there,
The wild mice cross them dry shod : deeper in
Shut thy soft eyes — now look — still deeper in !
This is the very heart of the woods all round
Mountain-like heaped above us ; yet even here
One pond of water gleams ; far off the river
Sweeps like a sea, barred out from land ; but one —
One thin clear sheet has over-leaped and wound
Into this silent depth, which gained, it lies
Still, as but let by sufferance ; the trees bend
O'er it as wild men watch a sleeping girl,
And through their roots long creeping plants stretch
    out
Their twined hair, steeped and sparkling ; farther on,
Tall rushes and thick flag-knots have combined
To narrow it ; so, at length, a silver thread,
It winds, all noiselessly through the deep wood
Till thro' a cleft way, thro' the moss and stone,
It joins its parent-river with a shout.
Up for the glowing day, leave the old woods !
See, they part, like a ruined arch, the sky !
Nothing but sky appears, so close the roots
And grass of the hill-top level with the air —
Blue sunny air, where a great cloud floats laden
With light, like a dead whale that white birds pick,
Floating away in the sun in some north sea.
Air, air, fresh life-blood, thin and searching air,

17

The clear, dear breath of God that loveth us,
Where small birds reel and winds take their delight !
Water is beautiful, but not like air :
See, where the solid azure waters lie
Made as of thickened air, and down below,
The fern-ranks like a forest spread themselves
As though each pore could feel the element ;
Where the quick glancing serpent winds his way,
Float with me there, Pauline ! — but not like air.
Down the hill !   Stop — a clump of trees, see, set
On a heap of rocks, which look o'er the far plains,
And envious climbing shrubs would mount to rest
And peer from their spread boughs ; there they wave,
          looking
At the muleteers who whistle as they go
To the merry chime of their morning bells, and all
The little smoking cots and fields and banks
And copses bright in the sun.   My spirit wanders :
Hedge-rows for me — still, living hedge-rows where
The bushes close and clasp above and keep
Thought in — I am concentrated — I feel ;
But my soul saddens when it looks beyond :
I cannot be immortal nor taste all.
O God, where does this tend — these struggling
          aims ? [1]

[1] Je crains bien que mon pauvre ami ne soit pas toujours parfaitement compris dans ce qui reste à lire de cet étrange frag-

What would I have ? What is this "sleep" which seems

To bound all ? Can there be a "waking " point

ment, mais il est moins propre que tout autre à éclaircir ce qui de sa nature ne peut jamais être que songe et confusion. D'ail· leurs je ne sais trop si en cherchant à mieux co-ordonner certaines parties l'on ne courrait pas le risque de nuire au seul mérite auquel une production si singulière peut prétendre, celui de donner une idée assez précise du genre qu'elle n'a fait qu'ébaucher. Ce début sans prétention, ce remuement des passions qui va d'abord en accroissant et puis s'appaise par degrés, ces élans de l'âme, ce retour soudain sur soi-même, et par-dessus tout, la tournne d'esprit tout particulière de mon ami, rendent les changemens presque impossibles. Les raisons qu'il fait valoir ailleurs, et d'autres encore plus puissantes, ont fait trouver grâce à mes yeux pour cet écrit qu'autrement je lui eusse conseillé de jeter au feu. Je n'en crois pas moins au grand principe de toute composition — à ce prin· cipe de Shakespeare, de Rafaelle, de Beethoven, d'où il suit que la concentration des idées est dûe bien plus à leur conception qu'à leur mise en execution : j'ai tout lieu de craindre que la première de ces qualités ne soit encore étrangère à mon ami, et je doute fort qu'un redoublement de travail lui fasse acquérir la seconde. Le mieux serait de brûler ceci ; mais que faire ?

Je crois que dans ce qui suit il fait allusion à un certain examen qu'il fit autrefois de l'âme ou plutôt de son âme, pour découvrir la suite des objets auxquels il lui serait possible d'atteindre, et dont chacun une fois obtenu devait former une espèce de plateau d'où l'on pouvait apercevoir d'autres buts, d'autres projets, d'autres jouissances qui, à leur tour, devaient être surmontés. Il en résultait que l'oubli et le sommeil devaient tout terminer. Cette idée, que je ne saisis pas parfaitement, lui est peutêtre aussi in intelligible qu'à moi. PAULINE.

Of crowning life ?   The soul would never **rule** ;
It would be first in all things, it would have
Its utmost pleasure filled, but, that complete,
Commanding, for commanding, sickens it.
The last point I can trace is, rest, beneath
Some better essence than itself, in weakness ;
This is " myself," not what I think should be :
And what is that I hunger for but God ?
My God, my God, let me for once look on thee
As though nought else existed, we alone !
And as creation crumbles, my soul's spark
Expands till I can say, — Even from myself
I need thee and I feel thee and I love thee :
I do not plead my rapture in thy works
For love of thee, nor that I feel as one
Who cannot die : but there is that in me
Which turns to thee, which loves, or which should
          love.
Why have I girt myself with this hell-dress ?
Why have I labored to put out my life ?
Is it not in my nature to adore,
And e'en for all my reason do I not
Feel him, and thank him, and pray to him — now ?
Can I forego the trust that he loves me ?
Do I not feel a love which only ONE . . .
O thou pale form, so dimly seen, deep-eyed !
I have denied thee calmly — do I not

Pant when I read of thy consummate deeds,
And burn to see thy calm pure truths out-flash
The brightest gleams of earth's philosophy?
Do I not shake to hear aught question thee?
If I am erring save me, madden me,
Take from me powers and pleasures, let me die
Ages, so I see thee! I am knit round
As with a charm by sin and lust and pride,
Yet though my wandering dreams have seen all
    shapes
Of strange delight, oft have I stood by thee —
Have I been keeping lonely watch with thee
In the damp night by weeping Olivet,
Or leaning on thy bosom, proudly less,
Or dying with thee on the lonely cross,
Or witnessing thy bursting from the tomb!

A mortal, sin's familiar friend, doth here
Avow that he will give all earth's reward,
But to believe and humbly teach the faith,
In suffering and poverty and shame,
Only believing he is not unloved.

And now, my Pauline, I am thine forever!
I feel the spirit which has buoyed me up
Deserting me, and old shades gathering on;
Yet while its last light waits, I would say much,

And chiefly, I am glad that I have said
That love which I have ever felt for thee
But seldom told ; our hearts so beat together
That speech is mockery ; but when dark hours come,
And I feel sad, and thou, sweet, deem'st it strange
A sorrow moves me, thou canst not remove,
Look on this lay I dedicate to thee,
Which through thee I began, and which I end,
Collecting the last gleams to strive to tell
That I am thine, and more than ever now
That I am sinking fast : yet though I sink,
No less I feel that thou hast brought me bliss
And that I still may hope to win it back.
Thou knowest, dear friend, I could not think all calm,
For wild dreams followed me and bore me off,
And all was indistinct ; ere one was caught
Another glanced ; so, dazzled by my wealth,
Knowing not which to leave nor which to choose,
For all my thoughts so floated, nought was fixed.
And then thou said'st a perfect bard was one
Who shadowed out the stages of all life,
And so thou bad'st me tell this my first stage.
'T is done, and even now I feel all dim the shift
Of thought ; these are my last thoughts ; I discern
Faintly immortal life and truth and good.
And why thou must be mine is, that e'en now
In the dim hush of night, that I have done,

With fears and sad forebodings, I look through
And say, — E'en at the last I have her still,
With her delicious eyes as clear as heaven
When rain in a quick shower has beat down mist,
And clouds float white in the sun like broods of
    swans.
How the blood lies upon her cheek, all spread
As thinned by kisses ! only in her lips
It wells and pulses like a living thing,
And her neck looks life marble misted o'er
With love-breath, — a dear thing to kiss and love,
Standing beneath me, looking out to me,
As I might kill her and be loved for it.

Love me — love me, Pauline, love nought but me,
Leave me not ! All these words are wild and weak,
Believe them not, Pauline !   I stooped so low
But to behold thee purer by my side,
To show thou art my breath, my life, a last
Resource, an extreme want : never believe
Aught better could so look to thee ; nor seek
Again the world of good thoughts left for me !
There were bright troops of undiscovered suns,
Each equal in their radiant course ; there were
Clusters of far fair isles which ocean kept
For his own joy, and his waves broke on them
Without a choice ; and there was a dim crowd

Of visions, each a part of the dim whole :
And one star left his peers and came with peace
Upon a storm, and all eyes pined for him ;
And one isle harbored a sea-beaten ship,
And the crew wandered in its bowers and plucked
Its fruits and gave up all their hopes for home ;
And one dream came to a pale poet's sleep,
And he said, " I am singled out by God,
No sin must touch me."   I am very weak,
But what I would express is, — Leave me not,
Still sit by me with beating breast and hair
Loosened, be watching earnest by my side,
Turning my books or kissing me when I
Look up — like summer wind !   Be still to me
A key to music's mystery when mind fails,
A reason, a solution and a clue !
You see I have thrown off my prescribed rules :
I hope in myself — and hope and pant and love.
You 'll find me better, know me more than when
You loved me as I was.   Smile not !   I have
Much yet to gladden you, to dawn on you.
No more of the past !   I 'll look within no more.
I have too trusted to my own wild wants,
Too trusted to myself, to intuition —
Draining the wine alone in the still night,
And seeing how, as gathering films arose,
As by an inspiration life seemed bare

And grinning in its vanity, and ends
Hard to be dreamed of, stared at one as fixed,
And others suddenly became all foul
As a fair witch turned an old hag at night.
No more of this ! We will go hand in hand,
I will go with thee, even as a child,
Looking no farther than thy sweet commands,
And thou hast chosen where this life shall be :
The land which gave me thee shall be our home,
Where nature lies all wild amid her lakes
And snow-swathed mountains and vast pines all girt
With ropes of snow — where nature lies all bare,
Suffering none to view her but a race
Most stinted and deformed, like the mute dwarfs
Which wait upon a naked Indian queen.
And there (the time being when the heavens are thick
With storms) I 'll sit with thee while thou dost sing
Thy native songs, gay as a desert bird
Who crieth as he flies for perfect joy.
Or telling me old stories of dead knights ;
Or I will read old lays to thee — how she,
The fair pale sister, went to her chill grave
With power to love and to be loved and live :
Or we will go together, like twin gods
Of the infernal world, with scented lamp
Over the dead, to call and to awake,
Over the unshaped images which lie

Within my mind's cave : only leaving all,
That tells of the past doubts. So, when spring comes,
And sunshine comes again like an old smile,
And the fresh waters and awakened birds
And budding woods await us, I shall be
Prepared, and we will go and think again,
And all old loves shall come to us, but changed
As some sweet thought which harsh words veiled be-
      fore ;
Feeling God loves us, and that all that errs
Is a strange dream which death will dissipate.
And then when I am firm, we 'll seek again
My own land, and again I will approach
My old designs, and calmly look on all
The works of my past weakness, as one views
Some scene where danger met him long before.
Ah that such pleasant life should be but dreamed !

But whate'er come of it, and though it fade,
And though ere the cold morning all be gone,
As it will be ; — tho' music wait for me,
And fair eyes and bright wine laughing like sin
Which steals back softly on a soul half saved,
And I be first to deny all, and despise
This verse, and these intents which seem so fair, —
Still this is all my own, this moment's pride,
No less I make an end in perfect joy.

E'en in my brightest time, a lurking fear
Possessed me : I well knew my weak resolves,
I felt the witchery that makes mind sleep
Over its treasures, as one half afraid
To make his riches definite : but now
These feelings shall not utterly be lost,
I shall not know again that nameless care
Lest, leaving all undone in youth, some new
And undreamed end reveal itself too late :
For this song shall remain to tell forever
That when I lost all hope of such a change,
Suddenly beauty rose on me again.
No less I make an end in perfect joy,
For I, having thus again been visited,
Shall doubt not many another bliss awaits,
And, though this weak soul sink and darkness come,
Some little word shall light it up again,
And I shall see all clearer and love better,
I shall again go o'er the tracts of thought
As one who has a right, and I shall live
With poets, calmer, purer still each time,
And beauteous shapes will come to me again,
And unknown secrets will be trusted me
Which were not mine when wavering ; but now
I shall be priest and lover as of old.

Sun-treader, I believe in God and truth
And love ; and as one just escaped from death

Would bind himself in bands of friends to feel
He lives indeed, so, I would lean on thee !
Thou must be ever with me, most in gloom
When such shall come, but chiefly when I die,
For I seem, dying, as one going in the dark
To fight a giant : and live thou forever,
And be to all what thou hast been to me !
All in whom this wakes pleasant thoughts of me,
Know my last state is happy, free from doubt
Or touch of fear.   Love me and wish me well !

DRAMATIC IDYLS.

FIRST SERIES.

MARTIN RELPH.

My grandfather says he remembers he saw when a
youngster long ago,
On a bright May day, a strange old man with a beard
as white as snow,
Stand on the hill outside our town like a monument of
woe,
And, striking his bare bald head the while, sob out the
reason — so !

If I last as long as Methuselah I shall never forgive
myself :
But — God forgive me, that I pray, unhappy Martin
Relph,
As coward, coward I call him — him, yes, him ! Away
from me !
Get.you behind the man I am now, you man that I
used to be !

What can have sewed my mouth up, set me a-stare, all
　　eyes, no tongue?
People have urged "You visit a scare too hard on a
　　lad so young!
You were taken aback, poor boy," they urge, "no
　　time to regain your wits:
Besides it had maybe cost you life." Ay, there is the
　　cap which fits!

So, cap me, the coward, — thus! No fear! A cuff
　　on the brow does good:
The feel of it hinders a worm inside which bores at
　　the brain for food.
See now, there certainly seems excuse: for a moment,
　　I trust, dear friends,
The fault was but folly, no fault of mine, or if mine,
　　I have made amends!

For, every day that is first of May, on the hill-top,
　　here stand I,
Martin Relph, and I strike my brow, and publish the
　　reason why,
When there gathers a crowd to mock the fool. No
　　fool, friends, since the bite
Of a worm inside is worse to bear: pray God I have
　　baulked him quite!

I 'll tell you. Certainly much excuse ! It came of the
    way they cooped
Us peasantry up in a ring just here, close huddling
    because tight-hooped
By the red-coats round us villagers all : they meant we
    should see the sight
And take the example, — see, not speak, for speech
    was the Captain's right.

" You clowns on the slope, beware ! " cried he : " This
    woman about to die
Gives by her fate fair warning to such acquaintance as
    play the spy.
Henceforth who meddle with matters of state above
    them perhaps will learn
That peasants should stick to their plough-tail, leave
    to the King the King's concern.

" Here 's a quarrel that sets the land on fire, between
    King George and his foes :
What call has a man of your kind — much less, a
    woman — to interpose ?
Yet you needs must be meddling, folks like you, not
    foes — so much the worse !
The many and loyal should keep themselves unmixed
    with the few perverse.

18

"Is the counsel hard to follow?   I gave it you plainly
    a month ago,
And where was the good?   The rebels have learned
    just all that they need to know.
Not a month since in we quietly marched : a week,
    and they had the news,
From a list complete of our rank and file to a note of
    our caps and shoes.

"All about all we did and all we were doing and like
    to do !
Only, I catch a letter by luck, and capture who wrote
    it, too.
Some of you men look black enough, but the milk-
    white face demure
Betokens the finger foul with ink : 't is a woman who
    writes, be sure !

"Is it 'Dearie, how much I miss your mouth !' —
    good natural stuff, she pens?
Some sprinkle of that, for a blind, of course : with talk
    about cocks and hens,
How 'robin has built on the apple-tree, and our
    creeper which came to grief
Through the frost, we feared, is twining afresh round
    casement in famous leaf.'

"But all for a blind ! She soon glides frank into
  'Horrid the place is grown
With Officers here and Privates there, no nook we
  may call our own :
And Farmer Giles has a tribe to house, and lodging
  will be to seek
For the second Company sure to come ('t is whis-
  pered) on Monday week.'

"And so to the end of the chapter ! There ! The
  murder, you see, was out :
Easy to guess how the change of mind in the rebels
  was brought about !
Safe in the trap would they now lie snug, had treachery made no sign :
But treachery meets a just reward, no matter if fools
  malign !

"That traitors had played us false, was proved — sent
  news which fell so pat :
And the murder was out — this letter of love, the
  sender of this sent that !
'T is an ugly job, though, all the same — a hateful, to
  have to deal
With a case of the kind, when a woman 's in fault :
  we soldiers need nerves of steel !

" So, I gave her a chance, despatched post-haste a
   message to Vincent Parkes
Whom she wrote to; easy to find he was, since one
   of the King's own clerks,
Ay, kept by the King's own gold in the town close by
   where the rebels camp :
A sort of a lawyer, just the man to betray our sort —
   the scamp !

" ' If her writing is simple and honest and only the
   lover-like stuff it looks,
And if you yourself are a loyalist, nor down in the
   rebels' books,
Come quick,' said I, 'and in person prove you are
   each of you clear of crime,
Or martial law must take its course : this day next
   week 's the time ! '

" Next week is now : does he come ? Not he ! Clean
   gone, our clerk, in a trice !
He has left his sweetheart here in the lurch : no need
   of a warning twice !
His own neck free, but his partner's fast in the noose
   still, here she stands
To pay for her fault. 'T is an ugly job : but soldiers
   obey commands.

"And hearken wherefore I make a speech !   Should
    any acquaintance share
The folly that led to the fault that is now to be pun-
    ished, let fools beware !
Look black, if you please, but keep hands white : and,
    above all else, keep wives —
Or sweethearts or what they may be — from ink !
    Not a word now, on your lives ! "

Black ? but the Pit's own pitch was white to the Cap-
    tain's face — the brute
With the bloated cheeks and the bulgy nose and the
    blood-shot eyes to suit !
He was muddled with wine, they say : more like, he
    was out of his wits with fear ;
He had but a handful of men, that 's true, — a riot
    might cost him dear.

And all that time stood Rosamund Page, with pin-
    ioned arms and face
Bandaged about, on the turf marked out for the
    party's firing-place.
I hope she was wholly with God : I hope 't was His
    angel stretched a hand
To steady her so, like the shape of stone you see in
    our church-aisle stand.

I hope there was no vain fancy pierced the bandage
    to vex her eyes,
No face within which she missed without, no ques-
    tions and no replies —
"Why did you leave me to die?"—"Because. . . ."
    Oh, fiends, too soon you grin
At merely a moment of hell, like that—such heaven
    as hell ended in!

Let mine end too! He gave the word, up went the
    guns in a line:
Those heaped on the hill were blind as dumb, — for,
    of all eyes, only mine
Looked over the heads of the foremost rank. Some
    fell on their knees in prayer,
Some sank to the earth, but all shut eyes, with a sole
    exception there.

That was myself, who had stolen up last, had sidled
    behind the group:
I am highest of all on the hill-top, there stand fixed
    while the others stoop!
From head to foot in a serpent's twine am I tight-
    ened: *I* touch ground?
No more than a gibbet's rigid corpse which the fetters
    rust around!

Can I speak, can I breathe, can I burst — aught else
    but see, see, only see ?
And see I do — for there comes in sight — a man, it
    sure must be ! —
Who staggeringly, stumblingly, rises, falls, rises, at
    random flings his weight
On and on, anyhow onward — a man that's mad he
    arrives too late !

Else why does he wave a something white high-flour-
    ished above his head ?
Why does not he call, cry, — curse the fool ! — why
    throw up his arms instead ?
O take this fist in your own face, fool ! Why does not
    yourself shout " Stay !
Here's a man comes rushing, might and main, with
    something he's mad to say ? "

And a minute, only a moment, to have hell-fire boil
    up in your brain,
And ere you can judge things right, choose heaven,
    — time's over, repentance vain !
They level : a volley, a smoke and the clearing of
    smoke : I see no more
Of the man smoke hid, nor his frantic arms, nor the
    something white he bore.

But stretched on the field, some half-mile off, is an
    object.   Surely dumb,
Deaf, blind were we struck, that nobody heard, not
    one of us saw him come !
Has he fainted through fright?   One may well be-
    lieve !   What is it he holds so fast?
Turn him over, examine the face !   Heyday !   What
    Vincent Parkes at last?

Dead ! dead as she, by the self-same shot : one bullet
    has ended both,
Her in the body and him in the soul.   They laugh at
    our plighted troth.
"Till death us do part ? "   Till death us do join past
    parting — that sounds like
Betrothal indeed !   O Vincent Parkes, what need has
    my fist to strike ?

I helped you : thus were you dead and wed : one
    bound, and your soul reached hers !
There is clenched in your hand the thing, signed,
    sealed, the paper which plain avers
She is innocent, innocent, plain as print, with the
    King's Arms broad engraved :
No one can hear, but if anyone high on the hill can
    see, she 's saved !

And torn his garb and bloody his lips with heart-break,
 — plain it grew
How the week's delay had been brought about : each
 guess at the end proved true.
It was hard to get at the folks in power : such waste
 of time ! and then
Such pleading and praying, with, all the while, his
 lamb in the lion's den !

And at length when he wrung their pardon out, no
 end to the stupid forms —
The license and leave : I make no doubt — what wonder if passion warms
The pulse in a man if you play with his heart ? — he
 was something hasty in speech ;
Anyhow, none would quicken the work : he had to beseech, beseech !

And the thing once signed, sealed, safe in his grasp,
 — what followed but fresh delays ?
For the floods were out, he was forced to take such a
 roundabout of ways !
And 't was "Halt there !" at every turn of the road,
 since he had to cross the thick
Of the red-coats : what did they care for him and his
 " Quick, for God's sake, quick ! "

Horse? but he had one : had it how long? till the
  first knave smirked "You brag
Yourself a friend of the King's? then lend to a King's
  friend here your nag!"
Money to buy another? Why, piece by piece they
  plundered him still
With their "Wait you must, — no help : if aught can
  help you, a guinea will!"

And a borough there was — I forget the name —
  whose Mayor must have the bench
Of Justices ranged to clear a doubt : for "Vincent,"
  thinks he, sounds French!
It well may have driven him daft, God knows! all
  man can certainly know
Is — rushing and falling and rising, at last he arrived
  in a horror — so!

When a word, cry, gasp, would have rescued both!
  Ay, bite me! The worm begins
At his work once more. Had cowardice proved —
  that only — my sin of sins!
Friends, look you here! Suppose . . . suppose . . .
  But mad I am, needs must be!
Judas the Damned would never have dared such a sin
  as I dream! For, see!

Suppose I had sneakingly loved her myself, my
    wretched self, and dreamed
In the heart of me " She were better dead than happy
    and his ! " — while gleamed
A light from hell as I spied the pair in a perfectest
    embrace,
He the saviour and she the saved, — bliss born of the
    very murder-place !

No ! Say I was scared, friends ! Call me fool and
    coward, but nothing worse !
Jeer at the fool and gibe at the coward ! 'T was ever
    the coward's curse
That fear breeds fancies in such : such take their
    shadow for substance still,
— A fiend at their back. I liked poor Parkes, — loved
    Vincent, if you will !

And her — why, I said " Good morrow " to her,
    " Good even," and nothing more :
The neighborly way ! She was just to me as fifty had
    been before.
So, coward it is and coward shall be ! There 's a
    friend, now ! Thanks ! A drink
Of water I wanted : and now I can walk, get home by
    myself, I think.

PHEIDIPPIDES.

χαίρετε, νικῶμεν.

———✦———

FIRST I salute this soil of the blessed, river and rock !
Gods of my birthplace, demons and heroes, honor to
all !
Then I name thee, claim thee for our patron, co-equal
in praise
— Ay, with Zeus the Defender, with Her of the ægis
and spear !
Also, ye of the bow and the buskin, praised be your
peer,
Now, henceforth and forever, — O latest to whom I
upraise
Hand and heart and voice ! For Athens, leave pas-
ture and flock !
Present to help, potent to save, Pan — patron I call !

Archons of Athens, topped by the tettix, see, I return !

See, 't is myself here standing alive, no spectre that
    speaks !
Crowned with the myrtle, did you command me, Ath-
    ens and you,
" Run, Pheidippides, run and race, reach Sparta for
    aid !
Persia has come, we are here, where is She ? " Your
    command I obeyed,
Ran and raced : like stubble, some field which a fire
    runs through,
Was the space between city and city : two days, two
    nights did I burn
Over the hills, under the dales, down pits and up
    peaks.

Into their midst I broke : breath served but for " Per-
    sia has come !
Persia bids Athens proffer slaves'-tribute, water and
    earth ;
Razed to the ground is Eretria — but Athens, shall
    Athens sink,
Drop into dust and die — the flower of Hellas utterly
    die,
Die, with the wide world spitting at Sparta, the stu-
    pid, the stander-by ?
Answer me quick, what help, what hand do you stretch
    o'er destruction's brink ?

How, — when?   No care for my limbs ! — there 's
  lightning in all and some —
Fresh and fit your message to bear, once lips give it
  birth ! "

O my Athens — Sparta love thee ?   Did Sparta respond ?
Every face of her leered in a furrow of envy, mistrust,
Malice, — each eye of her gave me its glitter of gratified hate !
Gravely they turned to take counsel, to cast for ex-
  cuses.   I stood
Quivering, — the limbs of me fretting as fire frets, an
  inch from dry wood :
" Persia has come, Athens asks aid, and still they debate ?
Thunder, thou Zeus !   Athene, are Spartans a quarry
  beyond
Swing of thy spear ?   Phoibos and Artemis, clang
  them ' Ye must ' ! "

No bolt launched from Olumpos !   Lo, their answer
  at last !
" Has Persia come, — does Athens ask aid, — may
  Sparta befriend ?
Nowise precipitate judgment — too weighty the issue
  at stake !

Count we no time lost time which lags through respect to the Gods !
Ponder that precept of old, 'No warfare, whatever the
odds
In your favor, so long as the moon, half-orbed, is un-
able to take
Full-circle her state in the sky !'   Already she rounds
to it fast :
Athens must wait, patient as we — who judgment suspend."

Athens, — except for that sparkle, — thy name, I had
mouldered to ash !
That sent a blaze through my blood ; off, off and
away was I back,
— Not one word to waste, one look to lose on the
false and the vile !
Yet " O Gods of my land ! " I cried, as each hillock
and plain,
Wood and stream, I knew, I named, rushing past
them again,
" Have ye kept faith, proved mindful of honors we
paid you erewhile ?
Vain was the filleted victim, the fulsome libation !
Too rash
Love in its choice, paid you so largely service so
slack !

"Oak and olive and bay, — I bid you cease to en-
    wreathe
Brows made bold by your leaf! Fade at the Per-
    sian's foot,
You that, our patrons were pledged, should never
    adorn a slave !
Rather I hail thee, Parnes, — trust to thy wild waste
    tract !
Treeless, herbless, lifeless mountain ! What matter
    if slacked
My speed may hardly be, for homage to crag and to
    cave
No deity deigns to drape with verdure, — at least I
    can breathe,
Fear in thee no fraud from the blind, no lie from the
    mute ! "

Such my cry as, rapid, I ran over Parnes' ridge ;
Gully and gap, I clambered and cleared till, sudden, a
    bar
Jutted, a stoppage of stone against me, blocking the
    way.
Right ! for I minded the hollow to traverse, the fis-
    sure across :
"Where I could enter, there I depart by ! Night in
    the fosse ?

Out of the day dive, into the day as bravely arise!
  No bridge
Better!"—when—ha! what was it I came on, of
  wonders that are?

There, in the cool of a cleft, sat he—majestical Pan!
Ivy drooped wanton, kissed his head, moss cushioned
  his hoof:
All the great God was good in the eyes grave-kindly
  —the curl
Carved on the bearded cheek, amused at a mortal's
  awe,
As, under the human trunk, the goat-thighs grand I
  saw.
"Halt, Pheidippides!"—halt I did, my brain of a
  whirl:
"Hither to me! Why pale in my presence?" he
  gracious began:
"How is it,—Athens, only in Hellas, holds me aloof?

"Athens, she only, rears me no fane, makes me no
  feast!
Wherefore? Than I what godship to Athens more
  helpful of old?
Ay, and still, and forever her friend! Put Pan to the
  test!

19

Go, bid Athens take heart, laugh Persia to scorn, have
    faith
In the temples and tombs !   Go, say to Athens, 'The
    Goat-God saith :
When Persia — so much as strews not the soil — is
    cast in the sea,
Then praise Pan who fought in the ranks with your
    most and least,
Goat-thigh to greaved-thigh, made one cause with the
    free and the bold ! '

" Say Pan saith : ' Let this, foreshowing the place, be
    the pledge ! ' "
(Gay, the liberal hand held out this herbage I bear
— Fennel, whatever it bode — I grasped it a-tremble
    with dew)
" While, as for thee . . . "   But enough ! He was
    gone. If I ran hitherto —
Be sure that, the rest of my journey, I ran no longer,
    but flew.
Here am I back.   Praise Pan, we stand no more on
    the razor's edge !
Pan for Athens, Pan for me ! myself have a guerdon
    too !

Then Miltiades spoke. "And thee, best runner of
    Greece,
Whose limbs did duty indeed, — what gift is promised
    thyself?
Tell it us straightway, — Athens the mother demands
    of her son!"
Rosily blushed the youth: he paused: but, lifting at
    length
His eyes from the ground, it seemed as he gathered
    the rest of his strength
Into the utterance — "Pan spoke thus: 'For what
    thou hast done
Count on a worthy reward! Henceforth be allowed
    thee release
From the racer's toil, no vulgar reward in praise or in
    pelf!'

"I am bold to believe, Pan means reward the most to
    my mind!
Fight I shall, with our foremost, wherever this fennel
    may grow, —
Pound — Pan helping us — Persia to dust, and, under
    the deep,
Whelm her away for ever; and then, — no Athens to
    save, —
Marry a certain maid, I know keeps faith to the
    brave, —

Hie to my house and home : and, when my children
    shall creep
Close to my knees, — recount how the God was awful
    yet kind,
Promised their sire reward to the full — rewarding
    him — so ! "

Unforeseeing one !   Yes, he fought on the Marathon
    day :
So, when Persia was dust, all cried " To Akropolis !
Run, Pheidippides, one race more ! the meed is thy
    due !
' Athens is saved, thank Pan,' go shout ! "   He flung
    down his shield,
Ran like fire once more : and the space 'twixt the
    Fennel-field
And Athens was stubble again, a field which a fire
    runs through,
Till in he broke : " Rejoice, we conquer ! "   Like wine
    through clay,
Joy in his blood bursting his heart, he died — the
    bliss !

So, to this day, when friend meets friend, the word of
    salute
Is still " Rejoice ! " — his word which brought rejoic-
    ing indeed.

So is Pheidippides happy forever, — the noble strong
  man
Who could race like a God, bear the face of a God,
  whom a God loved so well
He saw the land saved he had helped to save, and was
  suffered to tell
Such tidings, yet never decline, but, gloriously as he
  began,
So to end gloriously — once to shout, thereafter be
  mute :
" Athens is saved ! " — Pheidippides dies in the shout
  for his meed.

HALBERT AND HOB.

HERE is a thing that happened. Like wild beasts
    whelped, for den,
In a wild part of North England, there lived once two
    wild men
Inhabiting one homestead, neither a hovel nor hut,
Time out of mind their birthright : father and son,
    these — but —
Such a son, such a father ! Most wildness by degrees
Softens away : yet, last of their line, the wildest and
    worst were these.

Criminals, then ? Why, no : they did not murder and
    rob ;
But, give them a word, they returned a blow — old
    Halbert as young Hob :
Harsh and fierce of word, rough and savage of deed,
Hated or feared the more — who knows ? — the gen-
    uine wild-beast breed.

Thus were they found by the few sparse folk of the
    country-side ;

But how fared each with other ?   E'en beasts couch,
  hide by hide,
In a growling, grudged agreement : so, father and son
  lay curled
The closelier up in their den because the last of their
  kind in the world.

Still, beast irks beast on occasion.   One Christmas
  night of snow,
Came father and son to words — such words ! more
  cruel because the blow
To crown each word was wanting, while taunt matched
  gibe, and curse
Competed with oath in wager, like pastime in hell, —
  nay, worse :
For pastime turned to earnest, as up there sprang at
  last
The son at the throat of the father, seized him and
  held him fast.

"Out of this house you go !" — (there followed a
  hideous oath) —
"This oven where now we bake, too hot to hold us
  both !
If there's snow outside, there's coolness : out with
  you, bide a spell
In the drift and save the sexton the charge of a par-
  ish shell !"

Now, the old trunk was tough, was solid as stump of
    oak

Untouched at the core by a thousand years : much
    less had its seventy broke

One whipcord nerve in the muscly mass from neck to
    shoulder-blade

Of the mountainous man, whereon his child's rash
    hand like a feather weighed.

Nevertheless at once did the mammoth shut his eyes,

Drop chin to breast, drop hands to sides, stand stif-
    fened — arms and thighs

All of a piece — struck mute, much as a sentry stands,

Patient to take the enemy's fire : his captain so com-
    mands.

Whereat the son's wrath flew to fury at such sheer
    scorn

Of his puny strength by the giant eld thus acting the
    babe new-born :

And "Neither will this turn serve !" yelled he.
    "Out with you ! Trundle, log !

If you cannot tramp and trudge like a man, try all-
    fours like a dog ! "

Still the old man stood mute. So, logwise, — down to
    floor

Pulled from his fireside place, dragged on from hearth
    to door, —
Was he pushed, a very log, staircase along, until
A certain turn in the steps was reached, a yard from
    the house-door-sill.

Then the father opened his eyes — each spark of their
    rage extinct, —
Temples, late black, dead-blanched, — right-hand with
    left-hand linked, —
He faced his son submissive ; when slow the accents
    came,
They were strangely mild though his son's rash hand
    on his neck lay all the same.

"Halbert, on such a night of a Christmas long
    ago,
For such a cause, with such a gesture, did I drag —
    so —
My father down thus far : but, softening here, I heard
A voice in my heart, and stopped : you wait for an
    outer word.

" For your own sake, not mine, soften you too ! Un-
    trod
Leave this last step we reach, nor brave the finger of
    God !

I dared not pass its lifting : I did well.   I nor blame
Nor praise you.   I stopped here :   Halbert, do you
   the same ! "

Straightway the son relaxed his hold of the father's
   throat.
They mounted, side by side, to the room again : no
   note
Took either of each, no sign made each to either : last
As first, in absolute silence, their Christmas-night they
   passed.

At dawn, the father sate on, dead, in the self-same
   place,
With an outburst blackening still the old bad fighting-
   face :
But the son crouched all a-tremble like any lamb new-
   yeaned.

When he went to the burial, someone's staff he bor-
   rowed, — tottered and leaned.
But his lips were loose, not locked, — kept muttering,
   mumbling.   " There !
At his cursing and swearing ! " the youngsters cried :
   . but the elders thought " In prayer."
A boy threw stones : he picked them up and stored
   them in his vest.

So tottered, muttered, mumbled he, till he died, per-
  haps found rest.
" Is there a reason in nature for these hard hearts ? "
  O Lear,
That a reason out of nature must turn them soft,
  seems clear !

IVÀN IVÀNOVITCH.

"THEY tell me, your carpenters," quoth I to my friend
    the Russ,
"Make a simple hatchet serve as a tool-box serves
    with us.
Arm but each man with his axe, 't is a hammer and
    saw and plane
And chisel, and — what know I else? We should
    imitate in vain
The mastery wherewithal, by a flourish of just the
    adze,
He cleaves, clamps, dovetails in, — no need of our
    nails and brads, —
The manageable pine : 't is said he could shave him-
    self
With the axe, — so all adroit, now a giant and now an
    elf,
Does he work and play at once ! "
                   Quoth my friend the Russ to me,

"Ay, that and more besides on occasion ! It scarce
  may be
You never heard tell a tale told children, time out of
  mind,
By father and mother and nurse, for a moral that 's
  behind,
Which children quickly seize. If the incident happened at all,
We place it in Peter's time when hearts were great
  not small,
Germanized, Frenchified. I wager 't is old to you
As the story of Adam and Eve, and possibly quite as
  true."

————————

In the deep of our land, 't is said, a village from out
  the woods
Emerged on the great main-road 'twixt two great soli-
  tudes.
Through forestry right and left, black verst and verst
  of pine,
From village to village runs the road's long wide bare
  line.
Clearance and clearance break the else-unconquered
  growth
Of pine and all that breeds and broods there, leaving
  loth
Man's inch of masterdom, — spot of life, spirt of
  fire, —

To star the dark and dread, lest right and rule expire
Throughout the monstrous wild a-hungered to resume
Its ancient sway, suck back the world into its womb :
Defrauded by man's craft which clove from North to
    South
This highway broad and straight e'en from the Neva's
    mouth
To Moscow's gates of gold.   So, spot of life and spirt
Of fire aforesaid, burn, each village death-begirt
By wall and wall of pine — unprobed undreamed
    abyss.

Early one winter morn, in such a village as this,
Snow-whitened everywhere except the middle road
Ice-roughed by track of sledge, there worked by his
    abode
Ivàn Ivànovitch, the carpenter, employed
On a huge shipmast trunk ; his axe now trimmed and
    toyed
With branch and twig, and now some chop athwart
    the bole
Changed bole to billets, bared at once the sap and
    soul.
About him, watched the work his neighbors sheep-
    skin-clad ;
Each bearded mouth puffed steam, each gray eye
    twinkled glad

To see the sturdy arm which, never stopping play,
Proved strong man's blood still boils, freeze winter as
    he may.

Sudden, a burst of bells. Out of the road, on edge
· Of the hamlet — horse's hoofs galloping. " How, a
    sledge ?
What 's here ? " cried all as — in, up to the open
    space,
Workyard and market-ground, folks' common meet-
    ing-place, —
Stumbled on, till he fell, in one last bound for life,
A horse : and, at his heels, a sledge held — " Dmìtri's
    wife !
Back without Dmìtri too ! and children — where are
    they ?
Only a frozen corpse ! "

               They drew it forth : then — " Nay,
Not dead, though like to die ! Gone hence a month
    ago :
Home again, this rough jaunt — alone through night
    and snow —
What can the cause be ? Hark — Droug, old horse,
    how he groans :
His day 's done ! Chafe away, keep chafing, for she
    moans :

She 's coming to ! Give here : see, motherkin, your
    friends !
Cheer up, all safe at home ! Warm inside makes
    amends
For outside cold, — sup quick ! Don't look as we
    were bears !
What is it startles you? What strange adventure
    stares
Up at us in your face? You know friends — which is
    which ?
I 'm Vàssili, he 's Sergeì, Ivàn Ivànovitch " . . .

At the word, the woman's eyes, slow-wandering till
    they neared
The blue eyes o'er the bush of honey-colored beard,
Took in full light and sense and — torn to rags, some
    dream
Which hid the naked truth — O loud and long the
    scream
She gave, as if all power of voice within her throat
Poured itself wild away to waste in one dread note !
Then followed gasps and sobs, and then the steady
    flow
Of kindly tears : the brain was saved, a man might
    know.
Down fell her face upon the good friend's propping
    knee ;

His broad hands smoothed her head, as fain to brush
    it free
From fancies, swarms that stung like bees unhived.
    He soothed —
"Loukèria, Loùscha!" — still he, fondling, smoothed
    and smoothed.
At last her lips formed speech.

                 "Ivàn, dear — you indeed!
You, just the same dear you! While I . . . O inter-
    cede,
Sweet Mother, with thy Son Almighty — let his might
Bring yesterday once more, undo all done last night!
But this time yesterday, Ivàn, I sat like you,
A child on either knee, and, dearer than the two,
A babe inside my arms, close to my heart — that's
    lost
In morsels o'er the snow! Father, Son, Holy Ghost,
Cannot you bring again my blessed yesterday?"

When no more tears would flow, she told her tale:
    this way.
"Maybe, a month ago, — was it not? — news came
    here,
They wanted, deeper down, good workmen fit to rear
A church and roof it in. 'We'll go,' my husband
    said:

20

' None understands like me to melt and mould their
    lead.'

So, friends here helped us off — Ivàn, dear, you the
    first !

How gay we jingled forth, all five — (my heart will
    burst) —

While Dmìtri shook the reins, urged Droug upon his
    track !

" Well, soon the month ran out, we just were coming
    back,

When yesterday — behold, the village was on fire !

Fire ran from house to house. What help, as, nigh
    and nigher,

The flames came furious ? ' Haste,' cried Dmìtri,
    ' men must do

The little good man may : to sledge and in with you,

You and our three ! We check the fire by laying flat

Each building in its path, — I needs must stay for
    that, —

But you . . . no time for talk ! Wrap round you
    every rug,

Cover the couple close, — you 'll have the babe to
    hug.

No care to guide old Droug, he knows his way, by
    guess,

Once start him on the road : but chirrup, none the
    less !

The snow lies glib as glass and hard as steel, and
    soon
You 'll have rise, fine and full, a marvel of a moon.
Hold straight up, all the same, this lighted twist of
    pitch !
Once home and with our friend Ivàn Ivànovitch,
All 's safe : I have my pay in pouch, all 's right with
    me,
So I but find as safe you and our precious three !
Off, Droug ! ' — because the flames had reached us,
    and the men
Shouted ' But lend a hand, Dmìtri — as good as ten ! '

" So, in we bundled — I, and those God gave me
    once ;
Old Droug, that 's stiff at first, seemed youthful for
    the nonce :
He understood the case, galloping straight a-head.
Out came the moon : my twist soon dwindled, feebly
    red
In that unnatural day — yes, daylight, bred between
Moon-light and snow-light, lamped those grotto-depths
    which screen
Such devils from God's eye. Ah, pines, how straight
    you grow
Nor bend one pitying branch, true breed of brutal
    snow !

Some undergrowth had served to keep the devils blind
While one escaped outside their border !

                                        "Was that — wind ?
Anyhow, Droug starts, stops, back go his ears, he
        snuffs,
Snorts, — never such a snort ! then plunges, knows
        the sough 's
Only the wind : yet, no — our breath goes up too
        straight !
Still the low sound, — less low, loud, louder, at a rate
There 's no mistaking more !   Shall I lean out — look
        — learn
The truth whatever it be ?   Pad, pad !   At last, I
        turn —

"'T is the regular pad of the wolves in pursuit of
        the life in the sledge !
An army they are : close-packed they press like the
        thrust of a wedge :
They increase as they hunt : for I see, through the
        pine-trunks ranged each side,
Slip forth new fiend and fiend, make wider and still
        more wide
The four-footed steady advance.   The foremost —
        none may pass :
They are elders and lead the line, eye and eye —
        green-glowing brass !

But a long way distant still.   Droug, save us !   He
    does his best :
Yet they gain on us, gain, till they reach, — one
    reaches . . . How utter the rest ?
O that Satan-faced first of the band !   How he lolls
    out the length of his tongue,
How he laughs and lets gleam his white teeth !   He
    is on me, his paws pry among
The wraps and the rugs !   O my pair, my twin-pigeons,
    lie still and seem dead !
Stepàn, he shall never have you for a meal, — here 's
    your mother instead !
No, he will not be counselled — must cry, poor Sti-
    òpka, so foolish ! though first
Of my boy-brood, he was not the best : nay, neigh-
    bors have called him the worst :
He was puny, an undersized slip, — a darling to me,
    all the same !
But little there was to be praised in the boy, and a
    plenty to blame.
I loved him with heart and soul, yes — but, deal him
    a blow for a fault,
He would sulk for whole days.   ' Foolish boy ! lie still
    or the villain will vault,
Will snatch you from over my head !'   No use ! he
    cries, screams, — who can hold
Fast a boy in a frenzy of fear ?   It follows — as I fore-
    told !

The Satan-face snatched and snapped : I tugged, I
    tore — and then
His brother too needs must shriek ! If one must go,
    't is men
The Tsar needs, so we hear, not ailing boys ! Per-
    haps
My hands relaxed their grasp, got tangled in the
    wraps :
God, he was gone ! I looked : there tumbled the
    cursed crew,
Each fighting for a share : too busy to pursue !
That 's so far gain at least : Droug, gallop another
    verst
Or two, or three — God sends we beat them, arrive
    the first !
A mother who boasts two boys was ever accounted
    rich :
Some have not a boy : some have, but lose him, —
    God knows which
Is worse : how pitiful to see your weakling pine
And pale and pass away ! Strong brats, this pair of
    mine !

"O misery ! for while I settle to what near seems
Content, I am 'ware again of the tramp, and again
    there gleams —
Point and point — the line, eyes, levelled green brassy
    fire !

So soon is resumed your chase? Will nothing ap-
    pease, nought tire
The furies? And yet I think — I am certain the race
    is slack,
And the numbers are nothing like. Not a quarter of
    the pack !
Feasters and those full-fed are staying behind . . .
    Ah why?
We 'll sorrow for that too soon ! Now, — gallop, reach
    home, and die,
Nor ever again leave house, to trust our life in the
    trap
For life — we call a sledge ! Teriòscha, in my lap !
Yes, I 'll lie down upon you, tight-tie you with the
    strings
Here — of my heart ! No fear, this time, your mother
    flings . . .
Flings? I flung? Never! But think ! — a woman,
    after all,
Contending with a wolf! Save you I must and shall,
Terentiì !
       "How now ? What, you still head the race,
Your eyes and tongue and teeth crave fresh food, Sa-
    tan-face ?
There and there ! Plain I struck green fire out!
    Flash again ?
All a poor fist can do to damage eyes proves vain !

When, wretches, you danced round — not this, thank
    God — not this !
Hellhounds, we baulk you ! '

        " But — Ah, God above ! — Bliss, bliss —
Not the band, no !   And yet — yes, for Droug knows
    him !   One —
Of them all, only this has said ' She saves a son ! '
His fellows disbelieve such luck : but he believes,
He lets them pick the bones, laugh at him in their
    sleeves :
He 's off and after us, — one speck, one spot, one ball
Grows bigger, bound on bound, — one wolf as good
    as all !
O but I know the trick !   Have at the snaky tongue !
That 's the right way with wolves !   Go, tell your
    mates I wrung
The panting morsel out, left you to howl your worst !
Now for it — now !   Ah me !   I know him — thrice-
    accurst
Satan-face, — him to the end my foe !

        " All fight 's in vain :
This time the green brass points pierce to my very
    brain.
I fall — fall as I ought — quite on the babe I guard :
I overspread with flesh the whole of him.   Too hard

To die this way, torn piecemeal? Move hence? Not
    I — one inch !
Gnaw through me, through and through : flat thus I
    lie nor flinch !
O God, the feel of the fang furrowing my shoulder !
    — see !
It grinds — it grates the bone. O Kìrill under me,
Could I do more? Besides he knew wolf's-way to win :
I clung, closed round like wax : yet in he wedged and
    in,
Past my neck, past my breasts, my heart, until . . .
    how feels
The onion-bulb your knife parts, pushing through its
    peels,
Till out you scoop its clove wherein lie stalk and leaf
And bloom and seed unborn ?

                    " That slew me : yes, in brief,
I died then, dead I lay doubtlessly till Droug stopped
Here, I suppose. I come to life, I find me propped
Thus — how or when or why, — I know not. Tell
    me, friends,
All was a dream : laugh quick and say the nightmare
    ends !
Soon I shall find my house : 't is over there : in proof,
Save for that chimney heaped with snow, you 'd see
    the roof
Which holds my three — my two — my one — not one ?

" Life's mixed
With misery, yet we live — must live. The Satan
 fixed
His face on mine so fast, I took its print as pitch
Takes what it cools beneath. Ivàn Ivànovitch,
'T is you unharden me, you thaw, disperse the thing !
Only keep looking kind, the horror will not cling.
Your face smooths fast away each print of Satan.
 Tears
— What good they do ! Life's sweet, and all its
 after-years,
Ivàn Ivànovitch, I owe you ! Yours am I !
May God reward you, dear ! "

      Down she sank. Solemnly
Ivàn rose, raised his axe, — for fitly, as she knelt,
Her head lay : well-apart, each side, her arms hung, —
 dealt
Lightning-swift thunder-strong one blow — no need of
 more !
Headless she knelt on still : that pine was sound at
 core
(Neighbors were used to say) — cast-iron-kerneled —
 which
Taxed for a second stroke Ivàn Ivànovitch.

The man was scant of words as strokes. " It had to
 be :

I could no other: God it was bade 'Act for me!'"
Then stooping, peering round — what is it now he
    lacks?
A proper strip of bark wherewith to wipe his axe.
Which done, he turns, goes in, closes the door behind.
The others mute remain, watching the blood-snake
    wind
Into a hiding-place among the splinter-heaps.

At length, still mute, all move : one lifts, — from
    where it steeps
Redder each ruddy rag of pine, — the head : two
    more
Take up the dripping body : then, mute still as before,
Move in a sort of march, march on till marching
    ends
Opposite to the church ; where halting, — who sus-
    pends,
By its long hair, the thing, deposits in its place
The piteous head : once more the body shows no trace
Of harm done : there lies whole the Loùscha, maid
    and wife
And mother, loved until this latest of her life.
Then all sit on the bank of snow which bounds a
    space
Kept free before the porch for judgment : just the
    place !

Presently all the souls, man, woman, child, which
    make
The village up, are found assembling for the sake
Of what is to be done. The very Jews are there :
A Gipsy-troop, though bound with horses for the Fair,
Squats with the rest. Each heart with its conception
    seethes
And simmers, but no tongue speaks : one may say, —
    none breathes.

Anon from out the church totters the Pope — the
    priest —
Hardly alive, so old, a hundred years at least.
With him, the Commune's head, a hoary senior too,
Stàrosta, that 's his style, — like Equity Judge with
    you, —
Natural Jurisconsult : then, fenced about with furs,
Pomeschìk, — Lord of the Land, who wields — and
    none demurs —
A power of life and death. They stoop, survey the
    corpse.

Then, straightened on his staff, the Stàrosta — the
    thorpe's
Sagaciousest old man — hears what you just have
    heard,
From Droug's first inrush, all, up to Ivàn's last word
" God bade me act for him : I dared not disobey ! "

Silence — the Pomeschìk broke with "A wild wrong
    way
Of righting wrong — if wrong there were, such wrath
    to rouse !
Why was not law observed ? What article allows
Whoso may please to play the judge, and, judgment
    dealt,
Play executioner, as promptly as we pelt
To death, without appeal, the vermin whose sole fault
Has been — it dared to leave the darkness of its vault,
Intrude upon our day ! Too sudden and too rash !
What was this woman's crime ? Suppose the church
    should crash
Down where I stand, your lord : bound are my serfs
    to dare
Their utmost that I 'scape : yet, if the crashing scare
My children, — as you are, — if sons fly, one and all,
Leave father to his fate, — poor cowards though I call
The runaways, I pause before I claim their life
Because they prized it more than mine. I would each
    wife
Diéd for her husband's sake, each son to save his
    sire :
'T is glory, I applaud — scarce duty, I require.
Ivàn Ivànovitch has done a deed that 's named
Murder by law and me : who doubts, may speak un-
    blamed ! "

All turned to the old Pope. "Ay, children, I am
    old —
How old, I get myself to know no longer. Rolled
Quite round, my orb of life, from infancy to age,
Seems passing back again to youth. A certain stage
At least I reach, or dream I reach, where I discern
Truer truths, laws behold more lawlike than we learn
When first we set our foot to tread the course I trod
With man to guide my steps : who leads me now is
    God.
'Your young men shall see visions : ' and in my youth
    I saw
And paid obedience to man's visionary law :
'Your old men shall dream dreams : ' and, in my age,
    a hand
Conducts me through the cloud round law to where I
    stand
Firm on its base, — know cause, who, before, knew
    effect.

" The world lies under me : and nowhere I detect
So great a gift as this — God's own — of human life.
' Shall the dead praise thee ? ' No ! ' The whole live
    world is rife,
God, with thy glory,' rather ! Life then, God's best
    of gifts,
For what shall man exchange ? For life — when so
    he shifts

The weight and turns the scale, lets life for life re-
    store
God's balance, sacrifice the less to gain the more,
Substitute — for low life, another's or his own —
Life large and liker God's who gave it : thus alone
May life extinguish life that life may trulier be !
How low this law descends on earth, is not for me
To trace : complexed becomes the simple, intricate
The plain, when I pursue law's winding. 'T is the
    straight
Outflow of law I know and name : to law, the fount
Fresh from God's footstool, friends, follow while I re-
    mount.

" A mother bears a child : perfection is complete
So far in such a birth. Enabled to repeat
The miracle of life, — herself was born so just
A type of womankind, that God sees fit to trust
Her with the holy task of giving life in turn.
Crowned by this crowning pride, — how say you,
    should she spurn
Regality — discrowned, unchilded, by her choice
Of barrenness exchanged for fruit which made rejoice
Creation, though life's self were lost in giving birth
To life more fresh and fit to glorify God's earth ?
How say you, should the hand God trusted with life's
    torch

Kindled to light the world — aware of sparks that
    scorch,
Let fall the same?   Forsooth, her flesh a fire-flake
    stings :
The mother drops the child !   Among what monstrous
    things
Shall she be classed?   Because of motherhood, each
    male
Yields to his partner place, sinks proudly in the scale :
His strength owned weakness, wit — folly, and cour-
    age — fear,
Beside the female proved male's mistress — only here.
The fox-dam, hunger-pined, will slay the felon sire
Who dares assault her whelp : the beaver, stretched
    on fire,
Will die without a groan : no pang avails to wrest
Her young from where they hide — her sanctuary
    breast.
What 's here then ?   Answer me, thou dead one, as, I
    trow,
Standing at God's own bar, he bids thee answer now !
Thrice crowned wast thou — each crown of pride, a
    child — thy charge !
Where are they? Lost? Enough : no need that thou
    enlarge
On how or why the loss : life left to utter ' lost '
Condemns itself beyond appeal.   The soldier's post

Guards from the foe's attack the camp he sentinels :
That he no traitor proved, this and this only tells —
Over the corpse of him trod foe to foe's success.
Yet — one by one thy crowns torn from thee — thou
    no less
To scare the world, shame God, — livedst! I hold
    he saw
The unexampled sin, ordained the novel law,
Whereof first instrument was first intelligence
Found loyal here. I hold that, failing human sense,
The very earth had oped, sky fallen, to efface
Humanity's new wrong, motherhood's first disgrace.
Earth oped not neither fell the sky, for prompt was
    found
A man and man enough, head-sober and heart-sound,
Ready to hear God's voice, resolute to obey.
Ivàn Ivànovitch, I hold, has done, this day,
No otherwise than did, in ages long ago,
Moses when he made known the purport of that flow
Of fire athwart the law's twain-tables! I proclaim
Ivàn Ivànovitch God's servant!"   '
                          At which name
Uprose that creepy whisper from out the crowd, is
    wont
To swell and surge and sink when fellow-men con
    front
A punishment that falls on fellow flesh and blood,

Appallingly beheld — shudderingly understood,
No less, to be the right, the just, the merciful.
"God's servant!" hissed the crowd.

                 When that Amen grew dull
And died away and left acquittal plain adjudged,
"Amen!" last sighed the lord. "There's none shall
      say I grudged
Escape from punishment in such a novel case.
Deferring to old age and holy life, — be grace
Granted! say I. No less, scruples might shake a
      sense
Firmer than I boast mine. Law's law, and evidence
Of breach therein lies plain, — blood-red-bright, — all
      may see!
Yet all absolve the deed : absolved the deed must be!

"And next — as mercy rules the hour — methinks
    't were well
You signify forthwith its sentence, and dispel
The doubts and fears, I judge, which busy now the
      head
Law puts a halter round — a halo — you, instead!
Ivàn Ivànovitch — what think you he expects
Will follow from his feat? Go, tell him — law protects
Murder, for once : no need he longer keep behind
The Sacred Pictures — where skulks Innocence en-
      shrined,

Or I missay! Go, some! You others, haste and hide
The dismal object there : get done, whate'er betide!'"

So, while the youngers raised the corpse, the elders
    trooped
Silently to the house : where halting, someone stooped,
Listened beside the door ; all there was silent too.
Then they held counsel ; then pushed door and, pass-
    ing through,
    Stood in the murderer's presence.
                    Ivàn Ivànovitch
Knelt, building on the floor that Kremlin rare and
    rich
He deftly cut and carved on lazy winter nights.
Some five young faces watched, breathlessly, as, to
    rights,
Piece upon piece, he reared the fabric nigh complete.
Stèscha, Ivàn's old mother, sat spinning by the heat
Of the oven where his wife Kàtia stood baking bread.
Ivàn's self, as he turned his honey-colored head,
Was just in act to drop, 'twixt fir-cones, — each a
    dome, —
The scooped-out yellow gourd presumably the home
Of Kolokol the Big : the bell, therein to hitch,
— An acorn-cup — was ready : Ivàn Ivànovitch
Turned with it in his mouth.
                  They told him he was free
As air to walk abroad. "How otherwise?" asked he.

TRAY.

Sing me a hero! Quench my thirst
Of soul, ye bards!
                    Quoth Bard the first :
" Sir Olaf, the good knight, did don
His helm and eke his habergeon " . . .
Sir Olaf and his bard —— !

" That sin-scathed brow" (quoth Bard the second)
" That eye wide ope as though Fate beckoned
My hero to some steep, beneath
Which precipice smiled tempting Death " . . .
You too without your host have reckoned !

" A beggar-child " (let 's hear this third !)
" Sat on a quay's edge : like a bird
Sang to herself at careless play,
And fell into the stream.   ' Dismay !
Help, you the standers-by ! '   None stirred.

" Bystanders reason, think of wives
　And children ere they risk their lives.
　Over the balustrade has bounced
　A mere instinctive dog, and pounced
　Plumb on the prize. ‘ How well he dives !

" ‘ Up he comes with the child, see, tight
　In mouth, alive too, clutched from quite
　A depth of ten feet — twelve, I bet !
　Good dog ! What, off again ? There 's yet
　Another child to save ? All right !

" ‘ How strange we saw no other fall !
　It 's instinct in the animal.
　Good dog ! But he 's a long while under :
　If he got drowned I should not wonder —
　Strong current, that against the wall !

" ‘ Here he comes, holds in mouth this time
　— What may the thing be ? Well, that 's prime !
　Now, did you ever ? Reason reigns
　In man alone, since all Tray's pains
　Have fished — the child's doll from the slime ! ’

" And so, amid the laughter gay,
　Trotted my hero off, — old Tray, —
　Till somebody, prerogatived

With reason, reasoned : ' Why he dived,
His brain would show us, I should say.

" ' John, go and catch — or, if needs be,
Purchase that animal for me !
By vivisection, at expense
Of half-an-hour and eighteen pence,
How brain secretes dog's soul, we 'll see ! ' "

NED BRATTS.

'T was Bedford Special Assize, one daft Midsummer's
    Day :
A broiling blasting June, — was never its like, men
    say.
Corn stood sheaf-ripe already, and trees looked yellow
    as that ;
Ponds drained dust-dry, the cattle lay foaming around
    each flat.
Inside town, dogs went mad, and folks kept bibbing
    beer
While the parsons prayed for rain. 'T was horrible,
    yes — but queer :
Queer — for the sun laughed gay, yet nobody moved
    a hand
To work one stroke at his trade : as given to under-
    stand
That all was come to a stop, work and such worldly
    ways,
And the world's old self about to end in a merry
    blaze.

Midsummer's Day moreover was the first of Bedford
    Fair;
So, Bedford Town's tag-rag and bobtail lay bowsing
    there.

But the Court House, Quality crammed : through doors
    ope, windows wide,
High on the Bench you saw sit Lordships side by
    side.
There frowned Chief Justice Jukes, fumed learned
    Brother Small,
And fretted their fellow Judge : like threshers, one
    and all,
Of a reek with laying down the law in a furnace.
    Why?
Because their lungs breathed flame — the regular
    crowd forbye —
From gentry pouring in — quite a nosegay, to be sure !
How else could they pass the time, six mortal hours
    endure
Till night should extinguish day, when matters might
    haply mend ?
Meanwhile no bad resource was — watching begin and
    end
Some trial for life and death, in a brisk five minutes'
    space,
And betting which knave would 'scape, which hang,
    from his sort of face.

So, their Lordships toiled and moiled, and a deal of
  work was done
(I warrant) to justify the mirth of the crazy sun,
As this and 't other lout, struck dumb at the sudden
  show
Of red robes and white wigs, boggled nor answered
  " Boh ! "
When asked why he, Tom Styles, should not — be-
  cause Jack Nokes
Had stolen the horse — be hanged : for Judges must
  have their jokes,
And louts must make allowance — let 's say, for some
  blue fly
Which punctured a dewy scalp where the frizzles stuck
  awry —
Else Tom had fleered scot-free, so nearly over and
  done
Was the main of the job. Full-measure, the gentles
  enjoyed their fun,
As a twenty-five were tried, rank puritans caught at
  prayer
In a cow-house and laid by the heels, — have at 'em,
  devil may care ! —
And ten were prescribed the whip, and ten a brand
  on the cheek,
And five a slit of the nose — just leaving enough to
  tweak.

Well, things at jolly high-tide, amusement steeped in
　　fire,
While noon smote fierce the roof's red tiles to heart's
　　desire,
The Court a-simmer with smoke, one ferment of oozy
　　flesh,
One spirituous humming musk mount-mounting until
　　its mesh
Entoiled all heads in a fluster, and Serjeant Postle-
　　thwayte
— Dashing the wig oblique as he mopped his oily
　　pate —
Cried " Silence, or I grow grease !　No loophole lets
　　in air ?
Jurymen, — Guilty, Death !　Gainsay me if you
　　dare ! "
— Things at this pitch, I say, — what hubbub without
　　the doors ?
What laughs, shrieks, hoots and yells, what rudest of
　　uproars ?

Bounce through the barrier-throng a bulk comes roll-
　　ing vast !
Thumps, kicks, — no manner of use ! — spite of them
　　rolls at last
Into the midst a ball which, bursting, brings to view
Publican Black Ned Bratts and Tabby his big wife
　　too :

Both in a muck-sweat, both . . . were never such
    eyes uplift
At the sight of yawning hell, such nostrils — snouts
    that sniffed
Sulphur, such mouths a-gape ready to swallow flame !
Horrified, hideous, frank fiend-faces ! yet, all the same,
Mixed with a certain . . . eh ? how shall I dare style
    — mirth
The desperate grin of the guess that, could they break
    from earth,
Heaven was above, and hell might rage in impotence
Below the saved, the saved !

                " Confound you ! (no offence !)
Out of our way, — push, wife ! Yonder their Wor-
    ships be ! "
Ned Bratts has reached the bar, and " Hey, my
    Lords," roars he,
" A Jury of life and death, Judges the prime of the
    land,
Constables, javelineers, — all met, if I understand,
To decide so knotty a point as whether 't was Jack or
    Joan
Robbed the henroost, pinched the pig, hit the King's
    Arms with a stone,
Dropped the baby down the well, left the tithesman
    in the lurch,

Or, three whole Sundays running, not once attended
    church !

What a pother — do these deserve the parish-stocks
    or whip,

More or less brow to brand, much or little nose to
    snip, —

When, in our Public, plain stand we — that's we
    stand here,

I and my Tab, brass-bold, brick-built of beef and
    beer,

— Do not we, slut ?   Stand forth and show your
    beauty, jade !

Wife of my bosom — that's the word now !   What a
    trade

We drove !   None said us nay : nobody loved his life
So little as wag a tongue against us, — did they, wife ?

Yet they knew us all the while, in their hearts, for
    what we are

— Worst couple, rogue and quean, unhanged — search
    near and far !

Eh, Tab ?   The pedlar, now — o'er his noggin —
    who warned a mate

To cut and run, nor risk his pack where its loss of
    weight

Was the least to dread, — aha, how we two laughed
    a-good

As, stealing round the midden, he came on where I
    stood

With billet poised and raised, — you, ready with the
  rope, —
Ah, but that's past, that's sin repented of, we hope !
Men knew us for that same, yet safe and sound stood
  we !
The lily-livered knaves knew too (I've baulked a
  d——)
Our keeping the 'Pied Bull' was just a mere pre-
  tence :
Too slow make food, drink, lodging, the pounds from
  out the pence !
There's not a stoppage has chanced to travel, this ten
  long year,
No break into hall or grange, no lifting of nag or
  steer,
Not a single roguery, from the cutting of a purse
To the cutting of a throat, but paid us toll. Od's
  curse !
When Gipsy Smouch made bold to cheat us of our
  due,
— Eh, Tab ? the Squire's strong-box we helped the
  rascal to —
I think he pulled a face, next Sessions' swinging-time !
He danced the jig that needs no floor, — and, here's
  the prime,
'T was Scroggs that houghed the mare ! Ay, those
  were busy days !

"Well, there we flourished brave, like scripture-trees
    called bays,

Faring high, drinking hard, in money up to head

— Not to say, boots and shoes, when . . . Zounds, I
    nearly said —

Lord, to unlearn one's language ! How shall we la-
    bor, wife ?

Have you, fast hold, the Book ? Grasp, grip it, for ·
    your life !

See, sirs, here 's life, salvation ! Here 's — hold but
    out my breath —

When did I speak so long without once swearing ?
    'Sdeath,

No, nor unhelped by ale since man and boy ! And
    yet

All yesterday I had to keep my whistle wet

While reading Tab this Book : book ? don't say ' book '
    — they 're plays,

Songs, ballads and the like : here 's no such strawy
    blaze,

But sky wide ope, sun, moon, and seven stars out full-
    flare !

Tab, help and tell ! I 'm hoarse. A mug ! or — no,
    a prayer !

Dip for one out of the Book ! Who wrote it in the
    Jail

— He plied his pen unhelped by beer, sirs, I 'll be
    bail !

" I 've got my second wind.   In trundles she — that 's
    Tab.

' Why, Gammer, what 's come now, that — bobbing
    like a crab

On Yule-tide bowl — your head 's a-work and both
    your eyes

Break loose ?   Afeard, you fool ?   As if the dead can
    rise !

Say — Bagman Dick was found last May with fud-
    dling-cap

Stuffed in his mouth : to choke 's a natural mishap !'

' Gaffer, be — blessed,' cries she, ' and Bagman Dick
    as well !

I, you, and he are damned : this Public is our hell :

We live in fire : live coals don't feel ! — once quenched,
    they learn —

Cinders do, to what dust they moulder while they
    burn !'

" ' If you don't speak straight out,' says I — belike I
    swore —

' A knobstick, well you know the taste of, shall, once
    more,

Teach you to talk, my maid !'   She ups with such a
    face,

Heart sunk inside me.   ' Well, pad on, my prate
    apace !'

" ' I 've been about those laces we need for . . . never
    mind !
If henceforth they tie hands, 't is mine they 'll have to
    bind.
You know who makes them best — the Tinker in our
    cage,
Pulled-up for gospelling, twelve years ago : no age
To try another trade, — yet, so he scorned to take
Money he did not earn, he taught himself the make
Of laces, tagged and tough — Dick Bagman found
    them so !
Good customers were we !   Well, last week, you must
    know,
His girl, — the blind young chit, who hawks about his
    wares, —
She takes it in her head to come no more — such airs
These hussies have !   Yet, since we need a stoutish
    lace, —
" I 'll to the jail-bird father, abuse her to his face ! "
So, first I filled a jug to give me heart, and then,
Primed to the proper pitch, I posted to their den —
Patmore — they style their prison !   I tip the turnkey,
    catch
My heart up, fix my face, and fearless lift the latch —
Both arms a kimbo, in bounce with a good round oath
Ready for rapping out: no " Lawks " nor " By my
    troth ! "

" 'There sat my man, the father. He looked up :
    what one feels
When heart that leapt to mouth drops down again to
    heels !
He raised his hand . . . Hast seen, when drinking
    out the night,
And in, the day, earth grow another something quite
Under the sun's first stare ?   I stood a very stone.

" ' " Woman ! " (a fiery tear he put in every tone),
" How should my child frequent your house where lust
    is sport,
Violence — trade?   Too true !   I trust no vague re-
    port.
Her angel's hand, which stops the sight of sin, leaves
    clear
The other gate of sense, lets outrage through the ear.
What has she heard ! — which, heard shall never be
    again.
Better lack food than feast, a Dives in the — wain
Or reign or train — of Charles ! "   (His language was
    not ours :
'T is my belief, God spoke : no tinker has such pow-
    ers).
" Bread, only bread they bring — my laces : if we
    broke
Your lump of leavened sin, the loaf's first crumb would
    choke ! "

"'Down on my marrow-bones! Then all at once
    rose he :
His brown hair burst a-spread, his eyes were suns to
    see :
Up went his hands : "Through flesh, I reach, I read
    thy soul !
So may some stricken tree look blasted, bough and
    bole,
Champed by the fire-tooth, charred without, and yet,
    thrice-bound
With dreriment about, within may life be found,
A prisoned power to branch and blossom as before,
Could but the gardener cleave the cloister, reach the
    core,
Loosen the vital sap : yet where shall help be found?
Who says ' How save it ? ' — nor ' Why cumbers it the
    ground ? '
Woman, that tree art thou ! All sloughed about with
    scurf,
Thy stag-horns fright the sky, thy snake-roots sting
    the turf !
Drunkenness, wantonness, theft, murder gnash and
    gnarl
Thine outward, case thy soul with coating like the
    marle
Satan stamps flat upon each head beneath his hoof !
And how deliver such ? The strong men keep aloof,

Lover and friend stand far, the mocking ones pass by,
Tophet gapes wide for prey: lost soul, despair and
  die !
What then ? 'Look unto me and be ye saved !' saith
  God :
'I strike the rock, outstreats the life-stream at my
  rod !¹
Be your sins scarlet, wool shall they seem like, — al-
  though
As crimson red, yet turn white as the driven snow !' "

" ' There, there, there ! All I seem to somehow un-
  derstand
Is — that, if I reached home, 't was through the guid-
  ing hand
Of his blind girl which led and led me through the
  streets
And out of town and up to door again. What greets
First thing my eye, as limbs recover from their
  swoon ?
A book — this Book she gave at parting. " Father's
  boon —
The Book he wrote : it reads as if he spoke himself :

¹ They did not eat
His flesh, nor suck those c."; which thence outstreat.
DONNE's *Progress of the Soul*, line 344.

He cannot preach in bonds, so, — take it down from
　　shelf
When you want counsel, — think you hear his very
　　voice ! ”

“ ‘ Wicked dear Husband, first despair and then re-
　　joice !
Dear wicked Husband, waste no tick of moment more,
Be saved like me, bald trunk ! There 's greenness yet
　　at core,
Sap under slough ! Read, read ! ’
　　　　　　　　“ Let me take breath, my lords !
I 'd like to know, are these — hers, mine, or Bunyan's
　　words ?
I 'm ’wildered — scarce with drink, — nowise with
　　drink alone !
You 'll say, with heat : but heat 's no stuff to split a
　　stone
Like this black boulder — this flint heart of mine :
　　the Book —
That dealt the crashing blow ! Sirs, here 's the fist
　　that shook
His beard till Wrestler Jem howled like a just-lugged
　　bear !
You had brained me with a feather : at once I grew
　　aware
Christmas was meant for me. A burden at your back,

Good Master Christmas ?   Nay, — yours was that
    Joseph's sack,
— Or whose it was, — which held the cup, — com-
    pared with mine !
Robbery loads my loins, perjury cracks my chine,
Adultery . . . nay, Tab, you pitched me as I flung !
One word, I 'll up with fist . . . No, sweet spouse,
    hold your tongue !

" I 'm hasting to the end.   The Book, sirs — take and
    read !
You have my history in a nutshell, — ay, indeed !
It must off, my burden !   See, — slack straps and into
    pit,
Roll, reach the bottom, rest, rot there — a plague on
    it !
For a mountain 's sure to fall and bury Bedford Town,
' Destruction ' — that 's the name, and fire shall burn
    it down !
O 'scape the wrath in time !   Time 's now, if not too
    late.
How can I pilgrimage up to the wicket-gate ?
Next comes Despond the slough : not that I fear to
    pull
Through mud, and dry my clothes at brave House
    Beautiful —
But it 's late in the day, I reckon : had I left years
    ago

Town, wife, and children dear . . . Well, Christmas
    did, you know ! —
Soon I had met in the valley and tried my cudgel's
    strength
On the enemy horned and winged, a-straddle across
    its length !
Have at his horns, thwick — thwack : they snap, see !
    Hoof and hoof —
Bang, break the fetlock-bones ! For love's sake, keep
    aloof
Angels ! I 'm man and match, — this cudgel for my
    flail, —
To thresh him, hoofs and horns, bat's wing and ser-
    pent's tail !
A chance gone by ! But then, what else does Hope-
    ful ding
Into the deafest ear except — hope, hope 's the thing ?
Too late i' the day for me to thrid the windings : but
There 's still a way to win the race by death's short
    cut !
Did Master Faithful need climb the Delightful
    Mounts ?
No, straight to Vanity Fair, — a fair, by all accounts,
Such as is held outside,— lords, ladies, grand and
    gay, —
Says he in the face of them, just what you hear me
    say.

And the Judges brought him in guilty, and brought
    him out
To die in the market-place — St. Peter's Green's
    about
The same thing : there they flogged, flayed, buffeted,
    lanced with knives,
Pricked him with swords, — I 'll swear, he 'd full a
    cat's nine lives, —
So to his end at last came Faithful, — ha, ha, he !
Who holds the highest card ? for there stands hid, you
    see,
Behind the rabble-rout, a chariot, pair and all :
He 's in, he 's off, he 's up, through clouds, at trumpet-
    call,
Carried the nearest way to Heaven-gate ! Odds my
    life —
Has nobody a sword to spare ? not even a knife ?
Then hang me, draw and quarter ! Tab — do the
    same by her !
O Master Worldly-Wiseman . . . That 's Master In-
    terpreter,
Take the will, not the deed ! Our gibbet 's handy,
    close :
Forestall Last Judgment-Day ! Be kindly, not mo-
    rose !
There wants no earthly judge-and-jurying : here we
    stand —

Sentence our guilty selves : so, hang us out of hand !
Make haste for pity's sake ! A single moment's loss
Means — Satan 's lord once more : his whisper shoots
    across
All singing in my heart, all praying in my brain,
' It comes of heat and beer ! ' — hark how he guffaws
    plain !
' To-morrow you 'll wake bright, and, in a safe skin,
    hug
Your sound selves, Tab and you, over a foaming jug !
You 've had such qualms before, time out of mind ! '
    He 's right !
Did not we kick and cuff and curse away, that night
When home we blindly reeled, and left poor hump-
    back Joe
I' the lurch to pay for what . . . somebody did, you
    know !
Both of us maundered then ' Lame humpback, —
    never more
Will he come limping, drain his tankard at our door !
He 'll swing, while — somebody ' . . . Says Tab, ' No,
    for I 'll peach ! '
' I 'm for you, Tab,' cries I, ' there 's rope enough for
    each ! '
So blubbered we, and bussed, and went to bed upon
The grace of Tab's good thought : by morning, all
    was gone !

We laughed — 'What 's life to him, a cripple of no
  account?'
Oh, waves increase around — I feel them mount and
  mount!
Hang us! To-morrow brings Tom Bearward with his
  bears:
One new black-muzzled brute beats Sackerson, he
  swears:
(Sackerson, for my money!) And, baiting o'er, the
  Brawl
They lead on Turner's Patch, — lads, lasses, up tails
  all, —
I 'm i' the thick o' the throng! That means the Iron
  Cage,
— Means the Lost Man inside! Where 's hope for
  such as wage
War against light? Light 's left, light 's here, I hold
  light still,
So does Tab — make but haste to hang us both! You
  will?"

I promise, when he stopped you might have heard a
  mouse
Squeak, such a death-like hush sealed up the old
  Mote House.
But when the mass of man sank meek upon his knees,
While Tab, alongside, wheezed a hoarse "Do hang
  us, please!"

Why, then the waters rose, no eye but ran with tears,
Hearts heaved, heads thumped, until, paying all past
    arrears
Of pity and sorrow, at last a regular scream outbroke
Of triumph, joy and praise.
                My Lord Chief Justice spoke,
First mopping brow and cheek, where still, for one
    that budged,
Another bead broke fresh : " What Judge, that ever
    judged
Since first the world began, judged such a case as
    this ?
Why, Master Bratts, long since, folks smelt you out, I
    wis !
I had my doubts, i' faith, each time you played the fox
Convicting geese of crime in yonder witness-box —
Yea, much did I misdoubt, the thief that stole her
    eggs
Was hardly goosey's self at Reynard's game, i' feggs !
Yet thus much was to praise — you spoke to point,
    direct —
Swore you heard, saw the theft: no jury could sus-
    pect —
Dared to suspect, — I 'll say, — a spot in white so
    clear :
Goosey was throttled, true : but thereof godly fear
Came of example set, much as our laws intend ;

And, though a fox confessed, you proved the Judge's
    friend.

What if I had my doubts?   Suppose I gave them
    breath,

Brought you to bar: what work to do, ere 'Guilty,
    Death'

Had paid our pains!   What heaps of witnesses to
    drag

From holes and corners, paid from out the County's
    bag!

Trial three dog-days long!   *Amicus Curiæ* — that 's

Your title, no dispute — truth-telling Master Bratts !

Thank you, too, Mistress Tab !   Why doubt one word
    you say?

Hanging you both deserve, hanged both shall be this
    day !

The tinker needs must be a proper man.   I 've heard

He lies in Jail long since : if Quality's good word

Warrants me letting loose, — some householder, I
    mean —

Freeholder, better still, — I don't say but — between

Now and next Sessions . . . Well !   Consider of his
    case,

I promise to, at least : we owe him so much grace.

Not that — no, God forbid ! — I lean to think, as you,

The grace that such repent is any jail-bird's due :

I rather see the fruit of twelve years' pious reign —

Astræa Redux, Charles restored his rights again !
— Of which, another time ! I somehow feel a peace
Stealing across the world. May deeds like this in-
 crease !
So, Master Sheriff, stay that sentence I pronounced
On those two dozen odd : deserving to be trounced
Soundly, and yet, — well, well, at all events despatch
This pair of — shall I say, sinner-saints ? — ere we
 catch
Their jail-distemper too. Stop tears, or I 'll indite
All weeping Bedfordshire for turning Bunyanite ! "
So, happily hanged were they, — why lengthen out my
 tale ? —
Where Bunyan's Statue stands facing where stood his
 Jail.

DRAMATIC IDYLS.

SECOND SERIES.

" You are sick, that 's sure " — they say :
" Sick of what ? " — they disagree.
" 'T is the brain " — thinks Doctor A.,
   " 'T is the heart " — holds Doctor B.,
" The liver — my life I 'd lay ! "
   " The lungs ! "   " The lights ! "
                                        Ah me !

   So ignorant of man's whole
Of bodily organs plain to see —
So sage and certain, frank and free,
About what 's under lock and key —
   Man's soul !

23

ECHETLOS.

HERE is a story, shall stir you! Stand up, Greeks
    dead and gone,
Who breasted, beat Barbarians, stemmed Persia roll-
    ing on,
Did the deed and saved the world, since the day was
    Marathon!

No man but did his manliest, kept rank and fought
    away
In his tribe and file : up, back, out, down — was the
    spear-arm play :
Like a wind-whipt branchy wood, all spear-arms a-
    swing that day!

But one man kept no rank and his sole arm plied no
    spear,
As a flashing came and went, and a form i' the van,
    the rear,
Brightened the battle up, for he blazed now there,
    now here.

Nor helmed nor shielded, he ! but, a goat-skin all his
    wear,
Like a tiller of the soil, with a clown's limbs broad
    and bare,
Went he ploughing on and on : he pushed with a
    ploughman's share.

Did the weak mid-line give way, as tunnies on whom
    the shark
Precipitates his bulk ?   Did the right-wing halt when,
    stark
On his heap of slain lay stretched Kallimachos Pole-
    march ?

Did the steady phalanx falter?   To the rescue, at
    the need,
The clown was ploughing Persia, clearing Greek earth
    of weed,
As he routed through the Sakian and rooted up the
    Mede.

But the deed done, battle won, — nowhere to be de-
    scribed
On the meadow, by the stream, at the marsh, — look
    far and wide
From the foot of the mountain, no, to the last blood-
    plashed sea-side, —

Not anywhere on view blazed the large limbs thonged
    and brown,
Shearing and clearing still with the share before
    which — down
To the dust went Persia's pomp, as he ploughed for
    Greece, that clown !

How spake the Oracle ?   " Care for no name at all !
Say but just this : We praise one helpful whom we call
The Holder of the Ploughshare. The great deed
    ne'er grows small."

Not the great name ! Sing — woe for the great name
    Míltiadés
And its end at Paros isle ! Woe for Themistokles
— Satrap in Sardis court ! Name not the clown like
    these !

CLIVE.

I AND Clive were friends — and why not? Friends!
  I think you laugh, my lad.
Clive it was gave England India, while your father
  gives — egad,
England nothing but the graceless boy who lures him
  on to speak —
"Well, Sir, you and Clive were comrades" — with a
  tongue thrust in your cheek!
Very true : in my eyes, your eyes, all the world's eyes,
  Clive was man,
I was, am and ever shall be — mouse, nay, mouse of
  all its clan
Sorriest sample, if you take the kitchen's estimate for
  fame ;
While the man Clive — he fought Plassy, spoiled the
  clever foreign game,
Conquered and annexed and Englished!
                    Never mind! As o'er my punch
(You away) I sit of evenings, — silence, save for bis-
  cuit crunch,

Black, unbroken, — thought grows busy, thrids each
    pathway of old years,
Notes this forthright, that meander, till the long-past
    life appears
Like an outspread map of country plodded through,
    each mile and rood,
Once, and well remembered still, — I 'm startled in
    my solitude
Ever and anon by — what 's the sudden mocking light
    that breaks
On me as I slap the table till no rummer-glass but
    shakes
While I ask — aloud, I do believe, God help me ! —
    " Was it thus ?
Can it be that so I faltered, stopped when just one
    step for us " —
(Us, — you were not born, I grant, but surely some
    day born would be)
— " One bold step had gained a province " (figurative
    talk, you see)
" Got no end of wealth and honor, — yet I stood stock
    still no less ? "
— " For I was not Clive," you comment : but it needs
    no Clive to guess
Wealth were handy, honor ticklish, did no writing on
    the wall
Warn me " Trespasser, 'ware man-traps ! "   Him who
    braves that notice — call

Hero ! none of such heroics suit myself who read
    plain words,
Doff my hat, and leap no barrier. Scripture says, the
    land 's the Lord's :
Louts then — what avail the thousand, noisy in a
    smock-frocked ring,
All-agog to have me trespass, clear the fence, be Clive
    their king ?
Higher warrant must you show me ere I set one foot
    before
T'other in that dark direction, though I stand for
    evermore
Poor as Job and meek as Moses. Evermore ? No !
    By and by
Job grows rich and Moses valiant, Clive turns out less
    wise than I.
Don't object " Why call him friend, then ? " Power is
    power, my boy, and still
Marks a man, — God's gift magnific, exercised for
    good or ill.
You 've your boot now on my hearth-rug, tread what
    was a tiger's skin :
Rarely such a royal monster as I lodged the bullet in !
True, he murdered half a village, so his own death
    came to pass ;
Still, for size and beauty, cunning, courage — ah, the
    brute he was !

Why, that Clive, — that youth, that greenhorn, that
    quill-driving clerk, in fine, —
He sustained a siege in Arcot . . . But the world
    knows ! Pass the wine.

Where did I break off at ? How bring Clive in ? Oh,
    you mentioned " fear " !
Just so : and, said I, that minds me of a story you
    shall hear.

We were friends then, Clive and I : so, when the
    clouds, about the orb
Late supreme, encroaching slowly, surely, threatened
    to absorb
Ray by ray its noontide brilliance, — friendship might,
    with steadier eye
Drawing near, bear what had burned else, now no
    blaze all majesty.
Too much bee's-wing floats my figure ? Well, suppose
    a castle 's new :
None presume to climb its ramparts, none find foot-
    hold sure for shoe
'Twixt those squares and squares of granite plating
    the impervious pile
As his scale-mail's warty iron cuirasses a crocodile.
Reels that castle thunder-smitten, storm-dismantled ?
    From without

Scrambling up by crack and crevice, every cockney
      prates about
Towers — the heap he kicks now ! turrets — just the
      measure of his cane !
Will that do ?   Observe moreover — (same similitude
      again) —
Such a castle seldom crumbles by sheer stress of can-
      nonade :
'T is when foes are foiled and fighting 's finished that
      vile rains invade,
Grass o'ergrows, o'ergrows till night-birds congregat-
      ing find no holes
Fit to build in like the topmost sockets made for ban-
      ner-poles.
So Clive crumbled slow in London, crashed at last.

                                 A week before,
Dining with him, — after trying churchyard-chat of
      days of yore, —
Both of us stopped, tired as tombstones, head-piece
      foot-piece, when they lean
Each to other, drowsed in fog-smoke, o'er a coffined
      Past between.
As I saw his head sink heavy, guessed the soul's ex-
      tinguishment
By the glazing eyeball, noticed how the furtive fingers
      went

Where a drug-box skulked behind the honest liquor,
   — "One more throw
Try for Clive !" thought I : "Let 's venture some
   good rattling question ! " So —
"Come Clive, tell us " — out I blurted — " what to
   tell in turn, years hence,
When my boy — suppose I have one — asks me on
   what evidence
I maintain my friend of Plassy proved a warrior every
   whit
Worth your Alexanders, Cæsars, Marlboroughs and —
   what said Pitt? —
Frederick the Fierce himself ! Clive told me once "
   — I want to say —
" Which feat out of all those famous doings bore the
   bell away
— In his own calm estimation, mark you, not the
   mob's rough guess —
Which stood foremost as evincing what Clive called
   courageousness !
Come ! what moment of the minute, what speck-centre
   in the wide
Circle of the action saw your mortal fairly deified ?
(Let alone that filthy sleep-stuff, swallow bold this
   wholesome Port !)
If a friend has leave to question, — when were you
   most brave, in short ? "

Up he arched his brows o' the instant — formidably
    Clive again.

"When was I most brave? I 'd answer, were the in-
    stance half as plain

As another instance that 's a brain-lodged crystal —
    curse it ! — here

Freezing when my memory touches — ugh — the time
    I felt almost fear.

Ugh ! I cannot say for certain if I showed fear —
    anyhow,

Fear I felt, and, very likely, shuddered, since I shiver
    now."

"Fear !" smiled I. "Well, that 's the rarer : that 's
    a specimen to seek,

Ticket up in one's museum, *Mind-Freaks, Lord Clive's
    Fear, Unique !*"

Down his brows dropped. On the table painfully he
    pored as though

Tracing, in the stains and streaks there, thoughts en-
    crusted long ago.

When he spoke 't was like a lawyer reading word by
    word some will,

Some blind jungle of a statement, — beating on and
    on until

Out there leaps fierce life to fight with.

" This fell in my factor-days.

Desk-drudge, slaving at St. David's, one must game,
    or drink, or craze.

I chose gaming : and, — because your high-flown
    gamesters hardly take

Umbrage at a factor's elbow if the factor pays his
    stake, —

I was winked at in a circle where the company was
    choice,

Captain This and Major That, men high of color, loud
    of voice,

Yet indulgent, condescending to the modest juvenile

Who not merely risked but lost his hard-earned guin-
    eas with a smile.

Down I sat to cards, one evening, — had for my an-
    tagonist

Somebody whose name 's a secret — you 'll know why
    — so, if you list,

Call him Cock o' the Walk, my scarlet son of Mars
    from head to heel !

Play commenced : and, whether Cocky fancied that a
    clerk must feel

Quite sufficient honor came of bending over one green
    baize,

I the scribe with him the warrior, guessed no penman
    dared to raise

Shadow of objection should the honor stay but play-
    ing end

More or less abruptly, — whether disinclined he grew
    to spend
Practice strictly scientific on a booby born to stare
At — not ask of — lace-and-ruffles if the hand they
    hide plays fair, —
Anyhow, I marked a movement when he bade me
    ' Cut ! '
                                        " I rose.
' Such the new manœuvre, Captain ?   I' m a novice :
    knowledge grows.
What, you force a card, you cheat, Sir ? '
                             " Never did a thunder-clap
Cause emotion, startle Thyrsis locked with Chloe in
    his lap,
As my word and gesture (down I flung my cards to
    join the pack)
Fired the man of arms, whose visage, simply red be-
    fore, turned black.
When he found his voice, he stammered ' That expres-
    sion once again ! '

" ' Well, you forced a card and cheated ! '
                      " ' Possibly a factor's brain,
Busied with his all-important balance of accounts,
    may deem
Weighing words superfluous trouble : *cheat* to clerkiy
    ears may seem

Just the joke for friends to venture : but we are not
    friends, you see !
When a gentleman is joked with, — if he's good at re-
    partee,
He rejoins, as I do — Sirrah, on your knees, withdraw
    in full !
Beg my pardon, or be sure a kindly bullet through
    your skull
Lets in light and teaches manners to what brain it
    finds ! Choose quick —
Have your life snuffed out or, kneeling, pray me trim
    yon candle-wick ! '

" ' Well, you cheated ! '
    " Then outbroke a howl from all the friends
    around.
To his feet sprang each in fury, fists were clenched
    and teeth were ground.
' End it ! no time like the present ! Captain, yours
    were our disgrace !
No delay, begin and finish ! Stand back, leave the
    pair a space !
Let civilians be instructed : henceforth simply ply the
    pen,
Fly the sword ! This clerk's no swordsman ? Suit
    him with a pistol, then !
Even odds ! A dozen paces 'twixt the most and least
    expert

Make a dwarf a giant's equal : nay, the dwarf, if he 's
    alert,
Likelier hits the broader target ! '
                " Up we stood accordingly.
As they handed me the weapon, such was my soul's
    thirst to try
Then and there conclusions with this bully, tread on
    and stamp out
Every spark of his existence, that, — crept close to,
    curled about
By that toying tempting teazing fool-forefinger's mid-
    dle joint, —
Don't you guess ? — the trigger yielded.   Gone my
    chance ! and at the point
Of such prime success moreover : scarce an inch above
    his head
Went my ball to hit the wainscot.   He was living, I
    was dead.

" Up he marched in flaming triumph — 't was his right,
    mind ! — up, within
Just an arm's length.   ' Now, my clerkling,' chuckled
    Cocky with a grin
As the levelled piece quite touched me, ' Now, Sir
    Counting-House, repeat
That expression which I told you proved bad man-
    ners !   Did I cheat ? '

" ' Cheat you did, you knew you cheated, and, this
moment, know as well.
As for me, my homely breeding bids you — fire and
go to Hell ! '

" Twice the muzzle touched my forehead.   Heavy
barrel, flurried wrist,
Either spoils a steady lifting.   Thrice : then, 'Laugh
at Hell who list,
I can't !   God 's no fable either.   Did this boy's eye
wink once ?   No !
There 's no standing him and Hell and God all three
against me, — so,
I did cheat ! '
                        " And down he threw the pistol, out
rushed — by the door
Possibly, but, as for knowledge if by chimney, roof or
floor,
He effected disappearance — I 'll engage no glance
was sent
That way by a single starer, such a blank astonishment
Swallowed up the senses : as for speaking — mute
they stood as mice.

" Mute not long, though !   Such reaction, such a hubbub in a trice !
24

'Rogue and rascal! Who 'd have thought it? What 's
        to be expected next,
When His Majesty's Commission serves a sharper as
        pretext
For . . . But where 's the need of wasting time now?
        Nought requires delay :
Punishment the Service cries for : let disgrace be
        wiped away
Publicly, in good broad daylight! Resignation? No,
        indeed !
Drum and fife must play the Rogue's-March, rank and
        file be free to speed
Tardy marching on the rogue's part by appliance in
        the rear
— Kicks administered shall right this wronged civil-
        ian, — never fear,
Mister Clive, for — though a clerk — you bore your-
        self — suppose we say —
Just as would beseem a soldier !'
                    " ' Gentlemen, attention — pray !
First, one word ! '
                    " I passed each speaker severally in review.
When I had precise their number, names and styles,
        and fully knew
Over whom my supervision thenceforth must extend,
        — why, then ——

" 'Some five minutes since, my life lay — as you all
    saw, gentlemen,
At the mercy of your friend there.   Not a single voice
    was raised
In arrest of jugdment, not one tongue — before my
    powder blazed —
Ventured " Can it be the youngster blundered, really
    seemed to mark
Some irregular proceeding?   We conjecture in the
    dark,
Guess at random, — still, for sake of fair play — what
    if for a freak,
In a fit of absence, — such things have been ! — if our
    friend proved weak
— What 's the phrase ? — corrected fortune !   Look
    into the case, at least ! "
Who dared interpose between the altar's victim and
    the priest ?
Yet he spared me !   You eleven !   Whosoever, all or
    each,
Utters — to the disadvantage of the man who spared
    me — speech
— To his face, behind his back, — that speaker has to
    do with me :
Me who promise, if positions change and mine the
    chance should be,
Not to imitate your friend and waive advantage ! '

" Twenty-five

Years ago this matter happened : and 't is certain,"
added Clive,

" Never, to my knowledge, did Sir Cocky have a single breath

Breathed against him : lips were closed throughout his
life, or since his death,

For if he be dead or living I can tell no more than
you.

All I know is — Cocky had one chance more ; how he
used it, — grew

Out of such unlucky habits, or relapsed, and back
again

Brought the late-ejected devil with a score more in his
train, —

That 's for you to judge. Reprieval I procured, at
any rate.

Ugh — the memory of that minute's fear makes goose-
flesh rise ! Why prate

Longer? You 've my story, there 's your instance :
fear I did, you see ! "

" Well " — I hardly kept from laughing — "if I see it,
thanks must be

Wholly to your Lordship's candor. Not that — in a
common case —

When a bully caught at cheating thrusts a pistol in
one's face,

I should under-rate, believe me, such a trial to the
    nerve!

'T is no joke, at one-and-twenty, for a youth to stand
    nor swerve.

Fear I naturally look for — unless, of all men alive,

I am forced to make exception when I come to Robert
    Clive.

Since at Arcot, Plassy, elsewhere, he and death — the
    whole world knows —

Came to somewhat closer quarters."

                    Quarters? Had we come to blows,

Clive and I, you had not wondered — up he sprang
    so, out he rapped

Such a round of oaths — no matter! I 'll endeavor
    to adapt

To our modern usage words he — well, 't was friendly
    license — flung

At me like so many fire-balls, fast as he could wag his
    tongue.

"You — a soldier? You — at Plassy? Yours the
    faculty to nick

Instantaneously occasion when your foe, if lightning-
    quick,

— At his mercy, at his malice, — has you, through
    some stupid inch

Undefended in your bulwark? Thus laid open, — not
    to flinch

— That needs courage, you 'll concede me. Then,
    look here ! Suppose the man,
Checking his advance, his weapon still extended, not
    a span
Distant from my temple, — curse him ! — quietly had
    bade me 'There !
Keep your life, calumniator ! — worthless life I freely
    spare :
Mine you freely would have taken — murdered me and
    my good fame
Both at once — and all the better ! Go, and thank
    your own bad aim
Which permits me to forgive you ! ' What if, with
    such words as these,
He had cast away his weapon ? How should I have
    borne me, please ?
Nay, I 'll spare you pains and tell you. This, and
    only this, remained —
Pick his weapon up and use it on myself. I so had
    gained
Sleep the earlier, leaving England probably to pay on
    still
Rent and taxes for half India, tenant at the French-
    man's will."

"Such the turn " said I " the matter takes with you ?
    Then I abate

— No, by not one jot nor tittle, — of your act my
    estimate.
Fear — I wish I could detect there : courage fronts
    me, plain enough —
Call it desperation, madness — never mind ! for here 's
    in rough
Why, had mine been such a trial, fear had overcome
    disgrace.
True, disgrace were hard to bear : but such a rush
    against God's face
— None of that for me, Lord Plassy, since I go to
    church at times,
Say the creed my mother taught me ! Many years in
    foreign climes
Rub some marks away — not all, though ! We poor
    sinners reach life's brink,
Overlook what rolls beneath it, recklessly enough, but
    think
There 's advantage in what 's left us — ground to stand
    on, time to call
' Lord, have mercy ! ' ere we topple over — do not
    leap, that 's all ! "
Oh, he made no answer, — re-absorbed into his cloud.
    I caught
Something like " Yes — courage : only fools will call
    it fear."
        If aught

Comfort you, my great unhappy hero Clive, in that I
    heard,
Next week, how your own hand dealt you doom, and
    uttered just the word
" Fearfully courageous ! " — this, be sure, and nothing
    else I groaned.
I 'm no Clive, nor parson either : Clive's worst deed
    — we 'll hope condoned.

MULÉYKEH.

IF a stranger passed the tent of Hóseyn, he cried "A
    churl's ! "
Or haply "God help the man who has neither salt nor
    bread ! "
— "Nay," would a friend exclaim, "he needs nor
    pity nor scorn
More than who spends small thought on the shore-
    sand, picking pearls,
— Holds but in light esteem the seed-sort, bears in-
    stead
On his breast a moon-like prize, some orb which of
    night makes morn.

"What if no flocks and herds enrich the son of Sinán?
They went when his tribe was mulct, ten thousand
    camels the due,
Blood-value paid perforce for a murder done of old.
'God gave them, let them go ! But never since time
    began,

Muléykeh, peerless mare, owned master the match of
  you,
And you are my prize, my Pearl : I laugh at men's
  land and gold ! '

" So in the pride of his soul laughs Hóseyn — and
  right, I say.
Do the ten steeds run a race of glory?   Outstripping
  all,
Ever Muléykeh stands first steed at the victor's
  staff.
Who started, the owner's hope, gets shamed and
  named, that day,
' Silence,' or, last but one, is ' The Cuffed,' as we use
  to call
Whom the paddock's lord thrusts forth.   Right,
  Hóseyn, I say, to laugh."

" Boasts he Muléykeh the Pearl ? " the stranger re-
  plies : " Be sure
On him I waste nor scorn nor pity, but lavish both
On Duhl the son of Sheybán, who withers away in
  heart
For envy of Hóseyn's luck.   Such sickness admits no
  cure.
A certain poet has sung, and sealed the same with an
  oath,

' For the vulgar — flocks and herds ! The Pearl is a
    prize apart.' "

Lo, Duhl the son of Sheybán comes riding to Hóseyn's
    tent,

And he casts his saddle down, and enters and
    " Peace " bids he.

" You are poor, I know the cause : my plenty shall
    mend the wrong.

'T is said of your Pearl — the price of a hundred cam-
    els spent

In her purchase were scarce ill paid : such prudence
    is far from me

Who proffer a thousand. Speak ! Long parley may
    last too long."

Said Hóseyn " You feed young beasts a many, of fa-
    mous breed,

Slit-eared, unblemished, fat, true offspring of Múzen-
    nem :

There stumbles no weak-eyed she in the line as it
    climbs the hill.

But I love Muléykeh's face : her forefront whitens in-
    deed

Like a yellowish wave's cream-crest. Your camels —
    go gaze on them !

Her fetlock is foam-splashed too. Myself am the
    richer still."

A year goes by : lo, back to the tent again rides Duhl.
"You are open-hearted, ay — moist-handed, a very
    prince.
Why should I speak of sale ?   Be the mare your sim-
    ple gift !
My son is pined to death for her beauty : my wife
    prompts ' Fool,
Beg for his sake the Pearl !   Be God the rewarder,
    since
God pays debts seven for one : who squanders on
    Him shows thrift.' "

Said Hóseyn "God gives each man one life, like a
    lamp, then gives
That lamp due measure of oil : lamp lighted — hold
    high, wave wide
Its comfort for others to share ! once quench it, what
    help is left ?
The oil of your lamp is your son : I shine while Mu-
    léykeh lives.
Would I beg your son to cheer my dark if Muléykeh
    died ?
It is life against life : what good avails to the life-
    bereft ? "

Another year, and — hist !   What craft is it Duhl de-
    signs ?

He alights not at the door of the tent as he did last
    time,
But, creeping behind, he gropes his stealthy way by
    the trench
Half-round till he finds the flap in the folding, for
    night combines
With the robber — and such is he : Duhl, covetous
    up to crime,
Must wring from Hóseyn's grasp the Pearl, by what-
    ever the wrench.

" He was hunger-bitten, I heard : I tempted with half
    my store,
And a gibe was all my thanks. Is he generous like
    Spring dew ?
Account the fault to me who chaffered with such an
    one ! ·
He has killed, to feast chance comers, the creature he
    rode : nay, more —
For a couple of singing-girls his robe has he torn in
    two :
I will beg ! Yet I nowise gained by the tale of my
    wife and son.

" I swear by the Holy House, my head will I never
    wash
Till I filch his Pearl away. Fair dealing I tried, then
    guile,

And now I resort to force. He said we must live or
    die :
Let him die, then, — let me live ! Be bold — but not
    too rash !
I have found me a peeping-place : breast, bury your
    breathing while
I explore for myself ! Now, breathe ! He deceived
    me not, the spy !

" As he said — there lies in peace Hóseyn — how
    happy ! Beside
Stands tethered the Pearl : thrice winds her headstall
    about his wrist :
'T is therefore he sleeps so sound — the moon through
    the roof reveals.
And, loose on his left, stands too that other, known
    far and wide,
Buhéyseh, her sister born : fleet is she yet ever missed
The winning tail's fire-flash a-stream past the thunder-
    ous heels.

" No less she stands saddled and bridled, this second,
    in case some thief
Should enter and seize and fly with the first, as I
    mean to do.
What then ? The Pearl is the Pearl : once mount her
    we both escape."

Through the skirt-fold in glides Duhl, — so a serpent
   disturbs no leaf
In a bush as he parts the twigs entwining a nest :
   clean through,
He is noiselessly at his work : as he planned, he per-
   forms the rape.

He has set the tent-door wide, has buckled the girth,
   has clipped
The headstall away from the wrist he leaves thrice
   bound as before,
He springs on the Pearl, is launched on the desert
   like bolt from bow.
Up starts our plundered man : from his breast though
   the heart be ripped,
Yet his mind has the mastery: behold, in a minute
   more,
He is out and off and away on Buhéyseh, whose worth
   we know !

And Hóseyn — his blood turns flame, he has learned
   long since to ride,
And Buhéyseh does her part, — they gain — they are
   gaining fast
On the fugitive pair, and Duhl has Ed-Dárraj to cross
   and quit,
And to reach the ridge El-Sabán, — no safety till that
   be spied !

And Buhéyseh is, bound by bound, but a horse-length
    off at last,
For the Pearl has missed the tap of the heel, the touch
    of the bit.

She shortens her stride, she chafes at her rider the
    strange and queer :
Buhéyseh is mad with hope — beat sister she shall and
    must,
Though Duhl, of the hand and heel so clumsy, she
    has to thank.
She is near now, nose by tail — they are neck by
    croup — joy ! fear !
What folly makes Hóseyn shout " Dog Duhl, Damned
    son of the Dust,
Touch the right ear and press with your foot my Pearl's
    left flank ! "

And Duhl was wise at the word, and Muléykeh as
    prompt perceived
Who was urging redoubled pace, and to hear him was
    to obey,
And a leap indeed gave she, and evanished for ever
    more.
And Hóseyn looked one long last look as who, all be-
    reaved,

Looks, fain to follow the dead so far as the living
  may :
Then he turned Buhéyseh's neck slow homeward,
  weeping sore.

And, lo, in the sunrise, still sat Hóseyn upon the
  ground
Weeping : and neighbors came, the tribesmen of
  Bénu-Asád
In the vale of green Er-Rass, and they questioned him
  of his grief ;
And he told from first to last how, serpent-like, Duhl
  had wound
His way to the nest, and how Duhl rode like an ape,
  so bad !
And how Buhéyseh did wonders, yet Pearl remained
  with the thief.

And they jeered him, one and all : " Poor Hóseyn is
  crazed past hope !
How else had he wrought himself his ruin, in fortune's
  spite ?
To have simply held the tongue were a task for a boy
  or girl,
And here were Muléykeh again, the eyed like an ante-
  telope,

25

The child of his heart by day, the wife of his breast by
    night ! " —
" And the beaten in speed ! " wept Hóseyn : " You
    never have loved my Pearl."

PIETRO OF ABANO.

———◆———

Petrus Aponensis — there was a magician !
When that strange adventure happened, which I mean
    to tell my hearers,
Nearly had he tried all trades — beside physician,
Architect, astronomer, astrologer, — or worse :
How else, as the old books warrant, was he able,
All at once, through all the world, to prove the prompt-
    est of appearers
Where was prince to cure, tower to build as high as
    Babel,
Star to name or sky-sign read, — yet pouch, for pains,
    a curse ?

— Curse : for when a vagrant, — foot-sore, travel-tat-
    tered,
Now a young man, now an old man, Turk or Arab,
    Jew or Gypsy, —
Proffered folks in passing — O for pay, what mat-
    tered ? —

"I 'll be doctor, I 'll play builder, star I 'll name —
    sign read ! "
Soon as prince was cured, tower built, and fate pre-
    dicted,
"Who may you be?" came the question ; when he
    answered " *Petrus ipse,*"
"Just as we divined ! " cried folks — "A wretch con-
    victed
Long ago of dealing with the devil — you indeed ! "

So, they cursed him roundly, all his labor's payment,
Motioned him — the convalescent prince would — to
    vacate the presence :
Babylonians plucked his beard and tore his raiment,
Drove him from that tower he built : while, had he
    peered at stars,
Town howled " Stone the quack who styles our Dog-
    star — Sirius ! "
Country yelled "Aroint the churl who prophesies we
    take no pleasance
Under vine and fig-tree, since the year 's delirious,
Bears no crop of any kind, — all through the planet
    Mars ! "

Straightway would the whileom youngster grow a gri-
    sard,
Or, as case might hap, the hoary eld drop off and show
    a stripling.

Town and country groaned — indebted to a wizard !
" Curse — nay, kick and cuff him — fit requital of his
 pains !
Gratitude in word or deed were wasted truly !
Rather make the Church amends by crying out on,
 cramping, crippling
One who, on pretence of serving man, serves duly
Man's arch foe : not ours, be sure, but Satan's — his
 the gains ! "

Peter grinned and bore it, such disgraceful usage :
Somehow, cuffs and kicks and curses seem ordained
 his like to suffer :
Prophet's pay with Christians, now as in the Jews' age,
Still is — stoning : so, he meekly took his wage and
 went,
— Safe again was found ensconced in those old quar-
 ters,
Padua's blackest blindest byestreet, — none the worse,
 nay, somewhat tougher :
" Calculating " quoth he " soon I join the martyrs,
Since, who magnify my lore, on burning me are
 bent." [1]

  [1] " Studiando le mie cifre col compasso,
   Rilevo che sarò presto sotterra,
   Perchè del mio saper si fa gran chiasso,
   E gl'ignoranti m'hanno mosso guerra."

Now as, on a certain evening, to his alley
Peter slunk, all bruised and broken, sore in body, sick
    in spirit,
Just escaped from Cairo where he launched a galley
Needing neither sails nor oars nor help of wind or
    tide,
— Needing but the fume of fire to set a-flying
Wheels like mad which whirled you quick — North,
    South, where'er you pleased require it, —
That is — would have done so had not priests come
    prying,
Broke his engine up and bastinadoed him beside : —

As he reached his lodging, stopped there unmolested,
(Neighbors feared him, urchins fled him, few were
    bold enough to follow)
While his fumbling fingers tried the lock and tested
Once again the queer key's virtue, oped the sullen
    door, —
Some one plucked his sleeve, cried "Master, pray your.
    pardon !

Said to have been found in a well at Abano in the last century.
They were extemporaneously Englished thus : not as Father
Prout chose to prefer them :

    Studying my ciphers with the compass,
      I reckon — I soon shall be below-ground ;
    Because, of my lore folks make great rumpus,
      And war on myself makes each dull rogue round.

Grant a word to me who patient wait you in your arch-
    way's hollow !
Hard on you men's hearts are : be not your heart hard
    on
Me who kiss your garment's hem, O Lord of magic
    lore !

" Mage — say I, who no less, scorning tittle-tattle,
To the vulgar give no credence when they prate of
    Peter's magic,
Deem his art brews tempest, hurts the crops and cat-
    tle,
Hinders fowls from laying eggs and worms from spin-
    ning silk,
Rides upon a he-goat, mounts at need a broomstick :
While the price he pays for this (so turns to comic
    what was tragic)
Is — he may not drink — dreads like the Day of
    Doom's tick —
One poor drop of sustenance ordained mere men —
    that 's milk !

" Tell such tales to Padua ! Think me no such dul-
    lard !
Not from these benighted parts did I derive my breath
    and being !
I am from a land whose cloudless skies are colored

Livelier, suns orb largelier, airs seem incense, — while,
    on earth —
What, instead of grass, our fingers and our thumbs
    cull,
Proves true moly! sounds and sights there help the
    body's hearing, seeing,
Till the soul grows godlike : brief, — you front no
    numb-scull
Shaming by ineptitude the Greece that gave him birth!

" Mark within my eye its iris mystic-lettered —
That 's my name! and note my ear — its swan-shaped
    cavity, my emblem!
Mine 's the swan-like nature born to fly unfettered
Over land and sea in search of knowledge — food for
    song
Art denied the vulgar! Geese grow fat on barley,
Swans require ætherial provend, undesirous to resem-
    ble 'em —
Soar to seek Apollo, — favored with a parley
Such as, Master, you grant me — who will not hold
    you long.

" Leave to learn to sing — for that your swan peti-
    tions :
Master, who possess the secret, say not nay to such a
    suitor!

All I ask is — bless mine, purest of ambitions !
Grant me leave to make my kind wise, free, and
    happy !   How ?
Just by making me — as you are mine — their model !
Geese have goose-thoughts : make a swan their teacher
    first, then co-adjutor, —
Let him introduce swan-notions to each noddle, —
Geese will soon grow swans, and men become what I
    am now !

"That's the only magic — had but fools discern-
    ment,
Could they probe and pass into the solid through the
    soft and seeming !
Teach me such true magic — now and no adjourn-
    ment !
Teach your art of making fools subserve the man of
    mind !
Magic is the power we men of mind should practise,
Draw fools to become our drudges — docile hence-
    forth, never dreaming —
While they do our hests for fancied gain — the fact is
What they toil and moil to get proves falsehood :
    truth 's behind !

" See now ! you conceive some fabric — say, a man-
    sion

Meet for monarch's pride and pleasure : this is truth
    — a thought has fired you,
Made you fain to give some cramped concept expan-
    sion,
Put your faculty to proof, fulfil your nature's task.
First you fascinate the monarch's self : he fancies
He it was devised the scheme you execute as he in-
    spired you :
He in turn sets slaving insignificances
Toiling, moiling till your structure stands there — all
    you ask !

" Soon the monarch 's known for what he was — a
    ninny :
Soon the rabble-rout leave labor, take their work-day
    wage and vanish :   •
Soon the late puffed bladder, pricked, shows lank and
    skinny —
' Who was its inflator ? ' ask we ' whose the giant
    lungs ? '
Petri en pulmones ! What though men prove ingrates ?
Let them — so they stop at crucifixion — buffet, ban
    and banish !
Peter's power 's apparent : human praise — its din
    grates
Harsh as blame on ear unused to aught save angels'
    tongues.

"Ay, there have been always, since our world existed,
Mages who possessed the secret — needed but to
    stand still, fix eye
On the foolish mortal : straight was he enlisted
Soldier, scholar, servant, slave — no matter for the
    style !
Only through illusion ; ever what seemed profit —
Love or lucre — justified obedience to the *Ipse dixi :*
Work done — palace reared from pavement up to
    soffit —
Was it strange if builders smelt out cheating all the
    while ?

"Let them pelt and pound, bruise, bray you in a mor-
    tar !
What's the odds to you who seek reward of quite an-
    other nature ?
You've enrolled your name where sages of your sort
    are,
—Michael of Constantinople, Hans of Halberstadt !
Nay and were you nameless, still you've your convic-
    tion
You it was and only you — what signifies the nomen-
    clature ? —
Ruled the world in fact, though how you ruled be
    fiction
Fit for fools : true wisdom's magic you — if e'er ℞
    — had 't !

" But perhaps you ask me ' Since each ignoramus
While he profits by such magic persecutes the bene-
　　factor,
What should I expect but — once I render famous
You as Michael, Hans and Peter — just one ingrate
　　more ?
If the vulgar prove thus, whatsoe'er the pelf be,
Pouched through my beneficence — and doom me
　　dungeoned, chained, or racked, or
Fairly burned outright — how grateful will yourself be
When, his secret gained, you match your — master
　　just before ? '

" That 's where I await you !　Please, revert a little !
What do folks report about you if not this — which,
　　though chimeric,
Still, as figurative, suits you to a tittle —
That, — although the elements obey your nod and
　　wink,
Fades or flowers the herb you chance to smile or sigh
　　at,
While your frown bids earth quake palled by obscura-
　　tion atmospheric, —
Brief, although through nature nought resists your *fiat,*
There 's yet one poor substance mocks you — milk
　　you may not drink !

" Figurative language !   Take my explanation !
Fame with fear, and hate with homage, these your art
 procures in plenty.
All 's but daily dry bread : what makes moist the ra-
 tion ?
Love, the milk that sweetens man his meal — alas,
 you lack !
I am he who, since he fears you not, can love you.
Love is born of heart not mind, *de corde natus haud de*
 mente ;
Touch my heart and love 's yoúrs, sure as shines
 above you
Sun by day and star by night though earth should go
 to wrack !

" Stage by stage you lift me — kiss by kiss I hallow
Whose but your dear hand my helper, punctual as at
 each new impulse
I approach my aim ? Shell chipped, the eaglet callow
Needs a parent's pinion push to quit the eyrie's edge :
But once fairly launched forth, denizen of æther,
While each effort sunward bids the blood more freely
 through each limb pulse,
Sure the parent feels, as gay they soar together,
Fully are all pains repaid when love redeems its
 pledge ! "

Then did Peter's tristful visage lighten somewhat,
Vent a watery smile as though inveterate mistrust
    were thawing.
"Well, who knows?" he slow broke silence. "Mor-
    tals — come what
Come there may — are still the dupes of hope there 's
    luck in store.
Many scholars seek me, promise mounts and marvels :
Here stand I to witness how they step 'twixt me and
    clapperclawing !
Dry bread, — that I 've gained me : truly I should
    starve else :
But of milk, no drop was mine ! Well, shuffle cards
    once more !"

At the word of promise thus implied, our stran-
    ger —
What can he but cast his arms, in rapture of embrace,
    round Peter?
"Hold ! I choke !" the mage grunts. "Shall I in
    the manger
Any longer play the dog? Approach, my calf, and
    feed !
Bene . . . won't you wait for grace?" But sudden
    incense
Wool-white, serpent-solid, curled up — perfume grow-
    ing sweet and sweeter

Till it reached the young man's nose and seemed to
    win sense
Soul and all from out his brain through nostril : yes,
    indeed !

Presently the young man rubbed his eyes. "Where
    am I ?
Too much bother over books ! Some reverie has
    proved amusing.
What did Peter prate of ? 'Faith, my brow is clammy !
How my head throbs, how my heart thumps ! Can it
    be I swooned ?
Oh, I spoke my speech out — cribbed from Plato's
    tractate,
Dosed him with ' the Fair and Good,' swore — Dog of
    Egypt — I was choosing
Plato's way to serve men ! What 's the hour ? Exact
    eight !
Home now, and to-morrow never mind how Plato
    mooned !

" Peter has the secret ! Fair and Good are products
(So he said) of Foul and Evil : one must bring to
    pass the other.
Just as poisons grow drugs, steal through sundry odd
    ducts
Doctors name, and ultimately issue safe and changed.

You'd abolish poisons, treat disease with dainties

Such as suit the sound and sane? With all such kick-
        shaws vain you pother!

Arsenic's the stuff puts force into the faint eyes,

Opium sets the brain to rights — by cark and care de-
        ranged.

"What, he's safe within door? — would escape — no
        question —

Thanks, since thanks and more I owe, and mean to
        pay in time befitting.

What most presses now is — after night's digestion,

Peter, of thy precepts! — promptest practice of the
        same.

Let me see! The wise man, first of all, scorns riches:

But to scorn them must obtain them: none believes
        in his permitting

Gold to lie ungathered: who picks up, then pitches

Gold away — philosophizes: none disputes his claim.

" So with worldly honors : 't is by abdicating,

Incontestably he proves he could have kept the crown
        discarded.

Sylla cuts a figure. leaving off dictating:

Simpletons laud private life? 'The grapes are sour,'
        laugh we.

So, again — but why continue? All's tumultuous

Here : my head 's a-whirl with knowledge.   Speedily
   shall be rewarded
He who taught me !   Greeks prove ingrates ?   So insult you us ?
When your teaching bears its first-fruits, Peter — wait
   and see ! "

As the word, the deed proved ; ere a brief year's pas-
   sage,
Fop — that fool he made the jokes on — now he made
   the jokes for, *gratis :*
Hunks — that hoarder, long left lonely in his crass
   age —
Found now one appreciative deferential friend :
Powder-paint-and-patch, Hag Jezebel — recovered,
Strange to say, the power to please, got courtship till
   she cried *Jam satis !*
Fop be-flattered, Hunks be-friended, Hag be-lov-
   ered —
Nobody o'erlooked, save God — he soon attained his
   end.

As he lounged at ease one morning in his villa,
(Hag 's the dowry) estimated (Hunks' bequest) his
   coin in coffer,
Mused on how a fool's good word (Fop's word) could
   fill a

26

Social circle with his praise, promote him man of
    mark, —
All at once — " An old friend fain would see your
    Highness ! "
There stood Peter, skeleton and scarecrow, plain writ
    Phi-lo-so-pher
In the woe-worn face — for yellowness and dryness,
Parchment — with a pair of eyes — one hope their
    feeble spark.

" Did I counsel rightly ?   Have you, in accordance,
Prospered greatly, dear my pupil ?   Sure, at just the
    stage I find you
When your hand may draw me forth from the mad
    war-dance
Savages are leading round your master — down, not
    dead.
Padua wants to burn me : baulk them, let me linger
Life out — rueful though its remnant — hid in some
    safe hole behind you !
Prostrate here I lie : quick, help with but a finger
Lest I house in safety's self — a tombstone o'er my
    head !

" Lodging, bite and sup, with — now and then — a
    copper
— Alms for any poorer still, if such there be, — is all
    my asking.

Take me for your bedesman, — nay, if you think
    proper,
Menial merely, — such my perfect passion for repose !
Yes, from out your plenty Peter craves a pittance
— Leave to thaw his frozen hands before the fire
    whereat you 're basking !
Double though your debt were, grant this boon — re-
    mittance
He proclaims of obligation : 't is himself that owes ! "

" Venerated Master — can it be, such treatment
Learning meets with, magic fails to guard you from,
    by all appearance ?
Strange ! for, as you entered, — what the famous feat
    meant,
I was full of, — why you reared that fabric, Padua's
    boast.
Nowise for man's pride, man's pleasure, did you slyly
Raise it, but man's seat of rule whereby the world
    should soon have clearance
(Happy world) from such a rout as now so vilely
Handles you — and hampers me, for which I grieve
    the most.

" Since if it got wind you now were my familiar,
How could I protect you — nay, defend myself against
    the rabble ?

Wait until the mob, now masters, willy-nilly are
Servants as they should be : then has gratitude full
    play !
Surely this experience shows how unbefitting
'T is that minds like mine should rot in ease and
    plenty. Geese may gabble,
Gorge, and keep the ground : but swans are soon for
    quitting
Earthly fare — as fain would I, your swan, if taught
    the way.

" Teach me, then, to rule men, have them at my pleas-
    ure !
Solely for their good, of course, — impart a secret
    worth rewarding,
Since the proper life's-prize ! Tantalus's treasure
Aught beside proves, vanishes and leaves no trace at
    all.
Wait awhile, nor press for payment prematurely !
Over-haste defrauds you. Thanks ! since, — even while
    I speak, — discarding
Sloth and vain delights, I learn how — swiftly, surely —
Magic sways the sceptre, wears the crown and wields
    the ball !

" Gone again — what, is he ? 'Faith, he 's soon dis-
    posed of !

Peter's precepts work already, put within my lump
　　their leaven !
Ay, we needs must don glove would we pluck the rose
　　— doff
Silken garment would we climb the tree and take its
　　fruit.
Why sharp thorn, rough rind ?　To keep unvio-
　　lated
Either prize !　We garland us, we mount from earth
　　to feast in heaven,
Just because exist what once we estimated
Hindrances which, better taught, as helps we now
　　compute.

" Foolishly I turned disgusted from my fellows !
Pits of ignorance — to fill, and heaps of prejudice —
　　to level —
Multitudes in motley, whites and blacks and yel-
　　lows —
What a hopeless task it seemed to discipline the host !
Now I see my error.　Vices act like virtues
— Not alone because they guard — sharp thorns —
　　the rose we first dishevel,
Not because they scrape, scratch — rough rind —
　　through the dirt-shoes
Bare feet cling to bole with, while the half-mooned
　　boot we boast.

" No, my aim is nobler, more disinterested !

Man shall keep what seemed to thwart him, since it
    proves his true assistance,

Leads to ascertaining which head is the best head,

Would he crown his body, rule its members — lawless
    else.

Ignorant the horse stares, by deficient vision

Takes a man to be a monster, lets him mount, then,
    twice the distance

Horse could trot unridden, gallops — dream Elys-
    ian ! —

Dreaming that his dwarfish guide 's a giant, — jockeys
    tell 's."

Brief, so worked the spell, he promptly had a rid-
    dance :

Heart and brain no longer felt the pricks which passed
    for conscience-scruples :

Free henceforth his feet, — *Per Bacco*, how they did
    dance

Merrily through lets and checks that stopped the way
    before !

Politics the prize now, — such adroit adviser,

Opportune suggester, with the tact that triples and
    quadruples

Merit in each measure, — never did the Kaiser

Boast a subject such a statesman, friend, and some-
    thing more !

As he, up and down, one noonday, paced his closet
— Council o'er, each spark (his hint) blown flame, by
    colleagues' breath applauded,
Strokes of statecraft hailed with " *Salomo si nôsset !* "
(His the nostrum) — every throw for luck come
    double-six, —
As he, pacing, hugged himself in satisfaction,
Thump — the door went. " What, the Kaiser ? By
    none else were I defrauded
Thus of well-earned solace. Since 't is fate's exac-
    tion, —
Enter, Liege my Lord ! Ha, Peter, you here ? *Te-
neor vix !* "

" Ah, Sir, none the less, contain you, nor wax irate !
You so lofty, I so lowly, — vast the space which yawns
    between us !
Still, methinks, you — more than ever — at a high
    rate
Needs must prize poor Peter's secret since it lifts you
    thus.
Grant me now the boon whereat before you boggled !
Ten long years your march has moved — one triumph
    — (though *e* 's short) — *hactēnus,*
While I down and down disastrously have joggled
Till I pitch against Death's door, the true *Nec Ultra
Plus.*

"Years ago — some ten 't is — since I sought for
    shelter,
Craved in your whole house a closet, out of all your
    means a comfort.
Now you soar above these : as is gold to spelter
So is power — you urged with reason — paramount to
    wealth.
Power you boast in plenty: let it grant me refuge !
Houseroom now is out of question : find for me some
    stronghold — some fort —
Privacy wherein, immured, shall this blind deaf huge
Monster of a mob let stay the soul I 'd save by
    stealth !

"Ay, for all too much with magic have I tampered !
— Lost the world, and gained, I fear, a certain plâce
    I 'm to describe loth !
Still, if prayer and fasting tame the pride long pam-
    pered,
Mercy may be mine : amendment never comes too
    late.
How can I amend beset by cursers, kickers ?
Pluck this brand from out the burning ! Once away,
    I take my Bible-oath,
Never more — so long as life's weak lamp-flame flick-
    ers —
No, not once I 'll tease you, but in silence bear my
    fate ! "

" Gently, good my Genius, Oracle unerring !
Strange now ! can you guess on what — as in you
    peeped — it was I pondered ?
You and I are both of one mind in preferring
Power to wealth, but — here 's the point — what sort
    of power, I ask ?
Ruling men is vulgar, easy and ignoble :
Rid yourself of conscience, quick you have at beck
    and call the fond herd.
But who wields the crosier, down may fling the crow-
    bill :
That 's the power I covet now ; soul's sway o'er souls
    — my task !

" ' Well but,' you object, ' you have it, who by glamour
Dress up lies to look like truths, mask folly in the
    garb of reason :
Your soul acts on theirs, sure, when the people clamor
Hold their peace, now fight now fondle, — earwigged
    through the brains.'
Possibly ! but still the operation 's mundane,
Grosser than a taste demands which — craving
    manna — kecks at peason —
Power o'er men by wants material : why should one
    deign
Rule by sordid hopes and fears — a grunt for all one's
    pains ?

"No, if men must praise me, let them praise to pur-
pose !
Would we move the world, not earth but heaven must
be our fulcrum — *pou sto !*
Thus I seek to move it : Master, why intérpose —
Baulk my climbing close on what's the ladder's top-
most round ?
Statecraft 't is I step from : when by priestcraft hoisted
Up to where my foot may touch the highest rung
which fate allows toe,
Then indeed ask favor !   On you shall be foisted
No excuse : I 'll pay my debt, each penny of the
pound !

"Ho, my knaves without there !   Lead this worthy
down-stairs !
No farewell, good Paul — nay, Peter — what 's your
name remembered rightly ?
Come, he 's humble : out another would have flounced
— airs
Suitors often give themselves when our sort bow them
forth.
Did I touch his rags ?   He surely kept his distance :
Yet, there somehow passed to me from him — where'er
the virtue might lie —
Something that inspires my soul — Oh, by assistance
Doubtlessly of Peter ! — still, he 's worth just what
he 's worth !

" 'T is my own soul soars now : soaring — how ? By
    crawling !
I 'll to Rome, before Rome's feet the temporal-supreme
    lay prostrate !
' Hands ' (I 'll say) ' proficient once in pulling, hauling
This and that way men as I was minded — feet now
    clasp ! '
Ay, the Kaiser's self has wrung them in his fervor !
Now — they only sue to slave for Rome, nor at one
    doit the cost rate.
Rome's adopted child — no bone, no muscle, nerve or
Sinew of me but I 'll strain, though out my life I
    gasp ! "

As he stood one evening proudly — (he had traversed
Rome on horseback — peerless pageant ! — claimed
    the Lateran as new Pope) —
Thinking " All 's attained now ! Pontiff ! Who could
    have erst
Dreamed of my advance so far when, some ten years
    ago,
I embraced devotion, grew from priest to bishop,
Gained the Purple, bribed the Conclave, got the Two-
    thirds, saw my coop ope,
Came out — what Rome hails me ! O were there a
    wish-shop,
Not one wish more would I purchase — lord of all
    below !

" Ha — who dares intrude now — puts aside the ar-
    ras ?
What, old Peter, here again, at such a time, in such a
    presence ?
Satan sends this plague back merely to embarrass
Me who enter on my office — little needing you !
'Faith, I 'm touched myself by age, but you look
    Tithon !
Were it vain to seek of you the sole prize left — re-
    juvenescence ?
Well, since flesh is grass which Time must lay his
    scythe on,
Say your say and so depart and make no more ado ! "

Peter faltered — coughing first by way of prologue —
" Holiness, your help comes late : a death at ninety
    little matters.
Padua, build poor Peter's pyre now, on log roll log,
Burn away — I 've lived my day ! Yet here 's the
    sting in death —
I 've an author's pride : I want my Book's survival :
See, I 've hid it in my breast to warm me mid the rags
    and tatters !
Save it — tell next age your Master had no rival !
Scholar's debt discharged in full, be ' Thanks ' my
    latest breath ! "

" Faugh, the frowsy bundle — scribblings harum-sca-
    rum

Scattered o'er a dozen sheepskins ! What 's the name
    of this farrago ?

Ha — ' *Conciliator Differentiarum* ' —

Man and book may burn together, cause the world no
    loss !

Stop — what else ? A tractate — eh, ' *De Speciebus*

Ceremonialis Ma-gi-æ ? ' I dream sure ! Hence, away,
    go,

Wizard, — quick avoid me ! Vain you clasp my knee,
    buss

Hand that bears the Fisher's ring or foot that boasts
    the Cross !

" Help ! The old magician clings like an octopus !

Ah, you rise now — fuming, fretting, frowning, if I
    read your features !

Frown, who cares ? We 're Pope — once Pope, you
    can't unpope us !

Good — you muster up a smile : that 's better ! Still
    so brisk ?

All at once grown youthful ? But the case is plain !
    Ass —

Here I dally with the fiend, yet know the Word —
    compels all creatures

Earthly, heavenly, hellish. *Apage, Sathanas!*
Dicam verbum Salomonis" — "*— dicite!*"   When —
    whisk ! —

What was changed ?   The stranger gave his eyes a
    rubbing :
There smiled Peter's face turned back a moment at
    him o'er the shoulder,
As the black-door shut, bang !   " So he scapes a drub-
    bing ! "
(Quoth a boy who, unespied, had stopped to hear the
    talk).
"That 's the way to thank these wizards when they
    bid men
Benedicite !   What ails you ?   You, a man, and yet no
    bolder ?
Foreign Sir, you look but foolish ! "   " *Idmen, idmen !* "
Groaned the Greek.   " O Peter, cheese at last I know
    from chalk ! "

Peter lived his life out, menaced yet no martyr,
Knew himself the mighty man he was — such knowl-
    edge all his guerdon,
Left the world a big book — people but in part err
When they style a true *Scientiæ Com-pen-di-um :*
" *Admirationem incutit* " they sourly
Smile, as fast they shut the folio which myself was
    somehow spurred on

Once to ope : but love — life's milk which daily,
    hourly,
Blockheads lap — O Peter, still thy taste of love 's to
    come !

Greek, was your ambition likewise doomed to failure ?
True, I find no record you wore purple, walked with
    axe and fasces,
Played some antipope's part : still, friend, don't turn
    tail, you 're
Certain, with but these two gifts, to gain earth's prize
    in time !
Cleverness uncurbed by conscience — if you ransacked
Peter's book you 'd find no potent spell like these to
    rule the masses ;
Nor should want example, had I not to transact
Other business. Go your ways, you 'll thrive ! So
    ends my rhyme.

When these parts Tiberius, — not yet Cæsar, — trav-
    elled,
Passing Padua, he consulted Padua's Oracle of Ger-
    yon
(God three-headed, thrice wise) just to get unravelled
Certain tangles of his future. " Fling at Abano
Golden dice," it answered : " dropt within the fount
    there,

Note what sum the pips present !" And still we see
    each die, the very one,
Turn up, through the crystal, — read the whole account
    there
Where 't is told by Suetonius, — each its highest throw.

Scarce the sportive fancy-dice I fling show "Venus :"
Still — for love of that dear land which I so oft in
    dreams revisit —
I have — Oh, not sung ! but lilted (as — between us —
Grows my lazy custom) this its legend. What the lilt ?

DOCTOR ——.

A RABBI told me : On the day allowed
Satan for carping at God's rule, he came,
Fresh from our earth, to brave the angel-crowd.

"What is the fault now?" "This I find to blame :
Many and various are the tongues below,
Yet all agree in one speech, all proclaim

"'Hell has no might to match what earth can show :
Death is the strongest-born of Hell, and yet
Stronger than Death is a Bad Wife, we know.'

"Is it a wonder if I fume and fret —
Robbed of my rights, since Death am I, and mine
The style of Strongest? Men pay Nature's debt

"Because they must at my demand ; decline
To pay it henceforth surely men will please,
Provided husbands with bad wives combine

" To baffle Death.   Judge between me and these ! "
" Thyself shalt judge.   Descend to earth in shape
Of mortal, marry, drain from froth to lees

" The bitter draught, then see if thou escape
Concluding, with men sorrowful and sage,
A Bad Wife's strength Death's self in vain would
       ape ! "

How Satan entered on his pilgrimage,
Conformed himself to earthly ordinance,
Wived and played husband well from youth to age

Intrepidly — I leave untold, advance
Through many a married year until I reach
A day when — of his father's countenance

The very image, like him too in speech
As well as thought and deed, — the union's fruit
Attained maturity.   " I needs must teach

" My son a trade : but trade, such son to suit,
Needs seeking after.   He a man of war?
Too cowardly !   A lawyer wins repute —

" Having to toil and moil, though — both which are
Beyond this sluggard.   There's Divinity :
No, that 's my own bread-winner — that be far

" From my poor offspring ! Physic ? Ha, we 'll try
If this be practicable. Where 's my wit
Asleep ? — since, now I come to think. . . . Ay, ay !

" Hither, my son ! Exactly have I hit
On a profession for thee. *Medicus* —
Behold, thou art appointed ! Yea, I spit

" Upon thine eyes, bestow a virtue thus
That henceforth not this human form I wear
Shalt thou perceive alone, but — one of us

" By privilege — thy fleshly sight shall bear
Me in my spirit-person as I walk
The world and take my prey appointed there.

" Doctor once dubbed — what ignorance shall baulk
Thy march triumphant ? Diagnose the gout
As colic, and prescribe it cheese for chalk —

" No matter ! All 's one : cure shall come about
And win thee wealth — fees paid with such a roar
Of thanks and praise alike from lord and lout

" As never stunned man's ears on earth before.
' How may this be ? ' Why, that 's my sceptic ! Soon
Truth will corrupt thee, soon thou doubt'st no more !

" Why is it I bestow on thee the boon
Of recognizing me the while I go
Invisibly among men, morning, noon

" And night, from house to house, and — quick or
    slow —
Take my appointed prey ?   They summon thee
For help, suppose : obey the summons ! so !

" Enter, look round !   Where 's Death ?   Know — I
    am he,
Satan who work all evil : I 't is, bring
Pain to the patient in whate'er degree.

" I, then, am there : first glance thine eye shall
    fling
Will find me — whether distant or at hand,
As I am free to do my spiriting

" At such mere first glance thou shalt understand
Wherefore I reach no higher up the room
Than door or window, when my form is scanned.

" Howe'er friends' faces please to gather gloom,
Bent o'er the sick, — howe'er himself desponds, —
In such case Death is not the sufferer's doom.

" Contrariwise, do friends rejoice my bonds
Are broken, does the captive in his turn
Crow ' Life shall conquer ? ' Nip these foolish fronds

" Of hope a-sprout, if haply thou discern
Me at the head — my victim's head be sure !
Forth now ! This taught thee, little else to learn ! "

And forth he went. Folks heard him ask demure
" How do you style this ailment ? (There he peeps,
My father, through the arras !) Sirs, the cure

" Is plain as A. B. C. ! Experience steeps
Blossoms of pennyroyal half an hour
In sherris. *Sumat !* — Lo, how sound he sleeps —

" The subject you presumed was past the power
Of Galen to relieve ! " Or else " How's this ?
Why call for help so tardily ? Clouds lour

" Portentously indeed, Sirs ! (Nought's amiss :
He's at the bed-foot merely.) Still, the storm
May pass averted — not by quacks, I wis

" Like you, my masters ! You, forsooth, perform
A miracle ? Stand, sciolists, aside !
At ignorance blood, ne'er so cold, grows warm ! "

Which boasting by result was justified,
Big as might words be : whether drugged or left
Drugless, the patient always lived, not died.

Great the heir's gratitude, so nigh bereft
Of all he prized in this world : sweet the smile
Of disconcerted rivals : " Cure ? — say, theft

" From Nature in despite of Art — so style
This off-hand kill-or-cure work !   You did much,
I had done more : folks cannot wait awhile ! "

But did the case change ? was it — " Scarcely such
The symptoms as to warrant our recourse
To your skill, Doctor !   Yet since just a touch

" Of pulse, a taste of breath, has all the force
With you of long investigation claimed
By others, — tracks an ailment to its source

" Intuitively, — may we ask unblamed
What from this pimple you prognosticate ? "
" Death ! " was the answer, as he saw and named

The coucher by the sick man's head.   " Too late
You send for my assistance.   I am bold
Only by Nature's leave, and bow to Fate !

" Besides, you have my rivals : lavish gold !
How comfortably quick shall life depart
Cosseted by attentions manifold !

" One day, one hour ago, perchance my art
Had done some service.   Since you have yourselves
Chosen — before the horse — to put the cart,

" Why, Sirs, the sooner that the sexton delves
Your patient's grave, the better !   How you stare
— Shallow, for all the deep books on your shelves !

" Fare you well, fumblers ! "   Do I need declare
What name and fame, what riches recompensed
The Doctor's practice ?   Never anywhere

Such an adept as daily evidenced
Each new vaticination !   Oh, not he
Like dolts who dallied with their scruples, fenced

With subterfuge, nor gave out frank and free
Something decisive !   If he said " I save
The patient," saved he was : if " Death will be

" His portion," you might count him dead.   Thus
          brave,
Behold our worthy, sans competitor
Throughout the country, on the architrave

Of Glory's temple golden-lettered for
Machaon *redivivus !*   So, it fell
That, of a sudden, when the Emperor

Was smit by sore disease, I need not tell
If any other Doctor's aid was sought
To come and forthwith make the sick Prince well.

" He will reward thee as a monarch ought.
Not much imports the malady ; but then,
He clings to life and cries like one distraught

" For thee — who, from a simple citizen,
May'st look to rise in rank, — nay, haply wear
A medal with his portrait, — always when

" Recovery is quite accomplished.   There !
Pass to the presence ! "   Hardly has he crossed
The chamber's threshold when he halts, aware

Of who stands sentry by the head.   All 's lost.
"" Sire, nought avails my art : you near the goal,
And end the race by giving up the ghost."

" How ? " cried the monarch : " Names upon your roll
Of half my subjects rescued by your skill —
Old and young, rich and poor — crowd check by jowl

"And yet no room for mine ?   Be saved I will !
Why else am I earth's foremost potentate ?
Add me to these and take as fee your fill

" Of gold — that point admits of no debate
Between us : save me, as you can and must, —
Gold, till your gown's pouch cracks beneath the
     weight ! "

This touched the Doctor.   " Truly a home-thrust,
Parent, you will not parry !   Have I dared
Entreat that you forego the meal of dust

— "Man that is snake's meat — when I saw prepared
Your daily portion ?   Never !   Just this once,
Go from his head, then, — let his life be spared ! "

Whisper met whisper in the gruff response
" Fool, I must have my prey : no inch I budge
From where thou see'st me thus myself ensconce."

"Ah," moaned the sufferer, " by thy look I judge
Wealth fails to tempt thee : what if honors prove
More efficacious ?   Nought to him I grudge

"Who saves me.   Only keep my head above
The cloud that's creeping round it — I 'll divide
My empire with thee !   No ?   What 's left but — love ?

" Does love allure thee ?   Well then, take as bride
My only daughter, fair beyond belief !
Save me — to-morrow shall the knot be tied ! "

" Father, you hear him !   Respite ne'er so brief
Is all I beg : go now and come again
Next day, for aught I care : respect the grief

" Mine will be if thy first-born sues in vain ! "
" Fool, I must have my prey ! " was all he got
In answer.   But a fancy crossed his brain.

" I have it !   Sire, methinks a meteor shot
Just now across the heavens and neutralized
Jove's salutary influence : 'neath the blot

" Plumb are you placed now : well that I surmised
The cause of failure !   Knaves, reverse the bed ! "
" Stay ! " groaned the monarch, " I shall be cap-
    sized —

" Jolt — jolt — my heels uplift where late my head
Was lying — sure I 'm turned right round at last !
What do you say now, Doctor ? "   Nought he said

For why ?   With one brisk leap the Antic passed
From couch foot back to pillow, — as before,
Lord of the situation.   Long aghast

The Doctor gazed, then " Yet one trial more
Is left me " inwardly he uttered.   " Shame
Upon thy flinty heart !   Do I implore

" This trifling favor in the idle name
Of mercy to the moribund ?   I plead
The cause of all thou dost affect : my aim

" Befits my author !   Why would I succeed ?
Simply that by success I may promote
The growth of thy pet virtues — pride and greed.

" But keep thy favors ! — curse thee !   I devote
Henceforth my service to the other side.
No time to lose : the rattle 's in his throat.

" So, — not to leave one last resource untried, —
Run to my house with all haste, somebody !
Bring me that knobstick thence, so often plied

" With profit by the astrologer — shall I
Disdain its help, the mystic Jacob's-Staff ?
Sire, do but have the courage not to die

" Till this arrive !   Let none of you dare laugh !
Though rugged its exterior, I have seen
That implement work wonders, send the chaff

" Quick and thick flying from the wheat — I mean,
By metaphor, a human sheaf it thrashed
Flail-like. Go fetch it ! Or — a word between

" Just you and me, friend ! — go bid, unabashed,
My mother, whom you 'll find there, bring the stick
Herself — herself, mind ! " Out the lackey dashed

Zealous upon the errand. Craft and trick
Are meat and drink to Satan : and he grinned
— How else ? — at an excuse so politic

For failure : scarce would Jacob's-Staff rescind
Fate's firm decree ! And ever as he neared
The agonizing one, his breath like wind

Froze to the marrow, while his eye-flash seared
Sense in the brain up : closelier and more close
Pressing his prey, when at the door appeared

— Who but his Wife the Bad ? Whereof one dose,
One grain, one mite of the medicament,
Sufficed him. Up he sprang. One word, too gross

To soil my lips with, — and through ceiling went
Somehow the Husband. " That a storm 's dispersed
We know for certain by the sulphury scent !

" Hail to the Doctor !   Who but one so versed
In all Dame Nature's secrets had prescribed
The staff thus opportunely?   Style him first

"And foremost of physicians ! "   " I 've imbibed
Elixir surely," smiled the prince, — " have gained
New lease of life.   Dear Doctor, how you bribed

"Death to forego me, boots not : you 've obtained
My daughter and her dowry.   Death, I 've heard,
Was still on earth the strongest power that reigned,

" Except a Bad Wife ! "   Whereunto demurred
Nowise the Doctor, so refused the fee
— No dowry, no bad wife !

                         " You think absurd
This tale ? " — the Rabbi added : " True, our Talmud
Boasts sundry such : yet — have our elders erred
In thinking there 's some water there, not all mud ? "
I tell it, as the Rabbi told it me.

PAN AND LUNA.

Si credere dignum est. — *Georgic*, III. 390.

———◆———

O WORTHY of belief I hold it was,
Virgil, your legend in those strange three lines !
No question, that adventure came to pass
One black night in Arcadia : yes, the pines,
Mountains and valleys mingling made one mass
Of black with void black heaven : the earth's confines,
The sky's embrace, — below, above, around,
All hardened into black without a bound.

Fill up a swart stone chalice to the brim
With fresh-squeezed yet fast-thickening poppy-juice :
See how the sluggish jelly, late a-swim,
Turns marble to the touch of who would loose
The solid smooth, grown jet from rim to rim,
By turning round the bowl !   So night can fuse
Earth with her all-comprising sky.   No less,
Light, the least spark, shows air and emptiness.

And thus it proved when — diving into space,
Stript of all vapor, from each web of mist
Utterly film-free — entered on her race
The naked Moon, full-orbed antagonist
Of night and dark, night's dowry : peak to base,
Upstarted mountains, and each valley, kissed
To sudden life, lay silver-bright : in air
Flew she revealed, Maid - Moon with limbs all
    bare.

Still as she fled, each depth — where refuge seemed —
Opening a long pale chamber, left distinct
Those limbs : mid still-retreating blue, she teemed
Herself with whiteness, — virginal, uncinct
By any halo save what finely gleamed
To outline not disguise her : heaven was linked
In one accord with earth to quaff the joy,
Drain beauty to the dregs without alloy.

Whereof she grew aware. What help ? When, lo,
A succorable cloud with sleep lay dense :
Some pine-tree top had caught it sailing slow,
And tethered for a prize : in evidence
Captive lay fleece on fleece of piled-up snow
Drowsily patient : flake-heaped how or whence,
The structure of that succorable cloud,
What matter ? Shamed she plunged into its shroud.

Orbed — so the woman-figure poets call
Because of rounds on rounds — that apple-shaped
Head which its hair binds close into a ball
Each side the curving ears — that pure undraped
Pout of the sister paps — that . . . Once for all,
Say — her consummate circle thus escaped
With its innumerous circlets, sank absorbed,
Safe in the cloud — O naked Moon full-orbed !

But what means this ?   The downy swathes combine,
Conglobe, the smothery coy-caressing stuff
Curdles about her !   Vain each twist and twine
Those lithe limbs try, encroached on by a fluff
Fitting as close as fits the dented spine
Its flexile ivory outside-flesh : enough !
The plumy drifts contract, condense, constringe,
Till she is swallowed by the feathery springe.

As when a pearl slips lost in the thin foam
Churned on a sea-shore, and, o'er frothed, conceits
Herself safe-housed in Amphitrite's dome, —
If, through the bladdery wave-worked yeast, she meets
What most she loathes and leaps from, — elf from
        gnome
No gladlier, — finds that safest of retreats
Bubbles about a treacherous hand wide ope
To grasp her — (divers who pick pearls so grope) —

So lay this Maid-Moon clasped around and caught
By rough red Pan, the god of all that tract :
He it was schemed the snare thus subtly wrought
With simulated earth-breath, — wool-tufts packed
Into a billowy wrappage.   Sheep far-sought
For spotless shearings yield such : take the fact
As learned Virgil gives it, — how the breed
Whitens itself for ever : yes, indeed !

If one fore-father ram, though pure as chalk
From tinge on fleece, should still display a tongue
Black 'neath the beast's moist palate, prompt men
    baulk
The propagating plague : he gets no young :
They rather slay him, — sell his hide to caulk
Ships with, first steeped in pitch, — nor hands are
    wrung
In sorrow for his fate : protected thus,
The purity we love is gained for us.

So did Girl-Moon, by just her attribute
Of unmatched modesty betrayed, lie trapped,
Bruised to the breast of Pan, half god half brute,
Raked by his bristly boar-sward while he lapped
— Never say, kissed her ! that were to pollute
Love's language — which moreover proves unapt
28

To tell how she recoiled — as who finds thorns
Where she sought flowers — when, feeling, she touched
          — horns !

Then — does the legend say ? — first moon-eclipse
Happened, first swooning-fit which puzzled sore
The early sages ?   Is that why she dips
Into the dark, a minute and no more,
Only so long as serves her while she rips
The cloud's womb through and, faultless as before,
Pursues her way ?   No lesson for a maid
Left she, a maid herself thus trapped, betrayed ?

Ha, Virgil ?   Tell the rest, you !   " To the deep
Of his domain the wildwood, Pan forthwith
Called her, and so she followed " — in her sleep,
Surely ? — " by no means spurning him."   The myth
Explain who may !   Let all else go, I keep
— As of a ruin just a monolith —
Thus much, one verse of five words, each a boon :
Arcadia, night, a cloud, Pan, and the moon.

" Touch him ne'er so lightly, into song he broke :
Soil so quick-receptive, — not one feather-seed,
Not one flower-dust fell but straight its fall awoke
Vitalizing virtue : song would song succeed
Sudden as spontaneous — prove a poet-soul ! "

          Indeed ?

Rock 's the song-soil rather, surface hard and bare :
Sun and dew their mildness, storm and frost their rage
Vainly both expend, — few flowers awaken there :
Quiet in its cleft broods — what the after age
Knows and names a pine, a nation's heritage.

STANDARD AND POPULAR

Library Books

SELECTED FROM THE CATALOGUE OF

HOUGHTON, MIFFLIN AND CO.

*C*ONSIDER *what you have in the smallest chosen library. A company of the wisest and wittiest men that could be picked out of all civil countries, in a thousand years, have set in best order the results of their learning and wisdom. The men themselves were hid and inaccessible, solitary, impatient of interruptions, fenced by etiquette; but the thought which they did not uncover to their bosom friend is here written out in transparent words to us, the strangers of another age.* — Ralph Waldo Emerson

Library Books

OHN ADAMS and Abigail Adams.
Familiar Letters of John Adams and his wife, Abigail Adams, during the Revolution. Crown 8vo, $2.00.

Louis Agassiz.
Methods of Study in Natural History. 16mo, $1.50.
Geological Sketches. 16mo, $1.50.
Geological Sketches. Second Series. 16mo, $1.50.
A Journey in Brazil. Illustrated. 8vo, $5.00.

Thomas Bailey Aldrich.
Story of a Bad Boy. Illustrated. 16mo, $1.50.
Marjorie Daw and Other People. 16mo, $1.50.
Prudence Palfrey. 16mo, $1.50.
The Queen of Sheba. 16mo, $1.50.
The Stillwater Tragedy. $1.50.
Cloth of Gold and Other Poems. 16mo, $1.50.
Flower and Thorn. Later poems. 16mo, $1.25.
Poems. Complete. Illustrated. 8vo, $5.00.

American Men of Letters.
Edited by CHARLES DUDLEY WARNER.
Washington Irving. By Charles Dudley Warner. 16mo, $1.25.
Noah Webster. By Horace E. Scudder. 16mo, $1.25.
Henry D. Thoreau. By Frank B. Sanborn. 16mo, $1.25.
George Ripley. By O. B. Frothingham. 16mo, $1.25.
J. Fenimore Cooper. By Prof. T. R. Lounsbury.
(*In Preparation.*)
Nathaniel Hawthorne. By James Russell Lowell.
N. P. Willis. By Thomas Bailey Aldrich.
William Gilmore Simms. By George W. Cable.
Benjamin Franklin. By T. W. Higginson.
Others to be announced.

American Statesmen.

Edited by JOHN T. MORSE, Jr.

John Quincy Adams. By John T. Morse, Jr. 16mo, $1.25.
Alexander Hamilton. By Henry Cabot Lodge. 16mo, $1.25.
John C. Calhoun. By Dr. H. von Holst. 16mo, $1 25.
Andrew Jackson. By Prof. W. G. Sumner. 16mo, $1.25.
John Randolph. By Henry Adams. 16mo, $1.25.
James Monroe. By Pres. D. C. Gilman. 16mo, $1.25.
(In Preparation.)
Daniel Webster. By Henry Cabot Lodge. 16mo, $1.25.
Thomas Jefferson. By John T. Morse, Jr. 16mo, $1.25.
James Madison. By Sidney Howard Gay.
Albert Gallatin. By John Austin Stevens.
Patrick Henry. By Prof. Moses Coit Tyler.
Henry Clay. By Hon. Carl Schurz.
Lives of others are also expected.

Hans Christian Andersen.

Complete Works. 8vo.
1. The Improvisatore ; or, Life in Italy.
2. The Two Baronesses.
3. O. T. ; or, Life in Denmark.
4. Only a Fiddler.
5. In Spain and Portugal.
6. A Poet's Bazaar.
7. Pictures of Travel.
8. The Story of my Life. With Portrait.
9. Wonder Stories told for Children. Ninety-two illustrations.
10. Stories and Tales. Illustrated.
Cloth, per volume, $1.50 ; price of sets in cloth, $15.00.

Francis Bacon.

Works. Collected and edited by Spedding, Ellis, and Heath. In fifteen volumes, crown 8vo, cloth, $33.75.
The same. *Popular Edition.* In two volumes, crown 8vo, with Portraits and Index. Cloth, $5.00.

Bacon's Life.

Life and Times of Bacon. Abridged. By James Spedding.
2 vols. crown 8vo, $5.00.

Björnstjerne Björnson.

Norwegian Novels. 16mo, each $1.00.

Synnöve Solbakken.
Arne.
The Bridal March.

A Happy Boy.
The Fisher Maiden.
Captain Mansana.

Magnhild.

British Poets.

Riverside Edition. In 68 volumes, crown 8vo, cloth, gilt top, per vol. $1.75; the set, 68 volumes, cloth, $100.00.

Akenside and Beattie, 1 vol.
Ballads, 4 vols.
Burns, 1 vol.
Butler, 1 vol.
Byron, 5 vols.
Campbell and Falconer, 1 vol.
Chatterton, 1 vol.
Chaucer, 3 vols.
Churchill, Parnell, and Tickell, 2 vols.
Coleridge and Keats, 2 vols.
Cowper, 2 vols.
Dryden, 2 vols.
Gay, 1 vol.
Goldsmith and Gray, 1 vol.
Herbert and Vaughan, 1 vol.
Herrick, 1 vol.
Hood, 2 vols.

Milton and Marvell, 2 vols.
Montgomery, 2 vols.
Moore, 3 vols.
Pope and Collins, 2 vols.
Prior, 1 vol.
Scott, 5 vols.
Shakespeare and Jonson, 1 vol.
Shelley, 2 vols.
Skelton and Donne, 2 vols.
Southey, 5 vols.
Spenser, 3 vols.
Swift, 2 vols.
Thomson, 1 vol.
Watts and White, 1 vol.
Wordsworth, 3 vols.
Wyatt and Surrey, 1 vol.
Young, 1 vol.

John Brown, M. D.

Spare Hours. 3 vols. 16mo, each $1.50.

Robert Browning.

Poems and Dramas, etc. 14 vols. $19.50.
Complete Works. New Edition. 7 vols. (*In Press.*)

Wm. C. Bryant.

Translation of Homer. The Iliad. 2 vols. royal 8vo, $9.00. Crown 8vo, $4.50. 1 vol. 12mo, $3.00.
The Odyssey. 2 vols. royal 8vo, $9.00. Crown 8vo, $4.50. 1 vol. 12mo, $3.00.

John Burroughs.

Wake-Robin. Illustrated. 16mo, $1.50.
Winter Sunshine. 16mo, $1.50.
Birds and Poets. 16mo, $1.50.
Locusts and Wild Honey. 16mo, $1.50.
Pepacton, and Other Sketches. 16mo, $1.50.

Thomas Carlyle.

Essays. With Portrait and Index. Four volumes, crown
   8vo, $7.50. *Popular Edition.* Two volumes, $3.50.

Alice and Phœbe Cary.

Poems. *Household Edition.* 12mo, $2.00.
Library Edition. Portraits and 24 illustrations. 8vo, $4.00.
Poetical Works, including Memorial by Mary Clemmer.
   1 vol. 8vo, $3.50. Full gilt, $4.00.
Ballads for Little Folk. Illustrated. $1.50.

L. Maria Child.

Looking toward Sunset. 4to, $2.50.

James Freeman Clarke.

Ten Great Religions. 8vo, $3.00.
Common Sense in Religion. 12mo, $2.00.
Memorial and Biographical Sketches. 12mo, $2.00.
Exotics. $1.00.

J. Fenimore Cooper.

Works. *Household Edition.* Illustrated. 32 vols. 16mo.
   Cloth, per volume, $1.00 ; the set, $32.00.
Globe Edition. Illust'd. 16 vols. $20.00. (*Sold only in sets.*)
Sea Tales. Illustrated. 10 vols. 16mo, $10.00.
Leather Stocking Tales. *Household Edition.* Illustrated.
   5 vols. $5.00. *Riverside Edition.* 5 vols. $11.25.

Richard H. Dana.

To Cuba and Back. 16mo, $1.25.
Two Years Before the Mast. 16mo, $1.50.

Thomas De Quincey.

Works. *Riverside Edition.* In 12 vols. crown 8vo. Per volume, cloth, $1.50 ; the set, $18.00.
Globe Edition. Six vols. 12mo, $10.00. (*Sold only in sets.*)

Madame De Stael.
Germany. 1 vol. crown 8vo, $2 50.

Charles Dickens.
Works. *Illustrated Library Edition.* In 29 volumes, crown 8vo. Cloth, each, $1.50 ; the set, $43.50.
Globe Edition. In 15 vols. 12mo. Cloth, per volume, $1.25 ; the set, $18.75.

J. Lewis Diman.
The Theistic Argument as Affected by Recent Theories. 8vo, $2.00.
Orations and Essays. 8vo, $2.50.

F. S. Drake.
Dictionary of American Biography. 1 vol. 8vo, cloth, $6.00.

Charles L. Eastlake.
Hints on Household Taste. Illustrated. 12mo, $3.00.

George Eliot.
The Spanish Gypsy. 16mo, $1.50.

Ralph Waldo Emerson.
Works. 10 vols. 16mo, $1.50 each ; the set, $15.00.
Fireside Edition. 5 vols. 16mo, $10.00. (*Sold only in sets.*)
"Little Classic" Edition. 9 vols. Cloth, each, $1.50.
Prose Works. Complete. 3 vols. 12mo, $7.50.
Parnassus. *Household Ed.* 12mo, $2.00. *Library Ed.*, $4.00.

Fénelon.
Adventures of Telemachus. Crown 8vo, $2.25.

James T. Fields.
Yesterdays with Authors. 12mo, $2.00. 8vo, $3.00.
Underbrush. $1.25.
Ballads and other Verses. 16mo, $1.00.
The Family Library of British Poetry, from Chaucer to the Present Time (1350–1878). Royal 8vo. 1,028 pages, with 12 fine steel portraits, $5.00.
Memoirs and Correspondence. 1 vol. 8vo, gilt top, $2.00.

John Fiske.
Myths and Mythmakers. 12mo, $2.00.
Outlines of Cosmic Philosophy. 2 vols. 8vo, $6.00.
The Unseen World, and other Essays. 12mo, $2.00.

Goethe.
Faust. Metrical Translation. By Rev. C. T. Brooks 16mo, $1.25.
Faust. Translated into English Verse. By Bayard Taylor. 2 vols. royal 8vo, $9.00 ; cr. 8vo, $4.50 ; 1 vol. 12mo, $3.00.
Correspondence with a Child. Portrait of Bettina Brentano. 12mo, $1.50.
Wilhelm Meister. Translated by Thomas Carlyle. Portrait of Goethe. 2 vols. 12mo, $3.00.

Bret Harte.
Works. New complete edition. 5 vols. 12mo, each $2.00.
Poems. *Household Edition.* 12mo, $2.00.

Nathaniel Hawthorne.
Works. *"Little Classic"* Edition. Illustrated. 24 vols. 18mo, each $1.25 ; the set $30.00.
Illustrated Library Edition. 13 vols. 12mo, per vol. $2.00.
Fireside Edition. Illustrated. 13 vols. 16mo, the set, $21.00.
New Globe Edition. 6 vols. 16mo, illustrated, the set, $10.00

George S. Hillard.
Six Months in Italy. 12mo, $2.00.

Oliver Wendell Holmes.
Poems. *Household Edition.* 12mo, $2.00.
Illustrated Library Edition. Illustrated, full gilt, 8vo, $4.00.
Handy Volume Edition. 2 vols. 18mo, gilt top, $2.50.
The Autocrat of the Breakfast-Table. 18mo, $1.50 ; 12mo, $2.00.
The Professor at the Breakfast-Table. 12mo, $2.00.
The Poet at the Breakfast-Table. 12mo, $2.00.
Elsie Venner. 12mo, $2.00.
The Guardian Angel. 12mo, $2.00.
Soundings from the Atlantic. 16mo, $1.75.
John Lothrop Motley. A Memoir. 16mo, $1.50.

W. D. Howells.

Venetian Life. 12mo, $1.50.   Italian Journeys. $1.50.
Their Wedding Journey. Illus. 12mo, $1.50 ; 18mo, $1.25.
Suburban Sketches. Illustrated. 12mo, $1.50.
A Chance Acquaintance. Illus. 12mo, $1.50 ; 18mo, $1.25.
A Foregone Conclusion. 12mo, $1.50.
The Lady of the Aroostook. 12mo, $1.50.
The Undiscovered Country. $1.50.   Poems. $1.25.
Out of the Question. A Comedy. 18mo, $1.25.
A Counterfeit Presentment. 18mo, $1.25.
Choice Autobiography. Edited by W. D. Howells. 18mo,
  per vol. $1.25.
I., II. Memoirs of Frederica Sophia Wilhelmina, Margra-
  vine of Baireuth.
III. Lord Herbert of Cherbury, and Thomas Ellwood.
IV. Vittorio Alfieri. V. Carlo Goldoni.
VI. Edward Gibbon. VII., VIII. François Marmontel.

Thomas Hughes.

Tom Brown's School-Days at Rugby. $1.00.
Tom Brown at Oxford. 16mo, $1.25.
The Manliness of Christ. 16mo, gilt top, $1.00.

Henry James, Jr.

Passionate Pilgrim and other Tales. $2.00.
Transatlantic Sketches. 12mo, $2.00.
Roderick Hudson. 12mo, $2.00.
The American. 12mo, $2.00.
Watch and Ward. 18mo, $1.25.
The Europeans. 12mo, $1.50.
Confidence. 18mo, $1.50.
The Portrait of a Lady. $2.00.

Mrs. Anna Jameson.

Writings upon Art subjects. 10 vols. 18mo, each $1.50.

Sarah O. Jewett.

Deephaven. 18mo, $1.25.
Old Friends and New. 18mo, $1.25.
Country By-Ways. 18mo, $1.25.
Play-Days. Stories for Children. Sq. 16mo, $1.50.

Rossiter Johnson.

Little Classics. Eighteen handy volumes containing the choicest Stories, Sketches, and short Poems in English literature. Each in one vol. 18mo, $1.00; the set, $18.00 In 9 vols. square 16mo, $13.50. (*Sold in sets only.*)

Samuel Johnson.

Oriental Religions: India, 8vo, $5.00. China, 8vo, $5.00.

T. Starr King.

Christianity and Humanity. With Portrait. 12mo, $2.00. Substance and Show. 12mo, $2.00.

Lucy Larcom.

Poems. 16mo, $1.25. An Idyl of Work. 16mo, $1.25. Wild Roses of Cape Ann and other Poems. 16mo, $1.25 Childhood Songs. Illustrated. 12mo, $1.50; 16mo, $1.00. Breathings of the Better Life. 18mo, $1.25.

G. P. Lathrop.

A Study of Hawthorne. 18mo, $1.25. An Echo of Passion. 16mo, $1.25.

G. H. Lewes.

The Story of Goethe's Life. Portrait. 12mo, $1.50. Problems of Life and Mind. 5 vols. $14.00.

H. W. Longfellow.

Poems. *Cambridge Edition complete.* Portrait. 4 vols. cr. 8vo, $9.00. 2 vols. $7.00.
Octavo Edition. Portrait and 300 illustrations. $8.00.
Household Edition. Portrait. 12mo, $2.00.
Red-Line Edition. 12 illustrations and Portrait. $2.50.
Diamond Edition. $1.00.
Library Edition. Portrait and 32 illustrations. 8vo, $4.00.
Prose Works. *Cambridge Edition.* 2 vols. cr. 8vo, $4.50.
Hyperion. A Romance. 16mo, $1.50.
Outre-Mer. 16mo, $1.50. Kavanagh. 16mo, $1.50.
Christus. *Household Edition*, $2.00; *Diamond Edition*, $1.00
Translation of the Divina Commedia of Dante. 3 vols. royal 8vo, $13.50; cr. 8vo, $6.00; 1 vol. cr. 8vo, $3.00.
Poets and Poetry of Europe. Royal 8vo, $5.00.
In the Harbor. Steel Portrait. 16mo, gilt top, $1.00.

James Russell Lowell.

Poems. *Red-Line Ed.* 16 illustrations and Portrait. $2.50.
Household Edition. Portrait. 12mo, $2.00.
Library Edition. Portrait and 32 illustrations. 8vo, $4.00.
Diamond Edition. $1.00.
Fireside Travels. 16mo, $1.50.
Among my Books. 1st and 2nd Series. 12mo, $2.00 each.
My Study Windows. 12mo, $2 00.

T. B. Macaulay.

England. *New Riverside Edition.* 4 vols., cloth, $5.00.
Essays. Portrait. *New Riverside Edition.* 3 vols., $3.75.
Speeches and Poems. *New Riverside Ed.* 1 vol., $1.25.

Harriet Martineau.

Autobiography. Portraits and illus. 2 vols. 8vo, $6.00.
Household Education. 18mo, $1.25.

Owen Meredith.

Poems. *Household Edition.* Illustrated. 12mo, $2.00.
Library Edition. Portrait and 32 illustrations. 8vo, $4.00.
Shawmut Edition. $1.50.
Lucile. *Red-Line Edition.* 8 illustrations. $2.50.
Diamond Edition. 8 illustrations, $1.00.

Michael de Montaigne.

Complete Works. Portrait. 4 vols. crown 8vo, $7.50.

Rev. T. Mozley.

Reminiscences, chiefly of Oriel College and the Oxford
Movement. 2 vols. crown 8vo, $3.00.

E. Mulford.

The Nation. 8vo, $2.50.
The Republic of God. 8vo, $2.00.

D. M. Mulock.

Thirty Years. Poems. 1 vol. 16mo, $1.50.

T. T. Munger.

On the Threshold. 16mo, gilt top, $1.00.

J. A. W. Neander.

History of the Christian Religion and Church, with Index
volume, 6 vols. 8vo, $20.00; Index alone, $3.00.

C. E. Norton.

Notes of Travel and Study in Italy. 16mo, $1.25.
Translation of Dante's New Life. Royal 8vo, $3.00.

Francis W. Palfrey.

Memoir of William Francis Bartlett. 16mo, $1.50.

James Parton.

Life of Benjamin Franklin. 2 vols. 8vo, $4.00.
Life of Thomas Jefferson. 8vo, $2.00.
Life of Aaron Burr. 2 vols. 8vo, $4 00.
Life of Andrew Jackson. 3 vols. 8vo, $6.00.
Life of Horace Greeley. 8vo, $2.50.
General Butler in New Orleans. 8vo, $2.50.
Humorous Poetry of the English Language. 8vo, $2.00.
Famous Americans of Recent Times. 8vo, $2.00.
Life of Voltaire. 2 vols. 8vo, $6 00.
The French Parnassus. 12mo, $2.00; crown 8vo, $3.50.

Blaise Pascal.

Thoughts, Letters, and Opuscules. Crown 8vo, $2.25.
Provincial Letters. Crown 8vo, $2.25.

E. S. Phelps.

The Gates Ajar. 16mo, $1.50.
Men, Women, and Ghosts. 16mo, $1.50.
Hedged In. 16mo, $1.50.
The Silent Partner. 16mo, $1.50.
The Story of Avis. 16mo, $1.50.
Sealed Orders, and other Stories. 16mo, $1.50.
Friends : A Duet. 16mo, $1.25.
Dr. Zay. 16mo. (*In Press.*)
Poetic Studies. Square 16mo, $1.50.

Adelaide A. Procter.

Poems. *Diamond Edition.* $1.00.
Red-Line Edition. Portrait and 16 illustrations. $2.50.
Favorite Edition. Illustrated. 16mo, $1.50.

Henry Crabb Robinson.

Diary. Crown 8vo, $2.50.

A. P. Russell.
Library Notes. 12mo, $2.00.

John G. Saxe.
Works. Portrait. 16mo, $2.25.
Poems. *Red-Line Edition.* Illustrated. $2.50.
Diamond Edition. 18mo, $1.00.
Household Edition. 12mo, $2.00.

Sir Walter Scott.
Waverley Novels. *Illustrated Library Edition.* In 25 vols.
cr. 8vo, each $1.00; the set, $25.00.
Globe Edition. 13 vols. 100 illustrations, $16.25.
Tales of a Grandfather. *Library Edition.* 3 vols. $4.50.
Poems. *Red-Line Edition.* Illustrated. $2.50.
Diamond Edition. 18mo, $1.00.

Horace E. Scudder.
The Bodley Books. 6 vols. Each $1.50.
The Dwellers in Five-Sisters' Court. 16mo, $1.25.
Stories and Romances. $1.25.
Dream Children. Illustrated. 16mo, $1.00.
Seven Little People. Illustrated. 16mo, $1.00.
Stories from my Attic. Illustrated. 16mo, $1.00.
The Children's Book. 4to, 450 pages, $3.50.
Boston Town. Illustrated. 12mo, $1.50.

J. C. Shairp.
Culture and Religion. 16mo, $.125.
Poetic Interpretation of Nature. 16mo, $1.25.
Studies in Poetry and Philosophy. 16mo, $1.50.
Aspects of Poetry. 16mo, $1.50.

Dr. William Smith.
Bible Dictionary. *American Edition.* In four vols. 8vo,
the set, $20.00.

E. C. Stedman.
Poems. *Farringford Edition.* Portrait. 16mo, $2.00.
Victorian Poets. 12mo, $2.00.
Hawthorne, and other Poems. 16mo, $1.25.
Edgar Allan Poe. An Essay. Vellum, 18mo, $1.00.

Harriet Beecher Stowe.
Agnes of Sorrento. 12mo, $1.50.
The Pearl of Orr's Island. 12mo, $1.50.
Uncle Tom's Cabin. *Popular Edition.* 12m' $2.00.
The Minister's Wooing. 12mo, $1.50.
The May-flower, and other Sketches. 12mo, $1.50.
Nina Gordon. 12mo, $1.50.
Oldtown Folks. 12mo, $1.50.
Sam Lawson's Fireside Stories. Illustrated. $1.50.
Uncle Tom's Cabin. 100 Illustrations. 12mo, full gilt, $3.50

Bayard Taylor.
Poetical Works. *Household Edition.* 12mo, $2.00.
Dramatic Works. Crown 8vo, $2.25.
The Echo Club, and other Literary Diversions. $1.25.

Alfred Tennyson.
Poems. *Household Ed.* Portrait and 60 illustrations. $2.00
Illustrated Crown Edition. 48 illustrations. 2 vols. $5.00.
Library Edition. Portrait and 60 illustrations. $4.00.
Red-Line Edition Portrait and 16 illustrations. $2.50.
Diamond Edition. $1 00.
Shawmut Edition. Illustrated. Crown 8vo, $1.50.
Idylls of the King. Complete. Illustrated. $1.50.

Celia Thaxter.
Among the Isles of Shoals. $1.25.
Poems. $1.50.   Drift-Weed. Poems. $1.50.

Henry D. Thoreau.
Walden. 12mo, $1.50.
A Week on the Concord and Merrimack Rivers. $1.50.
Excursions in Field and Forest. 12mo, $1.50.
The Maine Woods. 12mo, $1.50.
Cape Cod. 12mo, $1.50.
Letters to various Persons. 12mo, $1 50.
A Yankee in Canada. 12mo, $1.50.
Early Spring in Massachusetts. 12mo, $1.50.

George Ticknor.
History of Spanish Literature. 3 vols. 8vo, $10.00.
Life, Letters, and Journals. Portraits. 2 vols. 8vo, $6.00
Cheaper edition. 2 vols. 12mo, $4.00.

J. T. Trowbridge.

A Home Idyl. $1.25.   The Vagabonds. $1.25.
The Emigrant's Story. 16mo, $1.25.

Voltaire.

History of Charles XII. Crown 8vo, $2.25.

Lew Wallace.

The Fair God. 12mo, $1.50.

George E. Waring, Jr.

Whip and Spur. $1.25.   A Farmer's Vacation. $3.00.
Village Improvements. Illustrated. 75 cents.
The Bride of the Rhine. Illustrated. $1.50.

Charles Dudley Warner.

My Summer in a Garden. 16mo, $1.00. *Illustrated.* $1.50
Saunterings. 18mo, $1.25.
Back-Log Studies. Illustrated. $1.50.
Baddeck, and that Sort of Thing. $1.00.
My Winter on the Nile. 12mo, $2.00.
In the Levant. 12mo, $2.00.
Being a Boy. Illustrated. $1.50.
In the Wilderness. 75 cents.

William A. Wheeler.

Dictionary of the Noted Names of Fiction. $2.00.

Edwin P. Whipple.

Works. Critical Essays. 6 vols., $9.00

Richard Grant White.

Every-Day English. 12mo, $2.00.
Words and their Uses. 12mo, $2.00.
England Without and Within. 12mo, $2.00.
Shakespeare's Complete Works. 3 vols. cr. 8vo. (*In Press.*)

Mrs. A. D. T. Whitney.

Faith Gartney's Girlhood. 12mo, $1.50.
Hitherto. 12mo, $1.50.
Patience Strong's Outings. 12mo, $1.50.
The Gayworthys. 12mo, $1.50.

Leslie Goldthwaite. Illustrated. 12mo, $1.50.
We Girls. Illustrated. 12mo, $1.50.
Real Folks. Illustrated. 12mo, $1.50.
The Other Girls. Illustrated. 12mo, $1.50.
Sights and Insights. 2 vols. 12mo, $3.00.
Odd or Even. $1.50.
Boys at Chequasset. $1.50.
Pansies. Square 16mo, $1.50.
Just How. 16mo, $1.00.

John G. Whittier.

Poems. *Household Edition.* Portrait. $2.00.
Cambridge Edition. Portrait. 3 vols. crown 8vo, $6.75.
Red-Line Edition. Portrait. 12 illustrations. $2.50.
Diamond Edition. 18mo, $1.00.
Library Edition. Portrait. 32 illustrations. 8vo, $4.00.
Prose Works. *Cambridge Edition.* 2 vols. $4.50.
John Woolman's Journal. Introduction by Whittier. $1.50.
Child Life in Poetry. Selected by Whittier. Illustrated.
   $2.25. Child Life in Prose. $2.25.
Songs of Three Centuries. Selected by J. G. Whittier.
   Household Edition. 12mo, $2.00. *Illustrated Library
   Edition.* 32 illustrations. $4.00.

Justin Winsor.

Reader's Handbook of the American Revolution. 16mo,
   $1.25.

_____

*A catalogue containing portraits of many of the above
authors, with a description of their works, will be sent
free, on application, to any address.*

HOUGHTON, MIFFLIN AND COMPANY, Boston, Mass

www.ingramcontent.com/pod-product-compliance
Lightning Source LLC
Chambersburg PA
CBHW031050110726
47900CB00003B/877